Pranks, Payback, & Poison

Mary Seifert

Books by Mary Seifert

Maverick, Movies, & Murder
Rescue, Rogues, & Renegade
Tinsel, Trials, & Traitors
Santa, Snowflakes, & Strychinine
Fishing, Festivities, & Fatalities
Diamonds, Diesel, & Doom
Creeps, Cache, & Corpses
Pranks, Payback, & Poison

Visit Mary's website and get a free recipe collection!
Scan the QR code

Pranks, Payback, & Poison

Katie & Maverick Cozy Mysteries, Book 8

Mary Seifert

Secret Staircase Books

Pranks, Payback, & Poison
Published by Secret Staircase Books, an imprint of
Columbine Publishing Group, LLC
PO Box 416, Angel Fire, NM 87710

Book layout and design by Secret Staircase Books
Cover images © BooksRme, Olenadesign, Pixelrobot, Cherezoff, Nfsphoto
First trade paperback edition: August, 2024
First e-book edition: August, 2024

* * *

Publisher's Cataloging-in-Publication Data

Seifert, Mary
Pranks, Payback, & Poison / by Mary Seifert.
p. cm.
ISBN 978-1649141927 (paperback)
ISBN 978-1649141934 (e-book)

1. Katie Wilk (Fictitious character). 2. Minnesota—Fiction. 3.
Amateur sleuths—Fiction. 4. Women sleuths—Fiction. 5. Dogs in
fiction. I. Title

Katie & Maverick Cozy Mystery Series : Book 8.
Siefert, Mary, Katie & Maverick cozy mysteries.

BISAC : FICTION / Mystery & Detective.

813/.54

Vengeance is the act of turning anger in on yourself.
On the surface, it may be directed at someone else,
but it is a surefire recipe for arresting emotional recovery.

Jane Goldman

ONE

Numbers shouldn't lie. My toes uncurled and my shoulders relaxed when I calculated the odds I couldn't possibly originate from the same genetic material as the young woman sitting across from me on the couch in our living room.

Ellen had burst in for another surprise visit, carelessly toting the mail as if she lived here. I cringed at her inappropriate sense of humor when she shuffled through the envelopes, reading our personal information. And she laughed as I grumbled about the postal worker who somehow managed to miss the large, black, block letters spelling out 'photograph — do not bend.'

"What do you find so funny? Look at this package." I waved it in front of her and groaned. "It's folded. Any picture inside will be ruined." My head fought to reconcile everything Ellen did with my heart's dream of the perfect family, and an exasperated moan escaped my lips. Until this person claiming to be my half-sister showed up on our doorstep a few weeks ago, I believed my mother had died when I was an infant.

Ellen smacked her gum. "Harry, I told you Katie's too intense." She reached across the coffee table and wobbled my knee. "Lighten up, Katie. Sheesh." She exaggerated a gulp, complete with sound effects.

"You swallowed your gum?" I shuddered, and she rolled her eyes. I flattened the packet and reread the addressee. "It looks like someone intentionally crinkled it. Look at the creases."

"Who sent it?" Dad asked quietly, trying to temper my growing frustration. He combed his strong fingers through his thinning, salt-and-pepper hair.

I flipped the envelope back and forth. "No return address." My thumb slid along the edge under the flap. I pinched the cardboard sandwich and tugged it loose. Although I appreciated geometric precision as much as the next person, the pleating in perfect thirds did nothing to pacify me.

My supposed half-sister stifled a chuckle, and the hairs on the back of my neck bristled. I expected her, at twenty-two, to have more sense.

I clamped the sheets between my thumb and forefinger. "Dad, did you order any photos?"

He turned, and his hands went up, palms forward. "Nope. Not me. Not this time."

"Oh, Harry," Ellen said and giggled. My lower lip jutted out when this woman, practically a stranger, addressed *my dad* with such familiarity. My head said I was acting jealous, but my heart didn't care.

I appreciated logic and order, analytically solving problems and methodically resolving puzzles. I wanted to know answers. Ellen only brought more questions. We were nothing alike—no relation.

But then I understood what Dad saw—a five-foot-two-inch mini-me. Wispy light brown hair framed a narrow face with crystal blue eyes and a pert nose. She had the familiar solitary cowlick, on the left side near her forehead, no amount of straightening could erase. Her ears looked like they'd amplify the slightest sounds—my students called mine 'teacher ears.' I supposed we looked like our mother, but my reference point so far in the past didn't bring up any clear images, and I had no way of knowing for certain.

I couldn't wrap my head around the idea of having a little sister, and the emotional roller coaster I rode made my stomach flip. Biting my upper lip to disguise the pout, I pressed the contents from the envelope, ironing the folds with the palm of my hand, and slipped my fingernail along the edge to sever the tape holding together the cardboard protectors.

Ellen plopped down on the cushions, swinging her feet above the carpet, and rubbed her hands together in anticipation before she leaned forward and said, "Okay. Let's see what you've got."

The hint of celebration evaporated as I peeled away the top and revealed …

"A full-page printed smiley-face emoji. How fun." Ellen applauded but her gleeful tone barely disguised an undercurrent of guilt.

I spotted a surreptitious glance between Dad and Ellen. He cleared his throat and said, "Katie—"

I spun on Ellen and sputtered. "This is from you? If

this is your idea of a joke, it's a pretty poor one."

"Katie," Dad began again. "I thought it would make you laugh. I told her to go ahead and send it. You've been a bit gloomy since—"

"Since the world saw fit to drop a sister on me after all this time."

Ellen interrupted. "Half-sister." She rose abruptly.

"Do you expect me to just accept everything and go on as though life is grand?" The constant reminder that my mother left me and began a new family stung.

Ellen grabbed her coat and shoved her fists through the sleeves. "I didn't mean to make life so difficult for you, Katie. I'll stay out of your hair."

Dad said, "Ellen, wait."

"I need to be off anyway. I've got a little shopping to do. Goodnight, Harry. Bye, Katie." She nodded at me and slipped through the door.

I rapidly blinked my eyes and hoped to hear words of comfort and encouragement. Instead, Dad bowed his head for a moment. When he looked up, he appeared disappointed.

"Katie, why are you taking it out on Ellen? It's not her fault. She's just trying to be friends. She isn't the one who hurt you. I am."

"No, Dad. You didn't hurt me. You never hurt me."

"I don't mean right here and now. I mean over the course of your life; I withheld information which has since become essential to you and Ellen."

"Did you know?" I couldn't inhale deeply enough. I'd been afraid to ask but I needed to understand. "Did you know my mother was still alive?"

"I did not. I lost track of her."

My sight blurred and tears overflowed, trailing down my cheeks. "You didn't know about Ellen?"

"How could I?" Dad shook his head. "But I do now. She's quite the fireball. Much like her older sister."

I swiped at my tears and picked up the buoyant emoji with shining royal blue eyes and pink circle cheeks. One corner of my mouth inched its way into a grin of sorts. The joke could elicit good feelings.

Dad said, "She's growing on you."

"Do you think I'm too intense?" Dad's eyebrows flew up. I blew out a puff of air. "The drawing could be funny I suppose, but I don't know what she wants from me, and I don't know if I can give her what she wants anyway."

"Aurora ran out on her too. She wants a family. I think you'd like her if you'd take the time to get to know her."

"I don't think I can, Dad."

"You, Katie, can do anything you put your mind to. The two of you could meet for coffee or go for a walk ..." He tipped his head, and our eyes met. "Or share a bottle of wine. Just think about it."

I sobered and sorted the rest of the mail, setting aside one piece addressed to our landlady. "Here's one for you, Dad." I read the front and cocked my head. "It's from the Monongalia County Traffic Department, Air Surveillance Unit, and says 'Final Notice.'" I tossed the white business envelope in front of him.

I watched him out of the corner of my eye. He sat up straighter and tugged at the collar of his shirt, and cleared his throat before he precisely sliced open one end. Swallowing hard, he removed the paperwork and peeled back the top third above the fold. His forehead crinkled and he unfolded the remainder. Scanning it from top to bottom, he exhaled, and turned it around for me to read.

Printed below a cross-eyed emoji were the words, 'Aren't you glad there is no Air Surveillance Unit of Monongalia County.'

My chuckle filled the space between us. "What do you think of Ellen now?"

TWO

I loved my job and began my school days early. Without the constant interruptions of colleagues, organizing took minutes in the morning quiet before my students converged on the classroom, but when I turned over the calendar cube on my desk, my throat closed up. April stared at me, and I cringed.

I didn't appreciate the allure of the gimmicks and jokes on April Fool's Day and avoided them as much as possible, careful of doors and drawers and chairs and food, a turn of phrase, or rotated images on my computer screen. I never answered my phone.

Dad loved the day, usually peppering our conversation with riddles and jokes. He once presented chicken wings prepared from cereal bars coated with a brown sugar glaze and baked a most realistic spice cake consisting entirely of meatloaf frosted with mashed potatoes. How could we have forgotten?

It dawned on me that Ellen's letter and drawing foreshadowed her ability to succeed at pulling a prank, I couldn't guess what I might be up against.

I made it through the day unscathed by creative and ingenious students and inspired teachers bent on catching anyone with their guard down but dropped my vigilance when our science club met after school.

Ashley Johannes, our club president, adjusted her blue cable knit sweater, twirled her blond locks around her finger, pounded her gavel, and called the meeting to order. "The first item on our agenda is a question for Ms. Wilk." She waited for an acknowledgment. "Is your computer running?" Her sincerity disarmed me.

"Yes, of course." I smiled and took a step toward my desk.

"Well, you'd better catch it." Her unexpected response barely registered until the rest of the kids began to chuckle.

"Good one, Ash." Galen Tonlenson tossed back a hank of chestnut colored hair and smirked, his dark eyes glittering. His girlfriend, Carlee Parks-Bluestone let her long black curtain of hair fall over her face. She shook her head, but when she looked up, she wore a smile.

"Do you have anything for us, Ms. Wilk?" Ashley asked. My reticence showed, and she said, "I promise—only one April Fool's joke a day."

"As a matter of fact, I have an experiment." I opened the cupboard and retrieved a small plastic tub, extracting the equipment I'd need: a candle, a plate, a glass with a small amount of water, and a fire starter. "Galen, place the plate in the middle of the table. Ashley, would you stand the candle upright in the center of the plate and light it? Carlee, please pour the water onto the plate and cover the candle with the glass. Can anyone predict what will happen?"

Galen crossed his bulky wrestler arms over his broad chest. "I think the candle uses up the oxygen and when the candle goes out, the air inside the glass cools and the pressure drops. The water will be drawn up to fill the space."

My jaw dropped. Galen usually kept his own counsel, preferring to listen and watch. The other students bit back a chortle.

"Boy Scouts," he admitted. "Watch and see for yourselves if you don't believe me."

As predicted, the flame petered out, and the water inched its way up inside the glass. "It appears we have a ghost."

"Good one, Ms. Wilk," said Ashley, giggling. "In other business, you'll notice we are missing forty percent of our regular members. I believe the confluence of paramount year-end school activities—"

"What language is that?" asked Galen with a snicker.

"Words you should know for the SAT exam." Ashley winked. "At any rate, all the stuff going on will preempt further attendance. There are AP finals and prom—"

"And track meets and baseball and softball games …" Galen rattled off what he knew of the athletic calendar.

"Concerts and contests," Carlee said. "And we have prep work for our mock trial competition."

Ashley lifted her left eyebrow and glared directly at Galen. "Some of us want to do well enough in the exams to earn college credit so rather than hold our weekly meetings, we could submit our ideas to you, Ms. Wilk." She blew strands of blond hair out of her face. "And you could let us know if we have another good opportunity to get together?"

"Rendezvous?" Galen said with air quotes and laughed. Ashley rolled her eyes.

"I can do that. That would definitely give you all a little leeway. I know the original reason some of you joined the science club was to be able to include this membership and the offices held on college applications and have it look good—"

"But you have made it enjoyable," said Ashley, "And thanks for that."

"Maybe we can plan an end of the year shindig, but I'm swamped right now," said Carlee. "And my head is spinning … in a good way." She smiled shyly.

Rather than hold the scheduled memorial during spring break for her mother, a woman thought to have died seventeen years ago, Carlee and her dad celebrated a reunion with her instead. The time and energy CJ, Carlee, and Danica invested in creating a family inspired me with awe, but not quite enough to warrant expanding my family with long lost relations yet. It hurt and made me angry at the same time.

Ashley's gavel struck the block and yanked me back to the moment. "Meeting adjourned." The students gathered their packs and books and raced out the door before I could even say goodbye.

My phone dinged and I glanced at the screen.

Can we talk?!?!?

Jane Mackey texted me at least twice a day since we returned from spring break. I had to admit, when it came to helping my best friend plan her wedding, I couldn't have been happier. Fortunately, my main job consisted of listening to her talk through her ideas. She'd be a gorgeous bride, fashion savvy, a bright blonde bombshell with huge brown eyes, a diminutive bundle of energy bursting with love, and I had her back. I punched in her number.

"Katie," she sniffled. "What am I going to do? You've got to help."

"Are you okay? Did something happen to Drew?"

"You're an easy mark, my friend. Happy April First," she said in a casual voice. "My hunk is perfectly fine. And how are you?"

I gritted my teeth. "I found out the hard way April Fool's is one of Ellen's favorite holidays too, and you know I don't like surprises."

"I know, but it doesn't stop us from trying. Anything else new on the half-sib front?" Jane understood the conflict going on in my head. We'd had conversations about what I could do, how I should feel, and how much had happened in such a short time.

"I've got to work on accepting her, but it's difficult. Sometimes it feels like she's trying to steal Dad away."

"Talk to Harry, Katie. He loves you more than anything. And speaking of men, aren't you and Pete going out Saturday, his first weekend night off from the ER since his partner resigned?"

"Yes, finally." Dr. Pete Erickson's delicious, bright brown eyes replaced the troubling thoughts of Ellen. "And he's stopping by tonight too. When will your perfectly fine hunk be back in town?"

Jane sighed. "His latest job has him investigating a series of burglaries in northern Minnesota, occurring over the last few months. It's very strange. At first, the victims thought, because the items weren't worth much, the articles had been lost or misplaced. However, three of the victims belong to the same card club and they discussed their annoyance at getting older and forgetful, but they exchanged enough information to conclude each had a similar encounter with a work crew in their homes."

As an undercover officer for the Minnesota Bureau of Criminal Affairs, Drew Kidd's erratic work schedule matched Pete's.

"That's odd. It almost sounds like someone is taking a trophy for getting in." Or, I thought, someone is testing the waters in preparation for a big heist. Before I could stop myself, a joke I'd read in my math journal last week jumped out of my mouth. "What percent of sailors are pirates?"

"3.14159%. π." My grin fell. "That's bad." She released a sigh. "If you're seeing Pete tonight, you'll have to do way better than that."

I pouted and nodded although she couldn't see me. "You don't think it's ingenious? Using the first few digits of π? Three point one four—"

"Ah, no. Let me give you one to use on Pete. Grab a pencil."

I couldn't wait to try it out. I rehearsed the April Fool's joke on my drive home, as I hung my jacket and put away my briefcase, and while I fed Maverick.

I concentrated so intently on my dog, nestled on the rug in front of the adjoining door to the front apartment and blinking with such sad eyes, I missed the knock. Dad strode into the room, sipping his cocoa. He brushed away a marshmallow moustache with the flick of his forefinger and set his cup on the table before flinging open the door.

"Good evening, Pete," he said, and my heart jumped to flutter-mode. "Welcome, Ellen." Ellen waltzed in, giggling at something Pete said. I felt the grin on my face droop.

Dad glanced my way with a look that said, 'I expect more from you,' and I contrived a smile of sorts. "Pete, did Ellen tell you about the ridiculous April Fool's gags she pulled on Katie and me? I've considered myself a capricious antic master for years, and now I've been demoted to a rank amateur."

"Do tell," Pete said and cast his gorgeous eyes to me. His long angular body leaned against the counter. The roller coaster pace of my first few months in Columbia, Minnesota hadn't deterred him. At least now we were on the same ride. I felt my face flush, and my heart danced to imagined music.

"About that," said Ellen sheepishly. "Maybe if you'd received your letter on April 1st, you wouldn't have been so discombobulated, Katie."

I crashed back to the present in time to hear Dad say, "Let me take your coats."

Ellen proceeded to relate my over-serious reaction to her wrinkled printed paper emoji, and Dad confessed to having heart palpitations when he thought a skyward law enforcement entity caught him speeding and the penalty he might have incurred if he didn't pay a traffic ticket.

"Magnolia County is the best place for gags," Ellen said with a self-satisfied grin. "But next year I'll do better."

"Monongalia. Monongalia County," I murmured as I cringed.

Dad hung their jackets. He gestured with his eyebrows, reminding me of my duties as a proper hostess, and I asked if I could get anyone something to drink.

"Coffee for me," said Pete. "You wouldn't have decaf, would you?"

"For you, anything." Reluctantly, I turned my attention

to Ellen.

"Champagne, if you have it," Ellen said. She grabbed my hands. "I figure it worked out so well for your friends, I got right to work, and I got a lead. I may have found her." Her enthusiasm surged.

"Found whom?"

With a toothy grin, she said, "Our mom."

THREE

I peeled my hands from her grasp and reached into the nearest cupboard to retrieve a mug for Pete's coffee. Fumbling with the coffee pod, refilling the water, and pushing the correct buttons gave me time to think.

"Isn't it great? I left a message on the genetic site—the same one where I found you—and I got a response. I realize the return email was generated by the company, probably some automated message, but the relationship percentages are too close to ignore. I didn't want to tell you before I knew for certain only to have your hopes dashed, but there's a ninety percent chance we have found a link to our mother."

A thought formed words and dashed from my lips. "Is this another April Fool's joke?"

"No, no." She grabbed my elbows and spun me around. "It's happening. We've got a family."

My insides churned. I *had* a family. Why did *we* have to be a family? Dad and I had done pretty well on our own, but I caught the solemn look on his face. I didn't want to let him down and reached deep inside for an appropriate level of interest.

"That's great. What are you going to do?"

"I thought we could check out the information and ask some questions—get the ball rolling."

We? "Just how close are you to finding her?"

"I've been in contact with sisla1955. She asked—at least I think it's a she—who I was, why I was looking, and what I intended to do with the information, and she implied she might know all about the person in the match."

The chair squawked as Dad dragged it across the floor and dropped into it with a heaviness his frame didn't support. I filled a glass with water and wrapped his fingers around it. Maverick padded close, sat, and nestled his chin on Dad's knees.

"I'm sorry, Harry," Ellen said. "I should have thought."

My ears burned. If anything more happened to Dad, I didn't know what I'd do. He'd been parent enough for me, both father and mother, and I loved him.

Pete stood behind him with a hand on his shoulder. "What can I do, Harry?"

Dad took a deep breath and let it out slowly. He continued the rhythmic in and out. I strained to hear him continue. "I didn't expect memories to have this effect. It's been ..."

"Forever." I completed his sentence and glared at Ellen. "Could we talk about this some other time?"

"No, Katie. We need to talk about it now," Dad sounded more assured. "You need to understand. It wasn't all your mother's fault."

Pete pulled out a chair and slid me closer to Dad. He

also held a chair for Ellen on Dad's other side. Pete sat and gripped my hand with both of his.

Dad gulped his water, then stared at the remaining contents in the glass, examining the liquid, and when he found what he was looking for, he placed the glass on the table and met my eyes. "AJ, Aurora Jeanne, and I met in a graduate statistics class. She was smart as a whip and always on the move. It didn't hurt that she was gorgeous. You both take after her." He peered at Ellen and me. "I latched onto her and asked if we could study together, but it was love at first sight. Ours was a whirlwind romance." A wan smile worked its way over his lips, and he sighed. "Within six months, we were married. I should have seen the signs, her flushed face and bright eyes, but I was blinded by how much I loved her. I didn't realize she was hooked on amphetamines. She'd never used anything when I was with her. We were married for a while before I found her stash, and she confessed she'd been diagnosed with ADHD which they treat with Adderall today."

He rubbed his hands over his face, stopping at his forehead. He dropped his hands and his eyes darkened with sadness. "She tried everything to get clean and did her best, as long as I was with her, but I couldn't be with her every second of the day, and anything could set her off. Her use escalated and changed. Looking back, I think she'd been hooked for a long time.

"But you need to know, Katie. Your mother stopped using drugs the second the pregnancy test came back positive. Because of you, she was drug-free for almost a year."

I turned away from Dad and blinked back the tears threatening to fall.

"She tried to stay clean. She went for help, but she

didn't want to become dependent on the new pills her doctor prescribed. Rather than take them, she started to self-medicate. Just a glass of wine to help her sleep instead of the sleeping pill, then a highball with dinner to relax. She had cocktail hour as she prepared dinner, but when the alcohol wasn't enough and she could no longer stay sober, she started using again, more potent drugs from less reputable sources.

"On her birthday, I thought I'd surprise her by going home for lunch." He took my hand, and I gazed into his glassy eyes. "I found you on the floor of your room, arranging pieces of a wooden puzzle. You'd climbed out by yourself. Three hours later, your mother came home, high. I still remember her astonishment. She said she'd been only gone a few minutes. She'd supposedly gone to a neighbor for a stick of butter. You can imagine the bewilderment when she realized she hadn't collected that stick of butter.

"Before she added insult to injury, and lied again, I gave her a choice. I told her it was you and me or the drugs, and she couldn't stay with us if she chose the drugs. We started divorce proceedings a month after she left, and once the decree was finalized, she disappeared. Although I maybe should have, I never looked for her."

"She never visited? She never called to find out how we were doing?" *How I was doing?* My chest was so tight I could only gasp at the air. Pete rubbed his thumb against my shoulder blade.

Ellen cleared her throat. "I was too young to understand at the time, but from what my mom, my adopted mother, read in my medical and social history, Aurora stayed off drugs longer. Maybe because I didn't have someone else to take care of me. I never knew my dad." She looked down at her fingers, weaving them together, in and out, reminding me of the ditty Dad and I used to share.

"This is the church, and this is the steeple," I said. I copied her, intertwining my fingers. Ellen's mouth fell and she joined me. "Open the doors and see all the people," we said together, curling our palms upward and wiggling our fingers.

"How did you know that?" Ellen asked, eyes wide.

"Dad taught me."

Dad's eyes never left the tabletop. "AJ used to do it all the time."

My hands dropped to my sides, and my throat closed up. I didn't want to have anything in common with Ellen.

"It's one of the few things I remember," Ellen said. "My mom handed me over to social services when I turned six and I spent the next two years in foster care. But my adoptive parents were spectacular. Looking back, I was extremely lucky. I was a bit on the wild side. Do you want me to continue the search, or will it be too painful?"

Three heads swiveled to look at her. *Incredulous.*

"Okay. You know I'll look into it anyway, but do you want me to share the results?"

It was up to Dad. I couldn't decide what I wanted to do with the information. Would I want to meet the woman who could choose drugs over me? When my eyes met Dad's, I saw his answer. "Let us know what you find out," I said. "And is there anything I can do to help?" I had tried to hold that comment in, but Dad almost smiled. I could read him like a book—sometimes non-fiction, more often a novel, and, most often, a mystery—but I could tell he still wondered what had happened to my mother, to our mother.

"Really? You're sure?" Her voice rose an octave. "Oh, Katie."

I knew I'd bitten off a big chunk. "I'm sure. Just let me know."

"I will. I will." She jumped from her chair and rushed around the table, grabbing Dad and me around the necks, and squeezing us in a three-way hug. "I'll let you know. Right now, though, I'm going to email sisla1955 and get this show on the road."

I staggered when she let me go. She grabbed her coat and rushed out the door.

Pete said gently, "Aurora might still be alive. You might be able to meet your mother. No matter what, I'll be here for you." A slow smile graced his handsome face. "And perhaps I might meet the main contributor of DNA for the most beautiful woman this side of the Mississippi. No offense, Harry."

"None taken. Pete, I think I'll have that champagne now. There's a bottle in the back of the fridge on the bottom shelf."

Pete rescued the bottle. "You never cease to amaze, Harry."

Pete peeled the foil and gently popped the cork. I retrieved four glasses, lining them up on the table. Dad's eyebrows rose, and I said, "Ida loves champagne. And this one's her favorite. We'd never hear the end of it if she doesn't get a glass. Besides, I haven't yet delivered her mail." I lifted the envelope that arrived with Ellen's April Fool's gags. "I didn't see her yesterday, and I haven't seen her today, but ..." I cocked my head and thought back to my drive home. "I'm sure her car is still in the garage."

I slipped the envelope into my back pocket and picked

up two champagne coupes. Maverick jumped to his feet so I could get around him, and he joined me. I tapped on the door with my foot, waited, and rapped again. Pete leaned around me and turned the knob. Ida Clemashevski's open-door policy began the day we moved into the apartment at the back of her spectacular Queen Anne residence. She took top honors in the landlady department and had rescued me from living out of a suitcase.

Little did I know I'd return the favor so soon.

FOUR

"Ida?" I called into the dark space. "Are you here?" Maverick's tail tickled my knee as he edged by me.

Pete flipped the switch on the wall inside the door, illuminating a kitchen in slight disarray. Ida loved to cook and took great pride in her superior fare, so a few things out of order weren't as bewildering as the macaroni-and-cheese congealing in a pan on the stovetop, and the garbage heaped with a pizza box and white cardboard cartons from Ho Wong's.

Pete had known Ida his entire life and seemed as befuddled as I was. He gestured, onward.

"Ida," he called. "Katie and I come bearing champagne."

A loud sigh sounded from her living room, and Pete hustled in front of me. The light went on, and we found Ida curled up on her couch under a quilt in shades of green, one of the many she'd hand stitched. Although this one caught the color in her lovely emerald eyes, her face sagged, and her rosy cheeks looked pale and slack.

Her fading hair had a pink tinge and stuck up on one side. She stared at a muted TV screen and scratched Maverick's forehead. He closed his eyes and eased into the magic at her fingertips, but she barely acknowledged us.

"Mrs. Clemashevski," Pete called out as if greatly surprised.

"Hello, dear." She heaved another great sigh. "What time is it?"

"It's time to celebrate, Ida." Pete held out a hand. Ida took it, and he hauled her to sitting. He relieved me of one of my coupes, handed it to her, and clinked glasses.

"What are we celebrating?" she asked, but didn't appear interested in Pete's response.

"The first of April? April showers? Halloween? Maverick's birthday?"

She reacted to the mention of my dog and lifted her glass. "At least you didn't use the champagne flute this time."

"I know, as a connoisseur of champagne," I said, "you like the bubbles to tickle your nose." Ida reveled in sharing her wealth of information, and I tipped my head in deference to her superior knowledge—of some things. "Cheers."

Before taking a sip, she sucked in a breath and lowered the champagne. She let the air out very slowly.

"What's wrong, Ida?" Pete asked. "Do you need a doctor?" He sat next to her and winked.

"I have you, don't I?" She slumped into the couch. "The years have finally caught up to me. I'm so tired and have no energy for anything. I guess I'll have to start acting my age."

"And what is that? Ida, you're ageless," I said.

Pete set his glass on the coffee table, held her wrist, and took her pulse. "Strong as ever." He smiled and asked gently, "Besides no energy, do you have other complaints? Is there anything bothering you? Any pain I should know about?"

"You scamp." She patted his hand. "Just getting old." The patting stopped, and she added, "And I just can't seem to remember as well as I used to."

"When's your birthday?"

"I know my own birthday." A bit of Irish ire colored her words. Pete raised his eyebrows and didn't back down. "June 18, year to be determined."

"And mine?"

"This is silly. Of course, I know your birthday. I've known you your entire life. It's …" At first, I was afraid she couldn't remember, but instead I witnessed a hint of her playacting. "… July 25."

"What about your anniversary?"

"I know all my dates, but it's like I'm in a fog. I feel like my head is covered in bubble wrap. I can see out but not clearly. I can hear, but the sounds are distant. I am becoming a bystander in my own life." She gazed at Pete with helplessness. "What's happening to me?" Her chin dropped to her chest, and she whispered. "Do you think it's the start of dementia?"

Pete snorted. "I seriously doubt it, Ida, but we can run some tests. Meanwhile, what would make you feel better, more secure, right now?"

She took a moment to collect her thoughts. "When I stayed with my cousin the week after her accident, I met the most helpful and interesting man. She hired him as her part-time nurse for her first two weeks of recuperation, and he set her on her road to recovery. We had a number of late night conversations about health and fitness and well-being and debated the benefits of natural and holistic medicine. He recommended I take an over-the-counter sleep aid for a good night's rest to help clear my mind and gave me turmeric capsules for inflammation. They seem to work. My cousin felt so comfortable with him, I applied to engage him as a caretaker of sorts. He travels around Minnesota, but I suppose he's in great demand and is too busy." She pouted before saying, "I haven't heard back."

The envelope I carried shot a bolt of lightning up my back. I snatched it from my pocket like Quick Draw McGraw. "You have mail."

Ida blinked rapidly, sat straighter, and reached for the envelope. Her lips moved as she silently read the return address. She scrutinized us with a look verging on hopeful. She tentatively tore off one end and removed the contents, showing the same lack of confidence and trepidation Dad exhibited opening his envelope from Ellen, a dread of the unknown.

"Would you like me to do the honors?" Pete asked as he reached out his hand.

"Would you? My cheaters are upstairs, and I'd hate to misread the letter." She placed the papers in his open palm and gingerly sipped the champagne but held back her usual effusive praise of the sparkling beverage.

"'Dear Ida.'" Pete looked up from the page and teased, "So far, so good." He scanned the page, silently reading ahead. She tapped him gently on his knee, and I saw the familiar spark in her eyes. "'You are truly a woman of many talents. I apologize for the delayed response, but I was seeking an employment opportunity sufficient to cover my expenses. I am pleased to inform you' …" Pete delivered the remaining words with good cheer and more speed. "… 'I've been hired by Columbia Home Health Care as a private caretaker-for-hire and would be honored to assist you in any way I can, should you still desire my help. Sincerely, Banning Rache. P.S. I might have openings for extra clients. Tell your friends.'"

Ida let out a huge breath. "I'm so relieved."

"If you are, so am I." Pete's face grew contemplative, and he tilted his head before saying, "Ida, do you think my dad would get along with your Banning Rache?"

Ida gasped and jerked upright. Pete acknowledged the alarm crossing her features with a shake of his head. "Don't worry. Dad's doing much better. We've fine-tuned his heart meds, and he's eating well and exercising. He'll never run another marathon, but he's still a force to reckon with. I should know."

Ida furrowed her brow. "I didn't know he ever ran a marathon."

Pete laughed and triggered a huge smile from Ida. "He didn't, but he'll never run another."

We finished our glasses of champagne and deliberated the logistics of a home health care nurse. After Ida yawned three times, I escorted her up the stairs and waited to help her if she needed anything.

"I'll be fine, dear." She grasped my hand. "And I want you to know I've spoken to my attorney. If anything should happen to me, you and your dad will be able to continue living in my home, in perpetuity."

The corners of my mouth turned down. "You don't have to do that. Nothing is going to happen to you."

"One way to assure that is to practice the Boy Scout

motto: Be Prepared." She released her grip and nestled deep under her covers. "I'm just going to rest a minute. Good night, kiddo."

"Sweet dreams, Ida." I flipped the light switch and exited quietly.

Dad had retired, but Maverick needed one more romp outside before he settled down. While Maverick completed his duties, Pete wrapped me in his arms, and under the night sky peppered with twinkling stars, the luscious good night kiss he gave before driving away topped off the evening perfectly.

As I held the door for Maverick, I smacked my forehead remembering Jane's April Fool's joke. It would only be effective in person, so I paged through the cache of math jokes I'd collected from a variety of online resources and texted one instead.

Eating too much cake is the sin of gluttony. However, eating too much pie is okay because the sin (π) = 0. April Fool's!

It took a long time for the three dots of doom to morph into a message. Pete returned a laughing emoji.

Trigonometry, huh? You just can't let it go, can you? 'Nite.

FIVE

Jane rushed through the door with our mock trial attorney coach, Dorene Dvorak. "Sorry we're late. We had to check in with the new office secretary. What did we miss?"

"We've only just begun …" I sang, a bit off key. With the exception of Jane, I don't think anyone recognized the lyrics, and I felt my face heat up. "We have a few things to cover today to help get you through sections and on to the state meet." I smiled, trying to allay their fears.

"Ms. Wilk, do you, in all honesty, believe we have a shot at getting there?" Carlee chewed on a fingernail. "I mean, this is our first year. We're newbies."

"I do," I said as optimistically as I knew how. "I think it's your acting ability as well as the studious observation of your characters. You project poise and confidence and have practiced like there's no tomorrow."

"You've lived through so much together; you read the nuances and understand each other so well. It shows," said

Jane. "I can't wait. The next meet date is a sign, don't you think?"

"To be honest," said Lorelei Calder, "I don't find the date of April 14 particularly auspicious. I mean, the *Titanic* sank during its first run too."

The students grumbled until Dorene spoke. "You are definitely the team to watch. I'm so fortunate to be able to assist in preparing this group. You listen and take guidance but ask intelligent questions when you don't understand. Keep up the good work. Let's get one more rehearsal under our belts."

At the conclusion of the practice trial, Jane and I had to curb our enthusiasm, putting up a nonchalant front lest we jinx our good fortune.

Dorene said, "In our remaining practices, we can run through some scenarios, but your knowledge of the material and vocabulary is spot on. You understand legal procedures. You can think on your feet, and I've noticed the improvement in your public speaking. Rest assured; you are ready for our upcoming meet." She reached her fist forward, and the students followed her lead, bumping knuckles and yelling our team's name, "EsqChoir."

A lone individual slowly applauded and tempered our ebullience. "My, my, what a performance." My fellow math teacher, ZaZa Lavigne, stood in the doorway and sneered. "You might make it after all."

What a way to spoil Dorene's pep talk, I thought. "Please excuse us, Ms. Lavigne. We're finishing up, and I have a few words of wisdom to impart."

"You don't have many to spare, so take it easy." She spun on her four-inch Manolos and left.

ZaZa had given our mock trial team some bad advice

and was *persona non grata* in Dorene's opinion. I welcomed her rapid departure and hoped my students took my silence as having the upper hand instead of showing my unpreparedness for her cutting remarks. At least I hadn't sputtered this time.

ZaZa and I attended the Royal Holloway in London together, studying mathematical cryptanalysis, and I thought we'd been friends until the man she'd wanted to claim for her own, fell in love with me. We never knew.

She'd been gone from my life since we finished our degrees. I didn't even hear from her when Charles was murdered, but when Columbia High School posted a position in mathematics at the end of last term, she applied. Charles would have been a great teacher. I chose my career by default, a way to remember my darling husband. She knew I taught here. She was overqualified, and I don't understand why she left her Paris job in security just to be a thorn in my side, poking every chance she had.

Brock Isaacson, one of my wise teen charges, who was only here to be with his girlfriend, said, "Don't mind her. She's just jealous."

The room emptied but for Jane. I finished rearranging the furniture and she primped in front of a small hand mirror she'd dug from her purse. She shook her head of long blond tresses and touched up her lipstick. "How do I look?" she said.

"Great. Like always. Who's the lucky fella?"

"Ha, ha, very funny." She tossed her shiny locks and straightened her collar. "Drew and I are meeting with a new photographer. I want to make a good impression. Fingers crossed. Do you want to come?"

An instant of icy fear seized my throat as I remembered

our encounter with Jane's first choice of photographer and all it entailed. We learned unscrupulous individuals used the internet as a tool to exaggerate reviews, make fraudulent claims, and outright lie about who and what they represented. We survived, and Danica Bluestone finally made it home, but it wasn't something I'd want to repeat any time soon.

"No, thanks. You and Drew will do a fine job."

"I'm glad Drew is willing to come with me. I'm not sure I'm the best person to make these choices alone." The smile dimmed and her shoulders fell.

"Jane, it could happen to anyone. How could you know what to expect when the only connection you had was a webpage filled with beautiful pictures and approving words from a long list of unknown individuals—"

"All of whom turned out to be phony."

"You're fortunate you found out before the wedding." I glanced atop my desk at the professional photograph of the goofy expression on Maverick's face, caught the precise moment before he snagged a very fishy, very tiny, very desirable treat. "However, Kimber Leigh does take great pet portraits."

Jane rallied and wrapped her arms around me in an unexpected hug. "Thanks, girlfriend."

I almost toppled when she released me. "Anytime. Now, don't you have places to be?"

She seized her jacket and bag, giggling and waving as she dashed through the exit.

I cowered when the door slammed. I hadn't realized I'd been as tense as my students. I plopped onto my chair and liberated a lungful of air. My head dropped back, and I closed my eyes to rest for a moment. My stomach turned over as the horrific vignettes flashed across my mind. We'd been riding bicycles at a leisurely pace on the trail when Dad yelled, "Gun," and sped ahead of us. He went down. My husband, Charles, crashed into me, knocking us into a shallow ditch. His body covered mine and jerked when the bullets struck. Again, I recalled the light leave his precious eyes and felt his fingers grow cold as they rested in my blood-slicked hand.

I promised him I'd live a good life, and at times I struggled, but I chased the bad memories with good and smiled as more pleasant thoughts sailed through me: Charles's dancing blue eyes and wicked grin, Dad's remarkable recovery, Ida's savory stew, a recent successful mock trial court scene, and Carlee's smiling face when she found her mother. I brought my head forward and opened my eyes. Everything worked out for CJ, Carlee, and Danica. I needed to think logically rather than emotionally.

A knock put my musings on hold, and I sat upright.

"Ellen." *Drat.* My positive thoughts scattered to the four corners of the room. "What can I do for you?"

She crept around the door frame, clutching a laptop and a bulging blue folder. Her staticky hair flew around her face. Her clothes clashed. She wore no makeup. For the first time, she looked ... unkempt.

"Ellen?"

"Katie, can you help me? When I was little, my violin teacher told me I was scatterbrained, and sometimes I still am. Would you check over what I've done? I want to make sure I don't lose anything or mix it up, and I don't know who else to ask."

"Sure," I said. I would do it because Dad would want me to. "What do you have there?"

She flopped the laptop on my desk and slid the folder to the right, hastily trapping the papers exploding from within.

"Could I hook up to the Wi-Fi here?" She opened the computer. I filled in the appropriate blanks and turned the screen in front of her. After a few keystrokes, she set the angle so I could read the display along with her.

She opened the latest email from sisla1955 and looked into my eyes with such hope. I wanted to cushion any possible failure.

"Ellen, you've never met this person?" She nodded." You don't know anything about them. You don't know where they are. It could be a hoax or an automated response. You never know what entity lurks at the end of that link. Promise me you won't give out any personal information."

She wrinkled her nose. "Too late."

SIX

I tried to ask my question gently, but I remembered, quite vividly, the fiasco Jane had stepped into, believing and blindly trusting information on the internet, and I couldn't temper my harshness. "Ellen, what have you done?"

"I connected with sisla1955. She's a nun—"

"Sisla1955 responded she's a nun. But you can't believe everything you read on the internet. She could be phishing. It could be a scam. She could be waiting for the right moment to steal your identity or ask you for money."

Ellen snorted. "As if. That's a laugh."

"She could be a he," I said on a puff of blistering air.

Ellen waited for me to cool down. "She's in charge of collecting data and recording the history of her convent. She kept DNA reports of those who wished to share with their families. That's how she discovered our match to an oblate at the convent." Ellen tapped a key and revealed a string of emails. "This nun works with Mom."

Red flags flew at high mast. How had this nun unearthed

the specific information Ellen needed?

"Why would she keep records like that? Why would she have DNA from Aurora?" It sounded suspicious to me, but of course, suspicious was my middle name.

"I did ask. I'm not a total blockhead." Ellen pouted and tapped a few keys while concentrating on the computer screen. "Her hobby in ancestry evolved into a history of the convent, but she included only those who wished to be part of the study. I even looked up what an oblate is." She read from her screen. "'Oblates are lay people who seek God with special guidance from a religious order to enrich their Christian way of life and bear witness to the teachings of Jesus. The word oblate means offering.' How can you be so skeptical?"

"*That* certainly sounds like Aurora," I said with such a heavy dose of sarcasm. Ellen cringed. I waited a moment before I added, "Tread carefully, Ellen. You want to make sure this *nun* is who she says she is and whether her information could possibly be true. Thoroughly think through how you want to proceed."

She turned toward me. "That's why I came to you. I don't have the foggiest idea how to prove or disprove Sister Lawrence's authenticity."

"She gave you her name?" My words sounded severe to my ears, but I couldn't help it.

Ellen swallowed hard. "She also gave me a phone number where I can reach her." Frustration blew through my lips, and I started to protest, but Ellen said, "I-I-I've only emailed her. I wanted to talk to you first. What do you think we need to do?"

"*You* need to figure out if she's really a nun. Where does she live or work or whatever she does?"

Ellen's forehead crinkled as she concentrated and hunched over the keyboard, her fingers poised to type into the search bar. "How do I do that?"

"Type in her name, at least as much of it as she gave you. Compare the results to the phone number she provided."

Her fingers flew over the keys until she finalized her query with a hard return. She waited a few seconds. I watched the scant information spew out, affirming a Sister Lawrence Evercrest.

"Here she is, and even the contact emails match. The bio provides the dates of her service at a Minnesota university. She taught music until her retirement and look at all the letters behind her name: BA, MA, PhD, MT-BC, CPT, MBA, ret. She's no dummy," Ellen said brightly.

She hadn't listened to a word I said. "And how are you so sure?"

Hot pink crawled up her neck, and she didn't answer. She made a few clicks, and the screen full of links morphed into a wide-angle interior photo of a beautiful church. She followed the arrows to more images of gorgeous grounds, fabulous structures, an enormous welcoming library, and an expansive performance hall. She found the personnel tab and scrolled through the names, zooming in on a picture of an intimidating woman.

The caption below identified someone as Sister Lawrence Evercrest, sitting on the piano bench. She held one hand in her lap and the other gripped the edge of a grand piano. She gazed into the camera with a raised chin and puckered lips, giving an aura of contempt, as if the photo had been an intrusion. Her short, fiery auburn hair curled around her face, framing violet eyes. Her softly draping white shirt buttoned to the collar, and her plain black skirt hung halfway down her shins over a pair of chunky black shoes.

"She sure looks real to me," said Ellen.

I had to admit, using such an unflattering portrait would be a poor technique to prey on the unaware. I tried to sound less overbearing. "Since you arrived at this photo by means other than those provided by Sister Lawrence, it does appear she could be real, but that doesn't mean she is any more trustworthy or that her motives are honorable."

Totally missing my point, she asked, "Now what?" She grinned, and her eyes widened with eagerness.

"We might want to contact someone at the convent. Where is it located?"

She pecked at the keys and brought up one of the earlier emails which had the convent logo printed at the bottom. As I read, I seethed.

"Aurora's in Minnesota? Less than an hour away this entire time and never thought to look for …" I broke off and pinched the bridge of my nose, warding off the headache beginning to pound behind my eyes. "Ellen, I don't know if I can do this."

Her voice quavered with concern. "I understand completely. I'm sorry. I guess this is a half-full/half-empty deal. But it seems like she's working on her life. Maybe she was afraid to contact you or me, realizing how she let us down, but she has support now and so do we. And give her credit. She might not have known you live here now. You moved in August."

Ellen looked so young and helpless, like I might have looked after I lost Charles. She folded her hands in her lap. "Please?" she implored. Did I care enough to quash her dream? I closed my eyes and heard Dad ask to give Ellen a chance. Guilt swung over my head like a guillotine.

I exhaled. "I'll help, but I don't know if I'm ready for—"

"If you don't know where you've come from, you don't know where you're going." Ellen's façade fell away. She gave a tiny cheer and tapped the keys on the computer. I gave in and read over her shoulder. The concise correspondence detailed our genetic connection and highlighted the probable familial relationship. Sister Lawrence assumed Ellen wanted to meet the woman whose genetic markers matched those of her mother with a ninety percent rate of accuracy and laid out a plan.

"But why is Sister Lawrence doing this? Why isn't Aurora initiating contact? What if she doesn't want to see you? Does Aurora know what's going on?"

Ellen frowned and clicked on another email. "I know you don't think you want to meet our mother."

"I never knew her. You did. If she wants to see me, I'll think about it. But if not, it's no skin off my back."

"Really?" Ellen scrunched up her face and focused on the computer screen. "What's next then?"

I rolled a chair next to her and fell into it, mentally canvassing the many topics we could cover. "You have to be careful and do your due diligence. Can you send Sister Lawrence an email asking more about why she has ... our mother's DNA?" Her fingers flew over the keys, almost faster than I asked the questions. "Ask her where she found the link to you—"

"And you."

"And me. Ask for their current locations and compare to the data you've discovered."

"We've discovered," she said while typing.

"Ask when you might meet with either of them. Request a very open populated place where you won't be alone. You can even insist on bringing someone with you if you'd like. I suppose it will depend on the meeting time and place. What else do you want to know?"

"She hinted she's checking our credentials to make sure we are who we say we are."

"You should continue to do the same, Ellen."

"I'd like to send a photo. Do you think that would be appropriate?" I nodded. "Can I send one of the two of us?"

I almost said no. What difference would it make? "Don't you already have one?"

"Let's take another one now. I don't know if, in any of the photos I have, we're both looking at the camera and not scowling." Her lips turned down at the corners for the briefest moment until she pulled out her phone and shoved her head near mine, snapping a half dozen shots. She swiped through the selections, comparing, and chose one. "How about this one? I think we both look pretty good, even if I do say so myself."

"You don't want to sound too eager."

Ellen nibbled on her bottom lip. "Yes, I think I do. I want to know how she is, where she's been, what she's been doing, and if she's found a way to stay off drugs and lead a normal life. I also want to know if she missed me."

I wondered if she missed Dad too or ever even thought about me. My heart pounded in my chest. Did I really want to know?

Ellen added more lines to her email, attached the photo, corrected a word here and there, and hit send. I stopped breathing for a second. Whether or not I wanted it, it was happening.

And my phone pinged.

"I copied you into the email list."

My mouth dropped.

"Blind carbon copy. Don't get your knickers in a bunch."

"It might take a while for her to answer," I said. I chewed on my bottom lip as I squared up the corners of loose papers and vehemently slashed the next day's information on the Smart Board.

A response gong sounded unexpectedly. Sister Lawrence must've been sitting at her computer. I rejoined Ellen, and she read the email aloud.

"Your likenesses are uncanny. I didn't realize Barb—"

"Barb? Who's Barb?" I jostled Ellen's arm and insisted she keep reading.

"I didn't realize Barb had any family and such a fine looking one at that. I'll try to answer your questions as succinctly as I can."

"Do you think Mom changed her name?" Ellen scratched her chin.

I puckered my lips. "Let's assume so. Keep reading."

"Barb has been with us for a little over five years now. She disclosed her difficulty with drugs, and it has haunted her, but she hasn't relapsed for the entire time she's been here. She teaches kids at our convent school who have a problem learning to read. She's popular with staff and students. As to your last question, I hope you two can get together soon and you can see the change in her. Perhaps you'll take her back into your life."

Ellen collapsed into the chair. "I feel like it was my fault she left."

"Don't ever think that. At the very least, it was Aurora's, or Barb's, inability to manage the drugs. You couldn't have made her do something any more than I could." My anger rose to the surface. I forced myself to soften. "It was never your fault. If you'd like to see how she's doing, I'll support you, but I don't know if I can follow you."

Ellen typed in a short response and a response email gong sounded again. She read, "How about April 14 at three?"

SEVEN

I chose my words with care. "The earliest possible meeting proposed by Sister Lawrence conflicted with our mock trial section competition on the same day at the same time. I couldn't commit, but Ellen is going to meet with Sister Lawrence." I couldn't read the mask on Dad's face. "Are you okay if she goes ahead with the plan?"

He shuddered, as if to wake himself. "Yes, absolutely." He looked into my face. "Katie, I always believed she'd died those many years ago. I thought I'd be able to feel if she were still on this earth. What if I could have done more? What if I should have done more?"

"Dad, she chose the drugs and left us. For twenty. Six. Years. She never contacted you, never let you know where she was or what she needed. I'm at fault too. I never asked about her. I guess I was afraid of the answer." Maverick nuzzled my hand. Sadness enveloped me and my heart clenched. I couldn't take a deep breath. I gasped and brushed at the tears I found coursing down my cheeks.

Dad wrapped his arms around me. "We'll be all right. Shhhhh." He ducked his head, scoured my face with his worried eyes, and lifted my chin with his knuckle. "It'll be all right, Darlin'. I promise." He tucked a lock of my hair behind my ear. "What a pair we make."

"I love you, Dad." When my racing heart calmed down, I asked, "Do you want to go with Ellen?"

"Aurora will have to ask me to come. I wouldn't think of imposing. After all this time, I think I'm the last person she'd want to see, but I'll be available if she should make the request." He stood and grabbed Maverick's leash. "Let's get this big boy outside and go for a walk."

After our two-mile trek, we joined Ida on the porch. She sat bundled in a thick quilt in shades of royal-blue and gold, Columbia High School's colors, staring into the evening sky.

"Earth to Ida. What are you thinking so intently about?" Dad asked.

"I'm wondering how long I'll be able to manage this old house; how long I'll be able to stay here."

"What are you talking about? Dad and I are always available."

She raised her eyebrows and gave us that incredulous look only Ida could form. "Thank you, my dear. Don't worry. You're not ever going to have to move," she said.

"That's not it. You must be in a bit of a funk. That's all. Have you talked to Pete?"

"Yes. I scheduled a checkup with my primary care physician, but it's three weeks away. I think I'm fine physically. It's my mind and the day-to-day operations I'm worried about. I seem to be forgetting more and more and feel like I'm walking around in a fog some days. I don't like it one bit. That's why I can't wait for Banning to get here. He called and I was certain he said he'd be arriving today, but he's hours late, so I probably mixed something else up."

The private caregiver, I reminded myself. "Did he leave a message?"

"No. I talked to the man himself. I can't wait for you to meet him." She shivered. "We'd better go in. It's a bit chilly with the sun setting so early."

Dad and I glanced at each other. He lent Ida his arm and she dragged herself to standing, not her usual spry self at all.

"Maybe you need to answer Cash's next call and get rid of the rest of your winter doldrums. Didn't you say he's back from his winter digs in Jacksonville, Florida and ready to kick up his heels? You won your last dance competition."

Ida shuffled to her door. "Katie, I don't think I can even kick up dust. Cash Schultz needs a partner who can keep up with him."

"Ida, he's eleven years older than you are."

"But I'm in no condition to dance."

I put it in my head to research memory loss, brain fog, and dementia. Although I didn't think she suffered from any of those maladies, she acted as though she believed it.

We entered via her front door and weren't surprised to find everything in its place. The floor gleamed. Prisms dangling from her glistening lampshades. She'd polished the furniture, and a bowl of fresh cut flowers took up space in the middle of the kitchen table. It looked like our old Ida had made an appearance to get ready for Banning's visit.

Ida melted into her sofa at the same time her phone chimed from the dining table. After two half-hearted attempts to rise from the couch, she said, "Can you get that, Katie? I don't think I can maneuver my way off the couch just yet."

I picked up her phone and read 'Banning RN' on the screen. "Hello."

A male voice pounced on my greeting before I could say anything more. "Ida, where've you been? I've been so worried. I thought I told you to stay by the phone so I could give you my arrival information. Do you have a pen and paper?" I scrambled for a pen and dug in Ida's desk drawer for a scrap of paper. "Ready?"

I had just enough time to grunt, "Uh huh."

He didn't wait for a response. "Here goes. We'll have a formal intake interview tomorrow morning at eleven, after which I'll give you the lowdown on what you can expect from me. My employer had calls out for someone in my line of work and, as of right now, I have two additional clients I need to review. I'll see you at ten."

"You said eleven."

He didn't answer right away. I thought he'd hung up until he said, "I apologize. You are correct. I'll see you at eleven."

And before I could correct his assumption about me being Ida, he was gone. I tore off the top sheet. "Banning will be here at eleven."

Ida unleashed a breath with so much velocity she sounded like the big, bad wolf from the story of the three little pigs. "Harry, will you be around to meet Banning? I'd like to make sure I correctly record all the information and having another set of ears can't hurt." She absentmindedly petted Maverick. When she slowed or stopped, he batted her hand with his nose. He'd give her no rest if she didn't pay attention.

"Of course, I'll be there. With bells on."

Ida blew out a steady stream of air. "I'm beat, and if I want to look presentable, I'd better call it a night and store up some extra winks. Thanks, you two. You can let yourselves out?"

Her contagious yawn started a chain reaction, first dad, and then me.

"Goodnight, Ida."

EIGHT

I arrived early, trekked through the quiet halls, unlocked the office door, turned on the lights, and lined up the materials I intended to use for the day. I rewarded myself with a sip of coffee and relished a nibble from one of Ida's flakey pastries, the supply of which was rapidly diminishing, before my students and colleagues arrived. The day progressed on schedule until Dad attempted an untimely communication, and I went on alert.

"What's wrong, Dad?"

"Hey, Darlin'. Banning just left."

I stole a look at the digital clock on the wall. "It's only ten fifty."

"He got here at nine forty-five. Ida wasn't quite ready although she looked fine to me. She was a bit unnerved, I guess, but she merely had to apply her makeup. You had eleven a.m. written on the message you took." I heard a question in his tone.

I thought back to our conversation. "Did he give any

reason for being early?"

"We never asked. When she got over her self-consciousness, she was so excited to see him, she didn't have anything else on her mind. He took basic information for a routine physical: blood pressure, heart rate, respiration, oxygen level, weight, and he pricked her finger for a sample of blood to analyze. The tasks he assigned sounded like they could help with memory decline and fogginess issues. The instructions make sense. Ida's on board, and we can help."

"What did he suggest?" The bell for our next class rang.

"Duty calls. I'll have Ida give you the lowdown when you get home."

Between classes for the rest of the day, I searched for information about the causes of memory loss and the best ways to halt decline and improve clarity. Everything made sense except the fact Ida had to worry about memory issues at all.

Jane lingered after our short mock trial meeting. "The students know their material, and I can't wait until the section meet. How many teams go to state?"

I was as new to the program as she and paged through the rules and regulations document, searching for the answer. "The winning team from each section is invited to the state tourney as well as the next two highest scoring teams across the state." I patted the pages in front of me. "It's like wild card teams in a sports matchup."

"Competition is competition. Are all of the section meets across the state held the same day?"

My finger trailed down the page. I stopped and tapped the comments. "It says this year all of the section meets must be completed by April 14." Jane beamed. "We'll know by the end of the day." She tried to contain her enthusiasm. "What?"

"Nationals are in Atlanta, and I can see my dad."

"Aren't you putting the cart before the horse there, girlfriend?"

"You don't understand the power of positive thinking."

A heavily accented voice sounded from the doorway. "I'm positively thinking you're putting the cart before the horse." ZaZa tossed her dark wavy locks over her shoulder and tugged at the front of her jacket.

"Hello, ZaZa," Jane said with artificial sweetness. "I almost didn't recognize you. I like your outfit. It's such a change from your normal cauldron black."

The gray pants, crimson-red silky blouse, and fitted gray bolero set off ZaZa's peaches-and-cream complexion. She looked down her nose and sneered at Jane through a stark slash of blood-red lipstick. "You think you're so smart."

"Our kids listened to your advice once and lost when you instigated an argument among them." Jane's grin stretched from ear to ear. "We'll try not to let that happen again."

"You'll see I was right all along. Your students will meet a superior group of individuals who know the ropes and use every stratagem at their disposal, and they will lose." She spun on her three-inch gray spikey heels and marched away.

"No matter how well they do, win or lose, I've enjoyed the entire ride," I said, hopefully loud enough for ZaZa to hear.

As Jane loaded her belongings in her backpack, she said, "Me, too. Now, I've got a supper guest to feed." She raised and lowered her eyebrows suggestively.

"Say hi to Drew for me."

She laughed. "See you tomorrow."

I believed ZaZa funneled her excess energy into making my life uncomfortable. A determined walk with Maverick might put my feelings back in perspective, so I raced home.

He sat at the back door, chomping on the leash in his mouth, as if he knew I needed him. His muscles rippled and his shiny black coat flashed as he shifted from foot to foot. I dropped my briefcase on the floor, secured his leash, and took him out for a fast two-mile head-clearing walk.

Upon our return, Maverick stood on his hind legs and pulled on the handle to open the back door, reacting to the enticing aromas emanating from within.

Dad peered through the steam rising from a pot on the stove. "Good walk?"

I said, removing my coat and shoes. "Yup. What are you making? It smells divine."

"It's a fancy soup Ida had frozen and decided she couldn't eat on her new diet, so she gave it to us."

"Why can't she have this? She only uses the finest ingredients and lots of good veggies."

"It's part of her new regimen. Calories have a way of sneaking into some cream-based soups, and she is taking Banning's recommendations very seriously. It's ready. Would you go get her, please? She's joining us, bringing a salad as her main course and our accompaniment."

Maverick scratched on her door. I knocked, and we heard a cheerful voice. "Coming."

I opened the door, and she breezed by me, her arms laden with a gigantic bowl of greens dotted with fresh vegetables in the colors of the rainbow, and a white crumbly cheese. I snatched one of the nuts from on top—pecans she'd most likely sugared herself, one of her salad signatures.

"You're rocking, Ida." What a great change—the way she dressed, her demeanor, and of course, her food.

Her hair had the vibrant color of the newly dyed. She'd applied makeup with the finesse of an artist, and she wore her flamboyant clothes like her old self. "I feel great. Banning has given me the best directions needed to make a full recovery, beginning with my diet." She caught my expression. I purposely lowered my eyebrows to hide my surprise. "I'll admit, I make tasty food, but it isn't necessarily always the healthiest fare."

"What else is in the plan designed by Banning?" Could she hear skepticism in my voice?

"I need to be active every day, walking or doing yoga." I nodded. "After Banning left, I called Cash, and we're registered for a dance exhibition in two weeks, so we'll have to hit the studio and brush up on our skills." She cupped her right elbow in her left palm and gestured an "Olé."

I almost felt guilty eating in front of her, but Ida never deviated from diligently chewing twenty times before swallowing. On occasion, she would longingly gaze at one of our bowls and draw a deep breath, clearly audible above the clinks of our utensils.

We cleared the dishes and as Ida wiped the tabletop, she bubbled with enthusiasm. "Let's play that game. You know the one, with the square letter tiles."

Dad filled the sink with soapy water and paused for a moment. "Scrabble?"

"Yes, that's it. Playing games fulfills another recommendation. You have it, don't you?"

I was already sliding the box from the game shelf. "Right here, Ida." I carried it to the kitchen table and unboxed the components.

"Can you remind me of the rules?" she said.

In the middle of my reading aloud from the box cover, a refresher for all three of us, Ida's bell rang. "You set up the game. I'll see who's at your door, Ida."

NINE

Maverick pranced next to me, my ever-ready escort. When I verified the visitor through the glass beside the door, I groaned, but only slightly. Ellen stood on the top step, rocking back and forth. She halted when I opened the door and caught her anxiously reaching for the bell again.

"Hi, um, Katie. Is Ida around?" She checked out her shoes before lifting her eyes. "I didn't want to bother you, but I wanted company tonight, and I don't know too many people in Columbia."

I breathed deeply and worked the corners of my mouth up. "Ida, Dad, and I are playing Scrabble. Are you up for a game?"

"Sure," she said with no enthusiasm at all. She hung her coat on the rack and followed me to our kitchen.

Dad drew his tiles, placed them on the rack, and said, "Good evening, Ellen. How's it going?"

"It's going well, Harry," she said, taking the empty seat

between Dad and me, pulling tiles from the pile of wooden squares in the middle of the table.

After playing thirty minutes, Dad had more points than the three of us put together, and the gong sounding from Ida's wrist granted us a reprieve. She tapped the smart watch. "My reminder to practice piano. I have to do that for thirty minutes, as if it's a hardship. Banning thought it could help. Then on to reading." She stood and gathered her belongings.

"Ida, do you have to do everything every day? Can you overdo it?"

She huffed as if my questions insulted her. "I'll have you know I'll do whatever it takes to recover my mind, and I like to do most of my assignments anyway. Oh." She flushed crimson. "I just remembered I didn't take my supplements today. Can you remind me later?"

I nodded and recalled a list from one of the resources of well-researched protocols touted by several highly acclaimed Ivy League schools. Banning's guidelines fit the treatment profile.

"Do you have an appointment with your doctor?"

"Of course, that's number one on my list. Tomorrow, Banning will start monitoring my daily compliance with his instructions."

"What else did he suggest?"

"Sleep is imperative. I am to use a sleep mask, and I have one scented with lavender. The calming app on my phone has a very seductive male voice, and I'm using a new silky pillowcase." She smiled and raised her eyes heavenward, patting her round cheeks. "Which is also very good for my complexion."

"That sounds dreamy," Ellen said. She scratched under

Maverick's chin. He closed his eyes and leaned in for more.

Ida's face dropped into her palms and matched her serious tone of voice. "Every morning …" Her bottom lip protruded. "… when I remember, I take a handful of vitamins and minerals." Her hands crossed in front of her and slid down her arms. She shivered and briskly rubbed up and down, manufacturing warmth. "Keeping track of what I eat and how I feel overall is on the to-do list too, but I find it counterintuitive to write I am eating a crisp green salad when I'd rather have a piece of chocolate cake."

"If you didn't make the best chocolate cake in the entire universe it might be a bit easier so cut yourself some slack."

Although Ida's litany of instructions came right off the page I'd researched, I started to worry. She had more concurrent assignments than I gave my students. And she was almost four times their age. "Who are you going to see for your checkup?"

Ida tilted her head. "I spoke to *Dr.* Pete." She winked. "He arranged an appointment with a family doctor …" She whispered the last words. "Specializing in geriatrics."

"Pete knows the ropes and won't steer you wrong," I said as I put the game pieces away.

Ida looped her arm through Ellen's and dragged her out of our kitchen. "Do you play piano, dear?"

"As a matter of fact, I took lessons for twelve years. I'm not very good, but I can read music, and I do like it."

Maverick and I squeezed through the doorway, with Dad close on our heels.

"I have some lovely duets I haven't been able to play in a very long time. No one will play with me." She gave me a disapproving eye. It was my turn to blush. I played but not often enough nor well enough. "Would you like to try one?"

"Okay." Ellen didn't sound too certain, but she settled in at the piano anyway. Dad and I plunked onto the couch and waited for the concert.

Ida retrieved a thick music book from her cabinet and arranged it on the music stand of the piano. She slid onto the seat to Ellen's left and thumbed through the pages, stopping occasionally to consult, looking for a satisfactory duet.

After they agreed and began to play, I recognized *Pure Imagination* from Willy Wonka and the Chocolate Factory, but before the end of the first page, Ida put her hands to her ears and screeched.

"No. No. No."

Confusion and a bit of apprehension filled Ellen's face. She snatched her hands away and leaned back before Ida slammed the piano cover. Ellen's eyes were the size of saucers. I shrugged, at a loss for words.

"It's so out of tune. I can't stand it." Ida's irascible tone caught me off guard. She might be domineering, direct, and confident, yes, but petulant and cantankerous? Not so much.

The sound hadn't irritated me, but I could enjoy music cranked out of a Jack-in-the-Box. Dad rescued Ida. He held her hand as she shifted her weight and rose from the piano bench.

"This will never do." Ida shook her head of flaming red curls. "Tomorrow, I find a tuner."

"There's no time like the present." Dad grabbed Ida's laptop and opened it. She logged in, and they skimmed over the short directory of piano tuners. "Who did you use before, Ida?"

"I don't recognize any of these names." Ida's face paled, and she began pacing behind the couch. "Every year, the week before Christmas, my neighbor, Grace, would engage a CPT. That's certified piano technician." She stopped in her tracks and turned to Ellen. "Grace Loehr was a magnificent musician. I knew she'd hire the best. He'd park his old truck with the musical staff logo painted on the side ..." She looked up, searching the ceiling. "I think it read George's Tuning, but that's not one of the choices, is it?"

Dad's eyes snapped back to the screen. He clicked, looked up and down, and shook his head.

Ida crossed her arms in front of her. "I'd dutifully wait for him to complete his task. When he finished, I'd *accidentally* be outside getting my mail or clearing the walkway. I'd greet him and ask if he had time to come by for another tuning. He never balked. I paid in cash. I think, after the second year, he expected it. He was such a nice man and always did an exceptional job, but I never had to initiate contact. I'm not even certain his name was George. With Grace gone ..." Sparkling pools threatened to spill over in her eyes. She sniffed and resumed her pacing. "It's too late."

Ellen cocked her head. She leaned forward and plucked an insert from the folded newspaper at the edge of the piano. She tapped it lightly with her fingernails. "Ida, look. Here's a flyer for new services including a tuner who's available at a moment's notice. Twenty-four seven." The impish look on her face coaxed a smile from Ida. "Her name is Redd Starr."

"Let me see that." Ida marched next to Ellen and tore

the paper from her hands. Her lips moved as she silently read the description. "She? She sounds perfect. I'll give her a call tomorrow."

Dad held out his phone. "Why not right now? It says twenty-four seven. If you have to, you can leave a message. At least you'll have a plan in place."

"And Banning will appreciate that. He said I have to work on my organizational skills. I think he might have been referring to my tardiness and unpreparedness today."

"But that wasn't your—" I wanted to tell her it wasn't her fault, but she cut me off with a shake of her head.

Ida punched in the numbers and put the phone to her ear. "This is … Oh, hello. I wasn't expecting a real person. I'm sorry to be calling so late."

I leaned forward, trying to catch Ida's side of the conversation.

"I need a grand piano tuned." She listened and gave her shimmy again. "Tomorrow at nine will be divine. That's 3141 North Maple Street and thank you. Thank you ever so much."

Ida ended the call and cupped the phone between her hands, folded in prayer. Her green eyes glowed and looked so much like they had the first time I met her, I forgot about her more pressing issues.

TEN

Maverick and I took advantage of the mild morning weather. As the pinks, yellows, and oranges blossomed in the sky, we jogged the neighborhood, returning at the same time a rusted, dusty-blue panel van pulled up in front of the lovely Queen Anne we called home.

The sizable man who popped out set a pair of glasses on his head, raised his arms, and stretched, grunting loudly. His dark hair curled around his ears and mingled with a neatly trimmed beard as he glanced over his shoulder. When he straightened the front of a short white coat, I caught a glimpse of faded rainbow-colored scrubs. He vigorously scrubbed his face and lowered the glasses. He reached across the front seat and pulled out a black bag, completing the overall picture of a man in the medical field.

Maverick dragged me closer. "Mr. Rache?" I asked, thumping along behind my dog.

He didn't answer immediately, taking careful stock of

muscles rippling on my sturdy black Labrador retriever.

"Sit, Maverick." Maverick raised his head. He let his tail meet the pavement.

The man hesitantly extended his hand. "I'm Rache, and you are?"

"Katie Wilk." I was so used to the strong grasps of the men in my life, I couldn't wait to release Mr. Rache's comparatively limp handshake. "I believe you met my dad yesterday."

"And heard a lot about you, Katie. How do you do?"

We began the short walk to Ida's door.

"Ida's so happy you were able to find employment locally and come to help her. She appreciated what you did for her cousin. Now she thinks there is something seriously wrong with her mind. She's fixated on the possibility of dementia, and it's making life more difficult for her. Actually, for all of us."

"Glad to be of service. Please, call me Banning. Everyone does. I'd have come to help Ida anyway. She's a sweet, retiring, little old lady and did a fine job assisting with her cousin's convalescence. Though she did share she was having a few issues remembering things."

I snorted. "Banning, we are talking about Ida Clemashevski, right?" I'd never before heard anyone refer to Ida in those terms. However, up close, I made out the Disney figures on his scrubs. If the man liked cartoon characters, he might be one to describe Ida as sweet. Maverick's head ping-ponged between us.

Banning slowly shook his head. "Be aware that her fears may not be unfounded. She's of an age, you know."

We mounted the steps to the front door. Banning's bell pressing was drowned out by spirited piano music, ricocheting around inside, a jazzy rendition of a familiar Chopin ballad.

"What on earth is that?" Banning asked. His forehead rippled above flashing dark eyes.

"Someone is playing piano, quite well. Maybe it's Ida." I wondered why Banning stiffened. Did her talent surprise him? "Or it could be my ..." I didn't want to have to explain the tenuous lines of our relationship. I said, "My friend, Ellen. She and Ida started to play duets last night, but Ida just couldn't get herself to shut off her perfect pitch gene. She couldn't play with the piano out of tune. Maybe Ellen returned to try again? Isn't playing piano one of the tasks you assigned Ida to facilitate her recuperation?"

His head nodded the tiniest bit. After a pause just long enough to take a breath, a spirited new song began before we could sneak in the gong of the doorbell.

Anxious to set my eyes on our sweet, retiring Ida, I tried the knob, and the door opened. The fun music charged the air. I tiptoed in so as not to disturb the artists practicing their craft, tripping on the footwear accumulated on the welcome mat. Ida sat on the bench next to a fair-skinned woman with streaky light-brown hair pulled high up on her head in a messy bun, eyeing us with luminous blue eyes through wire rim glasses—not Ellen. The slightly-over-middle-aged woman flashed a charming smile and nudged Ida, nodding at us as they continued to sway in tandem, flawlessly playing the four-handed *Pure Imagination*.

Banning dropped his black bag with a loud bump. He added his loafers to the collection and replaced them with polyurethane clogs he removed from his bag. At my questioning glance, he said, "They can be sterilized."

The music ended, and Ida said, "We have an audience."

She popped up from the seat and gestured for us to come closer. "Banning. Katie. Get over here and meet Redd Starr."

I applauded as I stepped up to the piano. "Great job. I love that song." I reached out. "I'm Katie." Maverick gave a yip. The woman leaned away.

"Sit, Maverick." His response was immediate. I praised him and gave him one of the tiny treats I kept on hand. "He's really quite friendly." Doubt filled her face. "But let me put him in my apartment." I discharged him to search for Dad and returned to the musicians.

A stiff red pinstriped shirt collar peeked through the open neck of Ms. Starr's crimson twill coveralls. She rose and extended her hand over the piano. She clasped mine with her long, strong sure fingers. Her beautiful, manicured, Caribbean Sea blue nails matched the large stone in the ring resting on her middle finger. "How do, Katie?"

"Great, thanks, and you are definitely Redd." She stopped shaking my hand and started to giggle as I read the insignia on her chest pocket, Redd's Piano Tuning. "We're sure glad to see you. Ida said the piano was too out of tune for her to play."

"And it was," she said. "Past tense."

Banning said, with a bit of admonishment in his voice, "Mrs. Clemashevski—"

Ms. Starr interrupted, laughing, "Mrs. What? If it's awright with you, I ain't callin' you that. Missus, I've gotta go, but I'll be back tomorrow to check the glue on the keytops. Around noon, okay?" Ida nodded. "Meanwhile, try not to play them too much. Wouldn't want that phony ivory to fall off."

"Perfect. I'll see you tomorrow," said Ida.

Redd stood. "Not if I see you first." Ida's eyes went wide. "Just joshing with ya. Tomorrow."

Redd threw up a hand and quickly skirted around the couch, dropping onto the floor. She wriggled the big toe popping through the end of her sock before sliding into her footwear, rose, and fled. Her tornadic exit left us reeling. Maverick scratched on the door but before I let him back in, I asked, "You don't mind dogs, do you Mr. Rache?"

"I don't want the dog to disturb Ida," he said hurriedly. Banning took several deep breaths and led Ida to the sofa. "How are you today? Have you taken your medication and completed your exercise routine?"

"I yoga'ed for twenty minutes until Starr arrived. But…" Ida hemmed and hawed. She looked everywhere but at Banning. "Last night the supplement bottle slid off the bathroom counter and into the toilet."

"You really shouldn't skip a day if you can possibly help it."

"Can't I get more?" She sounded contrite. Her shoulders rose around her ears and tensed. "I've been taking them religiously."

"I'll get you more after your physical," he said, and Ida shoulders relaxed. "When is it scheduled?"

She sat up as tall as she could, crossed her arms over her tummy, and sounded quite pleased with herself. "Pete pulled some strings and I have an appointment three weeks from Monday."

"Oh." It was a big empty sound, and Ida's face fell. "That's a fairly long time."

"Banning, what do I do?" Panic crept back into her voice.

"I think I can get you in to see the ancillary physician

working with Columbia Home Health Care if you'd like.
He has a direct primary care practice and doesn't take
insurance so you'd have to pay him upfront, but I can get
you the cost sheet ahead of the visit. A typical physical is
one hundred twenty-five dollars. Does that work for you?"

"Sounds perfectly reasonable. Just give me a time and a
place." She shifted her laughing green eyes to me, repeating
one of Dad's favorite lines. "I'll be there with bells on."

Banning's eyebrows rose above his horn-rimmed
glasses.

When Ida caught his disapproving glare, her face fell.
"I'll be there," Ida reiterated more seriously.

"If you'll excuse me, may I step outside to make the
call and see if he has an available slot? Does this afternoon
work?" Ida nodded, and Banning headed outside.

Her shoulders rounded until the door opened and
Maverick sauntered through the space Banning had
occupied and sat next to her, wriggling his nose beneath
her hand. She smiled and supplied him with a hefty scratch.
"At least you still remember me, and I still remember you."

The comment caught me off guard, but before I could
reassure her, Banning stuck his head in. "He usually doesn't
have office hours on Saturday, but he's doing us a favor. I
made the appointment for two this afternoon. His office is
in the Columbia Commerce building in Market Square. If
that doesn't work, I can call back, but it may take a while to
get an opening."

A shadow flitted across Ida's face, but she said, "That's
wonderful."

Pocketing his phone, he strode across the room,
avoiding Maverick, drew his black bag next to Ida, and
extracted a white plastic box. He wrapped a cuff around

Ida's arm and snapped an oximeter on her fingertip. After a few moments, he said, "The numbers on your vital signs aren't bad." He penciled his findings in a notebook and removed the devices. "There's nothing more I can do for you today. You look as well as can be expected." I thought she looked almost like her old self. Banning grinned. "If the doctor prescribes any medication, get started right away. I've asked him to replace your supplements too."

Ida nodded noncommittally at first, and then more vigorously.

"I have other clients to check on, but I can stop by tomorrow at eleven."

She carefully chose words for her response. "Of course, if it's not too much bother. With your schedule, are you sure you can work me in?"

I tried not to roll my eyes.

ELEVEN

I promised to provide Ida's transportation at two. Killing time, I cleaned our apartment, threw together a green salad for lunch, watched my phone for an update from Ellen, and reviewed my lesson plans for the upcoming week until Pete's ringtone played.

"Are we still on for dinner? Our reservation is set for six at Thai Fyre," he said.

"Absolutely. I've been dying to try that new restaurant. I'll be ready." A grin fixed itself on my face as I disconnected the call.

Maverick accompanied Ida and me an hour later, and while fending off sloppy dog kisses from the back seat, Ida kidded me about the eager love-sick look still visible on my face when we drove through town to Market Square. Large industrial warehouses dwarfed the Columbia Commerce building tucked behind a shipping company and a small manufacturing plant. It sat alone and next to a huge parking lot and grassy area.

We came to a stop and Ida fished a card out of her bag. "Suite 2001." She tapped on the card and scrutinized the building. She shrugged and spryly hopped out, then poked her head back in and said, "Thanks for the ride."

"Do you want me to come inside with you?"

"No, I've got this. I'll call when I finish."

The door slammed and she vanished inside, so I used the free time to walk my dog. He reminded me of the importance of stopping to smell the roses that might blossom, viewing the weeds breaking through the cracks in the concrete, the line of ants crawling along the edge of the pavement, the crunching gravel, the tar, and the scattering withered leaves leftover from winter. We even had time to locate a geocache spotlighting one of the town's founding fathers, Clarence Hamilton, prosperous owner and operator of the first grist mill in the county. The coordinates led us to a statue dedicated to the local amber waves of grain.

Ida's phone call put an end to our forty-one-minute three-block walk, and because Maverick already sniffed every scent along the path, the return didn't take as long.

She stopped pacing when we caught up to her. "His office takes up the entire second floor." We crammed into the car. "I'm so glad Dr. Riley fit me in today. He gave me a prescription and a refill of the supplements. Can we stop and pick up my meds? I'm supposed to take them today, if possible." She wiggled, adjusting her backside onto the seat. Deep furrows formed on her brow, and she clutched her bag handle so tightly, her knuckles went white.

"Absolutely." I concentrated on the meandering path out of Market Square.

"Where are we?" Ida said. "Where are you going?"

I thought she was kidding and eyed her curiously. "Where do you want to go? I'm taking us to the pharmacy."

She scoffed. "I knew that." She gazed out the window.

"What did the doctor say?" I managed to ask with nonchalance. I didn't want it to look like I was grilling her, digging into her private business.

She stared out the windshield, and I thought she might not have heard me. Maverick licked her ear. She squirmed in the seat. "I played a few games to measure my ..." She chewed on her lip. "... cerebral intelligence. Dr. Riley gave me a twelve-question gerocognitive memory exam, and I don't think I did as well as I should have."

"What did he have you do?"

Ida not only remembered the obscure name of the exam, but recalled her answers to the questions, line by line, in addition to drawing a cartoon face with ten different physical characteristics she had been asked to recreate.

"That sounds like it would have been difficult."

"Not really." At the bottom of the paper, she sketched two additional options for each trait. "The computer program gave only three choices, and when I was teaching, I always had my art students study faces, but I don't think I had the eyes right."

I began to worry about my own retention ability. It seemed I'd already forgotten what we'd had for lunch. "What did he say about your memory?"

"He didn't give any opinion but wrote me this prescription and took the cash."

We collected her meds from the drive-through at the pharmacy. I read the incomprehensible label, diphenhydramine, and rattled the pills before I handed it to her. She popped the top on the tan prescription bottle and shuddered as she dry-swallowed a capsule on our way home. "I want to get back on track as soon as possible. Banning believes this will do the trick. He said it might take a while for the medication to build up and have its desired effect." She let out a slow breath. "We'll see."

Ida's emotional roller coaster had taken its toll. Though she decided on a quiet evening and early to bed after a full day, she persuaded me to model my date outfit (a common occurrence) before Pete arrived.

"There's a pair of star sapphire earrings and a matching ring in the top drawer of my desk you simply must wear. They'll go a long way to make the blue in your eyes sparkle."

I retrieved the jewelry and bedazzled my ears.

Ida said, "See. They look much better on your lobes than in the desk drawer."

"Thank you, Ida. I love wearing your jewelry, but this ring …" My throat tightened. I had difficulty swallowing and returned it to the cradle in the palm of her hand.

"Too much? Casimer loved diamonds and star sapphires together." She smoothly fit it over the knuckles of her right hand and gazed in admiration. "It still fits my pinkie."

There was a brisk knock on the adjoining door, and an absolutely adorable Pete waltzed in wearing khakis pressed into razor sharp creases and a light-blue button-down shirt. "Good evening, Ida. Hi, Katie." After an appraising once over, he winked a luscious brown eye and added, "You look fabulous. You too, Ida."

She snickered.

He sat next to her and took her hand. "Katie said you had a checkup today. How'd that go?"

"My caretaker—you know, Banning—set me up with

Dr. Riley. He did an exam but never said whether the results were good or bad. I have some meds to take, and Banning is scheduled to check in and see how I'm faring."

"Ida, if you need anything—"

"I know you're always there for me, young man. Greet your dad for me and tell that old geezer he should come around for dinner." Around a huge yawn, she said, "Now, go have a good time and let an old woman get some shut eye."

I linked arms with Pete, and we strolled to his truck. He looked over his shoulder through the window to Ida's living room. "Old woman? I don't see her as often as you do and haven't witnessed the memory issues Ida claims to have. Could it be she's finally showing her age?"

"She's struggling a bit. It's probably a good idea to have someone she can depend on and not feel obligated in some way. It hurts her pride to have to ask for help or a repeat of something said. I read up on memory loss, dementia symptoms, and Alzheimer's. It seems like Banning is following the suggestions given by multiple sources. In fact, I don't think he's missed one item on the list, so maybe something will click." My eyes strayed to the sky and then to my handsome boyfriend. "Do you know Dr. Riley?"

"Can't say as I've ever met him, but I've heard of him."

"I thought the entire medical community knew one another. Columbia is not a very big place." I laughed. "Do you have any additional recommendations for Ida?"

"That's where the physician comes in. Together, Dr. Riley and Banning have a plan."

As I considered how best to help Ida, the rest of the short ride passed in silence. We searched the crowded lot and ended up parked on the street one block down.

Thai Fyre was hopping. Even with a reservation we had a ten-minute wait. We sat on the benches in the entry and the racket inside made communication impossible, so I concentrated on Pete's curling brown hair and teasing smile. I scoured the restaurant so it wouldn't look like I was staring, which I was, and almost didn't notice Banning, but his dark hair and wooly face were hard to miss.

I glimpsed him sitting with a pudgy balding man, and, given the intense looks and animated conversation passing between them, I wished I was close enough to hear what they were saying.

The hostess called, "Erickson, party of two." We rose, and I craned my neck around the forest of bodies to catch sight of Banning and his dinner mate and point them out to Pete, but my search was thwarted by the appearance of Susie and Tiny.

I respected her ability to care for patients—Susie was a phenomenal nurse, just sometimes a pain in the neck. During my first six months in Columbia, Nurse Susie Teasdale, nee Kelton, Pete's right hand, saw me as her rival. But when the love of her life returned to claim her, she called a truce. Gregory, better known as Tiny, though he was anything but, wore his trademark red plaid flannel shirt, flared and faded blue jeans, and scuffed cowboy boots. His huge arm rested possessively over Susie's shoulder, silently admonishing, 'Think twice if you mess with my wife because we come as a pair.' She glowed happily.

Susie took my hand and pulled me close. "Looks like you and Pete are enjoying the evening." She winked.

"You, too. How much longer?" Her right hand rested on her round belly and the luminescent smile assured me all was well.

"A little over two months, and this little munchkin will be all over this world."

Over Susie's shoulder, I thought I saw Banning's bald friend heading out, and Susie followed my gaze.

"Riley. What a charlatan. He should've stayed retired."

"Dr. Riley? Is that him?"

"Yes. That's him alright." She shook her head, hard enough to dislodge bad memories. "Two days ago, I had a patient come into the ER. She'd needed a routine physical for work as soon as possible. Everyone but Riley had a waiting list, so she made the appointment. His nurse, if you can call him that ..." She turned up her nose as if she'd smelled something toxic. "Supposedly took down information: weight, height, and vitals. Riley filled out the form without so much as one question asked, took his fee, and wrote her a prescription. Fortunately, she called her primary care physician with a question about the unfamiliar drugs. In the electronic notes, Riley noted she'd been crying, diagnosed her for depression, and gave her Prozac."

She snorted with derision. "The patient had an allergic reaction to dust mites in his office. She had swollen, red, watery eyes from an acute allergy and had trouble breathing. We confiscated the meds, treated her, and gave her instructions on using an epi-pen. Dr. Black almost filed a malpractice suit."

I felt my face scrunch up. *Thank goodness Pete was watching out for Ida too.*

TWELVE

I planned to check on Ida before Sunday Mass, but I had such an interesting, late evening, I overslept and rushed to make it on time myself. Since Ida rarely missed going to church, Dad and I fielded questions from her concerned (a nice way to say nosy) friends, but hadn't had a definitive answer to give them. It would've been better to see her in person rather than speculate, so we skipped the coffee, the doughnuts, and the snooping, and sped home to check on her.

As I drove down the driveway, movement in Ida's front window distracted me and the car veered off the pavement, ricocheting onto a small patch of lawn. Dad made a large production of clenching the overhead grab bar.

"Very funny," I said. I parked and followed Dad's eyes, turning to look over my shoulder. A blindingly red car with magnetic business signs clinging crookedly to the passenger door jerked to a stop behind Banning's van. Redd unfolded her long legs from the compact, and I waved. She traipsed around the side of the house, hauling a small leather satchel.

"Ain't it a be-yoo-tiful morning?" she said, swinging the bag as she twirled in a circle.

Dad hung back, and it dawned on me they hadn't met. "Dad, this is Redd Starr, Ida's piano tuner." I turned to Redd. "This is my dad, Harry Wilk."

He beamed. "Thank goodness you've been able to attend to her instrument. Ida's a bearcat when she can't play her music, and she's ultra-picky about who and what touches her lovely piano." He reached out to her. Redd seemed reticent at first but clasped his hand and pumped up and down, nearly pitching him off balance.

"How's the missus today?"

"We can see for ourselves."

Dad held the door. "After you, my lovely ladies."

Redd snickered and followed me into our kitchen.

"Who's that hunk?" she said, eyeing a photo of Pete and me stuck to the refrigerator door with a magnet in the shape of a Labrador retriever.

Dad answered, "Katie's beau, Dr. Pete Erickson."

I blushed and led Redd to the adjoining door. She cringed as Maverick tried to slip in front of us. I gave him the sign to sit. "No caterwauling, my friend. We've got work to do." I pulled the door closed.

Ida sat on the sofa and watched as Redd plopped down on the piano bench. "Hello, Redd."

Redd answered with a full-keyboard arpeggio, and an easy transition to *Danny Boy*.

"How'd you know my favorite?"

Redd gestured over her shoulder at a framed family tree. "There are a bunch of Donovans and Callahans on that paper hanging there. Sound Irish to me. When did your ancestors make the crossing?"

Ida stared into the past, her visage wistful, probably quietly remembering the story of her ancestors crossing in 1912. "I have *Titanic* casualty blood in me."

Redd dragged a red felt mute and wrench out of the tuning case and finessed a wonky key. "That so, Old Lady."

I stifled a snigger. No one in their right mind would call Ida old with her near enough to hear, but Ida didn't seem bothered. She rocked to her feet and trundled across the floor, settling next to Redd, with her back erect and her eyes closed. Her curved fingers hovered over the keys, but before she and Redd could strike up another animated duo, Banning pounded down the steps. "What do you think you're doing, Ida? You shouldn't be up." He glared at me. "No music today. Her stats aren't quite as good as yesterday."

Banning guided Ida back to the couch. "Let me rub this lotion into your hands." He pulled on nitrile gloves and squeezed a dab of cream onto his fingertips. "My technique is used to improve dexterity, and it'll make it easier for you when you are well enough to play." When her hands soaked up the lotion, he snapped off the gloves. "You stay here while I get your meds. I'll be right back." He patted her shoulder and disappeared into the kitchen.

Ida's eyes glistened, and she cleared her throat, attempting to talk, but struggled to string the right words together.

Redd pushed away from the piano. "I'll get you something to drink, Missus." She dashed to the kitchen and returned with a full glass of water. Ida's hands trembled as she accepted the drink, and water sloshed over the edge.

She secured the glass with a two-handed grip and brought it to her lips. After a few big swallows, Ida indicated she'd finished. Redd took the glass from her and placed it on the coffee table. On Redd's way back to the piano, she passed me, pointed to Ida's kitchen, and muttered, "Him and me? We don't see eye to eye."

Banning brought another glass of water and several capsules for Ida to down. She did as she was told and collapsed onto the sofa.

Banning checked his watch. "I need to visit my other clients, but please call if anything comes up or if you have any questions. Are you okay with me leaving, Ida?"

She nodded. "I'm just slowing down. I'll be fine."

"As long as you are stable, I'll be back the day after tomorrow and, if it's satisfactory, every other day thereafter."

She nodded. Her heavy eyelids fluttered closed.

Banning whispered to me, "She needs quiet. Don't let her get riled up or overdo it. And don't stay too long." He packed up his belongings and handed me a business card. "If you need me."

As soon as the door closed, Ida peeled open one eye. "Is he gone?"

I looked at her in disbelief.

Redd said, "Yup. Are we playing or what, Missus?"

"Just for a bit. My music makes me feel as good as when I finish a painting or make a savory Irish stew." Ida struggled, but I grabbed her arm and wrapped it around mine, towing her to standing.

"Piano bench," she said. "I can't hurt anything practicing, and I won't exert myself. I promise. I'll play just until I need a nap."

She waddled across the short span. "I'm not feeling as well as yesterday, but I want to do what I can to help my mind work better. I probably won't do much in the way of exercise today, but I'll read later and do some puzzles." She caught her foot on the nape of the carpet and almost tumbled, but righted herself, clenching my arm. She reached out and gently caressed the lid on the piano.

Ida had a few false starts but eventually she and Redd serenaded me with beautiful duets for twenty minutes before Ida's eyelids began to droop. Ida rubbed her eyes. "Playing piano is exhausting."

"Time for me to head out anyway, Missus," Redd said, wrapping up and securing her tools. "You wanna play again tomorrow? I don't have any tunings scheduled."

"Please," my dear friend said. "Let's plan for two o'clock."

"Can I help you get her up the stairs?" Redd asked, worry etched on her face.

Ida answered, "I don't want to get stuck upstairs, thank you. I have comfortable furniture, my water, my phone—"

"We'll bring food."

"Everything is close then. And I'm comfortable. I'll stay right here."

Redd nodded. "Katie, I want to say goodbye to your dad." Her eyes gleamed, and she whispered. "I'm going through the secret entrance." Redd vanished through the door between the apartments, and Maverick slipped by her to take his place next to Ida.

"Isn't she a card? I so enjoy our music." Ida yawned, scratching Maverick's ears. "Go on now. I'm going to take a nap."

I pulled the soft quilt up to her chin. "We're home all

day today, Ida. Call if you need anything. In fact, I'll leave the door open. We'll be listening for you, and if you so much as sneeze, one of us will come running."

She nodded, but her eyes had slammed shut. I had to peel Maverick away with the murmured promise of a stinky treat.

Redd and Dad sat at the kitchen table, having a pleasant conversation. When she saw me, she gave Dad one final word, and stood.

She took a discerning look at my dog. "Later, 'gator," she said and flapped her hand in a wave, lugging her tool bag behind her and marching out the door.

Dad stared off into the distance.

"What's wrong?" I asked.

"I'm beginning to think Ida may be right to worry."

THIRTEEN

Although sitting front and center, I didn't track much of our mock trial preparation on Monday and Tuesday, worrying about Ida, until the words exchanged took on a fierce edge.

"You're so righteous and serious," Allie said.

"This *is* serious. Lawyers can't be frivolous like actors, *ladling* it on thick with no thought to the consequence." Lorelei placed her hands on the desktop and leaned forward.

"Frivolous? You think dressing up like a British sailor with a chip on his shoulder and acting like he did everything he could while watching almost fifteen hundred people die is frivolous?"

"Hey guys, you've been working hard, maybe too hard." A text dinged on my phone. "We're finished for today and no practice tomorrow. Okay?"

I read the text as they trudged through the doorway.

Look what sisla says now.

Ellen forwarded an email containing information about the genetic matching process, but the questions Sister Lawrence asked sent up red flags. She fished for information about Ellen's childhood, her foster care and adoptive parents, and her life now. I couldn't quite wrap my head around her venture either.

Over an early dinner of seared green beans, juicy meatloaf, and a triple-tiered cream cheese frosted cake, Dad caught me up.

"Banning came by today, but it's a good thing he and Redd visit on alternate days. Avoiding each other will stave off a clash I feel coming. They have no tolerance for each other." He slurped his coffee, set it in front of him, and stared deep into the dark liquid. "Ida's the same today as yesterday. For a little while, she seems like her old self and then she withdraws. She remembers the day you moved in and then looks at me as if I'm from outer space. She's depressed one minute and elated the next, the hold on her recollections ebbing and flowing throughout the day."

I cleared the dinner dishes—my job because Dad provided the sustenance—and stacked them in the dishwasher. The cake begged to be eaten so I picked up the knife. Lovely music floating through the walls accompanied my actions, a culinary choreography.

"It's a Bach prelude. She plays it every day to assure herself she's still here." Dad tapped the side of his head. "Unfortunately, if she forgets, it will be only you and me who'll realize the loss."

I pinched the sticky frosting off the end of the knife so I could make a second clean cut, but one taste of the delicious cake and my questions about Ida went off the rails. "When did you start to bake, Dad?"

"Not me. During Ida's more lucid moments this morning, she baked. In fact, she put together the entire meal."

"Whatever she's doing must be working." I sliced the airy confection in front of me, sliding one large piece onto a glass plate and reached for the second when we heard a bang. Dad's eyes flashed open. It sounded like Ida slammed the piano cover again.

He took a deep breath. "I wish we could help."

"She's been doing everything on Banning's list, right?"

Dad shrugged noncommittally and looked at the clock. "Why don't you go check on her? I promised her leftovers, and you can ask if she wants to play a game." A wily smile cracked the solemn look on Dad's face. "Let's try Scrabble again."

I headed toward our adjoining door and rapped quickly, waited a beat, and turned the knob. Thinking the mechanism had jammed, I tried again. And again.

"Dad, it's locked." Maverick, roused from his spot on the carpet, woofed.

"It can't be. When Ida gave me the meatloaf and cake this afternoon, I promised she'd get leftovers, and I didn't lock it. Why would she?"

I tried again. Dad tried. He pounded on the door hard enough to rattle the windows.

"Do we have a key?" he asked.

"I don't know. It's never been locked before." In the catch-all drawer in the cupboard by the back door I found old receipts and grocery lists. I rooted among pencils, pens, paper clips, markers, and scissors for the ring of keys she gave me months ago. "I know they're in here if I have them," I said before lifting the clinking keys in triumph.

I handed the ring to Dad. He rapped on the door again and said loudly, "Ida, we're coming in," before trying the first unsuccessful key in the lock. When the third key turned, he edged the door open slowly. "In case she needs privacy," he said in an apologetic voice.

Maverick didn't have those qualms. He bolted through the narrow entrance Dad had made and dashed into the kitchen. We followed.

"Ida, where are you?" We stopped to listen and heard humming. Peeking around the corner we located the melody coming from under a pile of quilts on the couch. With the exception of the pale arm jutting out, Ida resembled a heap of fabric.

Fearing the worst, we hovered in the doorway. Maverick wriggled his nose beneath her hand, begging for a scratch. Ida acquiesced, still humming. It took a moment for me to recognize *How Much Is That Doggie in the Window*, and I released the breath I'd held. She was alive and knew Maverick.

I knelt on the floor next to her, gently shaking her shoulder. "Ida? Dad has supper. Are you up for it?"

Movement stopped as did the humming. "What did he make?"

Dad snickered and said, "Meatloaf and green beans, your work, remember?"

"Maybe." The bundle of coverings slid to the floor. She rocked to sitting but required a hand to rise. "I'm starved. No more salad for me today. Katie, will you grab my pills while I make another quick trip to the little girl's room?"

I hefted the bottle in my hand. It felt heavier than when we picked it up from the pharmacy. I tucked it into my back pocket as Ida clutched my elbow, and we trundled to the table, cleared and reset for one.

"You ate without me?" My face reddened with a pang of embarrassment, and she dug her bony fingers into my arm. "Just kidding, but I'm starting with the red velvet cake."

We set up the game next to her, and she wolfed down her food, cake first.

"You don't need to rush."

She mumbled an affirmative I think, gulped her water, and said, "I want to make things happen while I can. It seems like my mind and body come and go at different speeds and right now they're together."

Ida froze when her doorbell rang, and she had a deer-in-the-headlights look about her.

"Stay here with Dad. I'll get it."

"I don't want anyone to see me," Ida said.

Maverick pranced to the door, dutifully sat, and barked.

I peeked through the window at the side. Redd startled me peering in at the same time. Eye to eye, I couldn't very well not answer the door. I hooked Maverick's collar and turned the knob.

"Hey, Redd. What's up?"

She barreled past Maverick and me, scanned the living room, and stomped through the kitchen.

Dad and Ida had just finished straightening the Scrabble tiles when Redd stormed in and dropped onto a chair.

"Hey, Missus. I know today isn't my day to visit, but I stopped by earlier to see if I could do anything for you and ran into Banning. I caught that guy fiddling with your pills."

FOURTEEN

I think that's part of his job," said Dad. He grinned and added 'quixo' to Ida's 'try,' and she groaned. We should have given up when he placed the tiles to spell 'quixotry.'

"Banning's been most patient and supportive," Ida grumbled. "I know you're just trying to help, but you don't know what you're talking about."

Although often opinionated, Ida was unusually curt. Redd fidgeted. "He tried to hide what he was doing. I think you should get the meds tested."

"Why would I do that and jeopardize my relationship with a genuine caregiver when I need one?" She inhaled sharply. "I wouldn't know how to get the meds checked anyway."

Redd sat back in the chair. "Duh. Talk to the doctor hottie." She used her chin to point to Pete's photo on the fridge. "It wouldn't take much." She leaned forward and caught me in her laser glare. "Couldn't you just take one pill somewhere? I'd sure feel better if I knew that guy was on the up and up."

"Actually, so would I." I checked for the bottle in my back pocket.

"Listen, I really like you, Missus, and I've worked with a lot of old ladies. But you're different."

I almost laughed. That she was.

"Your ups and downs are driving me crazy."

Me too.

"Your ideas bubble to the surface like the colorful blob in a lava lamp, joining up with more until sinking to the underworld. Your memory is like a steel trap and then a flap opens and washes everything out to sea at weird times. Have you checked out your symptoms?"

Dad referred to his phone, scrolling up and down. "Ida, you do have a few unusual, noteworthy indicators: lacking motivation, mood swings, and persistent confusion. It says here they can be evidence of dementia but also multiple other maladies. You trust Pete, don't you? It can't hurt, can it?"

"What if Banning finds out and thinks I don't trust him."

Redd mumbled, "I wouldn't."

Bewilderment crossed Ida's features.

Redd sat up straight. "Missus, it's hard for you to read the sheet music after twenty minutes of playing. And then you get jittery and angry. You could say manic."

"Banning says he's managing your memory issues with conventional methods," Dad paused, deliberating. "But this list suggests other treatments that effect retention. Maybe Banning would be willing to look at them."

Redd huffed.

Dad placed his hand over Ida's. "You've appreciated

what he's done, but maybe he doesn't have the latest and greatest knowledge he needs to treat a one-in-a-million Ida Clemashevski."

"Let's call Pete." I started to panic. Why didn't we get a second opinion? What had we missed? My heart thudded. What if we were too late? How could we have been so careless?

In a very small voice Ida added, "And Lance. They'll know what to do."

The ex-chief of police and his emergency room doctor son would most certainly know what to do.

Redd rose and exhaled. "My work here is done." She aimed for the door but looked over her shoulder. "Missus, I'll be back tomorrow, and I expect you to be on top of your game. We're gonna finish that song." And she was gone.

My head spun. I couldn't imagine what it felt like for Ida. Fortunately, Pete's dad had wanted to visit Ida too. We invited them under the guise of taste testing Ida's cake, and for me to see Pete, of course.

When the last morsel of dessert had disappeared, I determinedly set the pill bottle in the middle of the table. Dad explained our concern and the need to make certain she had the correct prescription.

Pete patted Ida's hand and said gently, "You know it can take a while for a medication to produce the intended results." Ida nodded insecurely. He read the label on the prescription bottle. "We'll check it out. Speaking of which, did you ever get in to see your primary care physician?"

"I have my follow-up appointment scheduled for next week."

"Dr. Matt Lannie is on call in the hospital pharmacy

tonight. When it's slow, he's always up for an enigma. I'll have him check this out. It'll make us all feel better, and I'll touch base as soon as he has something to tell you."

Lance Erickson and I helped Ida trundle to her living room. She dropped onto the couch and closed her eyes. He settled himself in the wingback chair across from his dozing friend, his face a mask of concern. They'd become acquainted during Ida's first-year teaching in Columbia, and until they lost their respective spouses, Christa and Lance and Ida and Casimer spent time together cooking, dining, playing games, sharing life, and creating memories. Aside from letting his hair grow longer, he looked the same as when I'd met him in September over our first body. Then, he barely tolerated my interference—his words, but we'd worked together a few times, and both loved his son. Now he smiled at me. He brushed at his draping mustache and tilted his white head back against the blue crushed velvet. His eyes closed. I tiptoed out, allowing them peace.

Waiting gave rise to tension, but as Ida taught us, cooking provided temporary relief. Dad followed her instructions to the letter, and though he still charred plain grilled cheese, he never screwed up Ida's tasty long-cooking recipes. He pulled out a big pot, and cut up tomatoes, onions, parsley, and garlic, poured in broth, and stood stirring the sauce. I added the first cup of red wine to the pot and filled two glasses.

When Pete returned an hour later, the indignant look on his face justified our deviousness. "How long has she been taking these?"

"We picked up this prescription last week, but Ida said Banning started supplements when she was with her cousin. She complained of fatigue and forgetfulness, and he provided some natural, holistic concoctions known to boost brain power."

"This pill has twice the dose it's supposed to have. Taking too many might not kill anyone, but can cause symptoms mimicking those of a patient with memory issues. It could happen accidently, but I called Amanda, and she ran prints Matt located on the plastic capsule. Rache is not his real name. He's—"

The floor creaked behind us. Lance Erickson's strong arm held Ida upright. "Who is he, Pete?" she asked in her schoolmarm voice.

Caught like a boy with his hand in the cookie jar, Pete glanced at me and back at this dad. He tilted his head and with a quizzical expression said, "His name is Gerhard Weber."

Ida gasped, turned white, and sank against Lance. "It can't be. I thought they put Weber away for good."

Lance let loose an uncharacteristic blue streak.

Maverick yapped and I turned my attention in his direction. He sat in front of Ida. His neck stretched, his nose pointed to the ceiling, and his black ears flapped with each warning bark. Ida's face had taken on a tinge of yellow. She blinked rapidly and pointed into the dining room. "Casimer, I've missed you." She stiffened, and her head flew back. Her arms flailed and jerked at her sides. Frothy saliva bubbled from the corner of her mouth. Her knees gave out.

Pete caught her before she hit the ground, calmly diagnosing her condition. "She's hallucinating and seizing." He cradled a trembling Ida like a child and uttered encouraging words.

"I'll call 911," said Lance.

Ida gripped Lance's arm. "Wait." After a few heart-stopping moments, she wiped her lips with the back of her hand. "Stop fussing and let me sit up." She slurred the last words. She pulled in her legs and attempted to stand.

"Stay right where you are," said Pete, holding her in place. "We need to know precisely what's going on."

Lance added, "And that's an order."

Dad smiled reassuringly. "Doctor knows best."

After Pete checked her out, he and Lance led her to the table and, with tenderness that made me sigh, guided her to the chair Dad pulled out. I thought twice and filled a tumbler with two fingers of bourbon. Pete calmly replaced the glass with a tumbler of water. Ida gulped the contents.

"Weber's gained weight and has longer hair, a beard, and glasses." Ida looked up in bewilderment. "He looks so different."

"It's been almost forty years, old friend," said Lance.

Ida thumped his elbow. "Who're you calling old?" Ida's feisty self peeked through.

"Who is he, Dad?" Pete asked.

"Do you remember when Grace was murdered …" I shuddered and Lance continued. "A story broke, claiming Ida had been accused of murder before?"

My throat tightened and breathing became more difficult.

"I discovered the identity of the murdered victim's boyfriend—Weber." He gave Ida an introspective look. "Ida helped me perpetrate a sting. She hit on Weber in the airport bar and got him drunk enough to brag he got rid of his ex." He screwed up his face. "As they led him out of the courtroom, Weber said we'd get our just due."

Ida trembled. "He's come back."

"But we're ready for him, Ida," said Lance. He pulled out his phone, punched in some numbers, and stepped away from the table.

"It isn't all in my head. It's in the medication?" She gulped, and I squeezed her shoulder.

"It appears so. I'll get you in to be checked out by your regular physician, not that quack Riley. Matt says many of your symptoms can be attributed to the drug and he'll need to inspect the supplements too." Pete gently laid his hand on her arm.

She quaked and pounded two fists on the table. "I'm so angry." The fire in her eyes almost matched her hair. "He's had full access to everything."

FIFTEEN

I've never secured my passwords. They are all in a notebook in the desk drawer under my laptop. I thought if I began to fail, someone would be able to use my resources, but I don't know if Weber found them."

"Contact any financial institution where you might be vulnerable. Tell them what happened. Check your balances," said Lance.

"I recently consolidated my retirement accounts. That could be good or bad." Overwhelming fear replaced the fire in Ida's eyes.

Pete broke up the staring contest she had with her phone screen. He gave her shoulders a reassuring squeeze. "Ida, start with your bank and retirement accounts, and your most often used credit cards."

She blinked rapidly and nodded.

"I'll help." I refilled her glass of water, and shepherded her to the office where she retrieved the notebook.

Sitting at her desk she punched in numbers and begged

to speak with human representatives who transferred her calls to the fraud departments. After identifying herself and answering the extra layer of security questions, she directed me to dig in the filing cabinet and locate statements she could use for comparison. She ascertained she had preempted all unlawful use of the data, but a one hundred dollar bankcard withdrawal. After changing the passwords, her burst of energy waned. Her head dropped onto her hands, and she rubbed the back of her head. "How could I have been so blind?"

"It can happen to anyone," said Pete. "Do we have any idea where he's living? They could pick him up for questioning."

She closed her eyes and sighed. "No idea."

"Amanda will be searching for him, but we'll be ready when he comes tomorrow."

As if a light went on, Ida groaned. "He won't be here. He's said he's taking a class. Do you think Compassionate Care might know where he is?"

Lance's voice rose. After a few terse words, Lance clamped his jaw and shook his head. He mimed writing and Ida provided a pen and notepad. He turned away from us and furiously scribbled for what seemed like forever. He clicked off, took a moment, and let his head drop back. He gathered his notes and marched next to Ida. "I explained the situation to Chief West. She didn't find a background check nor a Columbia address for Rache or Weber in her system. Amanda is going to contact the prison and get whatever information they have on him. She'll have a car patrolling this neighborhood, but she was wondering how you felt about undercover work for a second time. Act normally." He eyed his friend. "Well, you just be you, but you don't have to, you know."

"If you're in Lance, I'm in," Ida said quickly.

"I'm in," he said and laid out Amanda's plan which would require a bit of groundwork.

When Lance finished, Ida searched his face. "Why weren't we notified of his release? I thought that was always done for anyone threatened by a convict."

Lance put his hand on her shoulder, dropped to one knee, and looked into her eyes. "I would imagine this is a relatively new development. He's been out for only a few weeks. Granted, they didn't look very hard, but you changed your name when you married Casimer, who has also since passed away. I've been the chief of police here until recently, and the department is still collecting messages for me. It might not have looked exigent, probably one notification among many."

"What can we do?" asked Dad. "That guy has wormed his way too far into our lives and I, for one, would like to take him out."

Lance said, "The most important part of our plan is to look casual, keep to a normal routine, and not give away what we know. We want to make sure we catch him committing a crime and send him back to prison. So far, since he was a nurse and he retained certification by taking courses while behind bars—"

"He could do that?" Ida shook her head in disbelief.

"Yes. He can claim someone else doctored the pills, and he was just doing what he was told to aid a dear, respected friend, one who set him on the right path so many years ago."

"There's no dear about it," Ida bristled. She plodded back to her spirited self.

Lance rose. "Ida, I'm your new roommate."

Ida wriggled forward and stood on wobbly legs. She jutted out her chin. "I don't need—" She faltered.

Lance stood next to her, ignoring her misstep, and lowered her back into the chair. "I need to know we have all our bases covered. Pete can bring some clothes and toiletries by, but I'm not leaving your side until Weber is under lock and key. I won't let him have another chance to do anything, Ida." His old chief of police persona came through like gangbusters and gave us the confidence to accommodate the plan Chief West wanted set into motion.

"What's Riley's part in this charade?" I asked.

"He may be the scapegoat, or he may be the lynchpin for all I know. Any way you look at it, he'll not be practicing in Columbia again," said Lance.

Pete squatted next to Ida and examined her bright green eyes. "Ida, promise me you won't take any medications or supplements at all until you see Dr. Cline, and we get this cleared up."

"Promise." She crossed her heart and held up three fingers. "Easy." She covered a yawn.

"Let's get you to bed," Lance said innocently.

One eyebrow rose, and she attempted a tentative smile.

"Singular. You. Alone." Lance said, turning crimson.

Lance and Ida retired to her apartment. Dad said goodnight. Maverick and I walked Pete to the door. Pete dragged his feet.

"This guy could be dangerous. I don't want to leave you here, unprotected."

"He's not after me. Your dad and Amanda will keep Ida safe until we can put this guy away. And Dad's here. I won't get into trouble."

An eyebrow rose over one disbelieving eye, and I smiled. He wrapped me in a tight hug, and this time Maverick did not try to wriggle between us. "Do everything you normally do. Don't draw undue attention to yourself. Don't go anywhere alone. He might be observing Ida instead of taking that class. We can't believe anything he's said. Dad will stay with Ida, and Amanda is having her watched. We just have to make it until we can draw him out and nail him."

I stepped back. "Redd is stopping by tomorrow at two to play piano with Ida. Do you think that's okay?"

"As long as it was already in the works, Ida should continue with any scheduled activity in case Banning, I mean Weber, overheard her. Dad and Amanda have a good plan, and we don't want him to disappear." He tipped my chin up and kissed me lightly. My heartrate picked up speed, and I almost missed his admonition. "Don't do anything to get Weber's guard up. I'll stop by in the morning. It might look suspicious if I come back this evening. 'Night, Katie. Be careful."

I closed the door behind him, sank against it, and slid down next to Maverick with a sappy grin on my face. "'Night, handsome."

SIXTEEN

Maverick met the knock on the door at five forty-five the next morning with one soft howl and snuffled along the bottom of the door until Dad reached out and hauled Pete through the entry. The five of us gave a quiet greeting, and he handed off a small duffle to Lance. His dark eyes filled with concern, but he didn't want to get caught doing anything out of the ordinary, so he gave me a very satisfactory hug to start my day and tramped to his truck.

Dad accompanied me on Maverick's short morning constitutional, constantly shushing me because every word on my lips was part of a question I couldn't ask and keep my composure intact. Actually seeing the patrol car guarding Ida would have set my mind at ease, but that didn't happen either.

The clock ticked down to my regular departure time, though my thoughts filled with the possible dangers Ida and Lance faced.

I stuck my head into Ida's apartment and called in a lighthearted voice, "Be safe today." I didn't get a response. Gripped with fear of the horrible images my mind conjured up, I crept in and searched, finding Ida and Lance engrossed in a cribbage game on the dining room table, oblivious to my presence.

"Be safe today," I repeated and received mumbled replies.

I sleepwalked through the day, teaching lessons, correcting problems, assigning new homework, waiting for bad news, and temporarily relaxed at the end of the day when Jane came by to review costumes for our mock trial team.

"Ashley Johannes did a good job studying the fashion of 1912. The kids could wear these great old pieces and get into their roles without donning an entire costume."

Allie played our best Reginald Lee, and Ashley scoured Goodwill and rescued a cute cap and cropped, navy-blue wool jacket, resembling a sailor's pea coat, for her. She also found slightly longer, double-breasted men's suitcoats to let the boys indulge in the *Titanic* fantasy—white for Captain Rostron, blue for Second Officer Lightoller, and brown for the military attaché. Whoever played our widow, Maggie Murphy, could wear a softly flowing mid-calf shirt dress cut from blue muslin, sporting a white Peter Pan collar. And for our Molly Brown, Ashley discovered a maroon satin jacket and white shirt adorned with ruffles and lace. The pieces looked vintage but weren't.

Our attorneys polished their shoes and wore business attire to look and play their professional parts realistically, elevating their game.

Jane had so much fun talking about their apparel, the

entertaining diversion helped me forget about the peril facing Ida. Jane helped me return the costume carton to my closet. "How did your day go?"

It all came flooding back and I dropped onto the nearest desktop, spilling the information and mixing it all up. "Oh, Jane. I'm a wreck. There's a wacko after Ida, so Lance is living with her until he's caught. She hired a nurse to help her out, but her caregiver gave her meds to induce memory loss instead, simulating dementia. Amanda has a police car patrolling the neighborhood even though I've never seen it. Ida and Lance are pretending they don't know who he is in order to catch him doing something illegal to put him away again. I don't think they've captured him yet, or Dad would have called. And I'm sure I'll screw it up and get someone hurt. I'm a horrible actress."

Her brown eyes grew to the size of half dollars. "Start over, girlfriend."

When I finished the retelling, Jane dropped onto a desk next to me and threw her arm over my shoulder. "You had a busy yesterday. And you didn't mention Ellen once."

My head fell to my chest. "She's still working the lead on our mother."

She pulled me into an embrace. "Katie." Then she held me at arm's length and looked into my eyes. I tried to portray satisfaction, but it didn't work. "What's wrong? Aren't you curious?"

"My mother left us and never looked back. I'm afraid."

She pulled me close. "There's a reason for everything. I know you, Katie. Your mother's another puzzle for you to decode and you will. Give yourself peace of mind and room to breathe, and you'll know what to do."

She gave me a gentle shove, and I couldn't help but

smile. "I want to know what happened. I'd love to be part of her life, but Ellen's initial meeting is slated for April 14. I can't attend because of our mock trial meet, and to be honest, I don't want to. I don't want to hear she hasn't room in her busy life for us."

"Ellen is all gung ho. Let her do the leg work and when they're ready for you, you'll be ready for them. And since it's so normal for me to come over to your apartment, I'd better make an appearance." She hopped off the desk. "Ready?"

I mirrored her actions. "Yes. Can you stay for supper?"

She nodded slowly. "I don't suppose Ida's cooking, but as long as you're not doing the honors, I'm all in."

"I take it Drew's back on the job, and you don't want to eat alone."

"Maybe, or maybe I want to be in on the action."

She followed me home and stayed for the supper Lance helped prepare. We devoured juicy barbecue pork chops, Dad's take on a deconstructed Caesar salad, and a cheesy broccoli casserole, laughing, talking about the Redd and Ida piano practice, and acting as if nothing were amiss.

But I stabbed the lettuce leaves with a death grip on my fork.

Dad gnawed on his lower lip, and said, "Katie, lighten up. You're going to give away the plan. Trust Lance and Amanda."

* * *

After a fitful night of sleep, I peeled my eyelids open with just enough time to walk Maverick before spending a day in front of my classes teaching on auto pilot. I have a few students who would've liked nothing better than to call me out for behaving oddly, so I must've done a fair job, but acting normal wiped me out. I prepared to leave and closed the snaps on my briefcase when Jane entered the math office with our mock trial team in tow.

"Ms. Wilk, Lorelei has something she wants to say." Jane took Lorelei by the shoulders and marched her to the front of the group. "Go on," she urged.

Lorelei inhaled, and her words flew out on the exhale. "We're sorry we've all been so crotchety."

Someone in back blew a raspberry and repeated, "Crotchety."

She ignored the interruption and said quickly. "Chalk it up to nerves and inexperience, but the competition is fierce, and the meet is coming up quickly. I know you called off the practices this week to let us calm down, but if it's okay with you, we'd like to have a rehearsal now—just a run through. Our section opposition has been unbeatable, and we'd like to give them a run for their money." She finally took a deep breath. "We don't need to use the costumes or anything."

Jane inclined her head, and I could see in her eyes what she wanted me to say. "Of course."

For the next hour the kids presented winning cases as both plaintiff and defendant, and I lost myself in their presentation. If another team beat them, I'd bow to the superior ability.

"Monday is my day to tutor AP Calc exam takers, so our final formal meeting is tomorrow after school. We'll have information and assignment sheets. It'll be a very short meeting," I said as we reorganized my classroom. "You are ready."

When they cleared out of the department, Jane exited with me. "Anything new on the home front?"

"I was hoping to hear they'd caught Banning, or whatever his name is, and Ida was safe, but nothing yet." I flipped off the lights and accompanied Jane out the door. "How's Drew?"

"They've narrowed down the why and what but need to determine the who. He believes the thief has left the area or caught wind of the investigation. Drew will soon be on his way home … until the next case." Jane beamed.

SEVENTEEN

When I turned the last corner onto Maple Street, my heart jumped in my chest. Vehicles lined both sides of the road and patrol cars filled our driveway. Uniformed officers crawled all over Ida's lovely property. As I drove closer, my pulse raced, and my mind gyrated, imagining all types of bad outcomes: Ida sicker, Lance or Dad hurt, Weber holding hostages or trapping a snarling Maverick in his kennel.

I jammed my Focus into park at the first open space I came across and slammed the car door upon exiting. Afraid of what I might find, my stomach clenched as I wended my way across the yard and came face-to-face with a rigid, steely-eyed police officer guarding my back door.

His face hardened. "What do you want?" He rested his hand on the butt of a gun at his waist.

"My name is Katie Wilk." Chills ran up my arms, and my voice sounded hoarse. I cleared my throat. "I live here." He didn't budge. "With my dad, Harry Wilk." No recognition. "Ida's my landlady." The policeman stood his ground.

Amanda West stepped onto Ida's front stoop. She hooked her thumbs on her belt, stretched, and breathed deeply, lifting her clear, dark complexion to the sky, drinking in what remained of the daylight.

"Amanda. Chief West," I called, craning my neck so she might determine where the voice originated. The unmoving officer followed the exchange. I raised both arms, crisscrossing them over my head, and when she spotted me, she waved me through. As I trotted past, I caught a hint of amusement from the officer.

"What's happened? Where's Banning? Did you get him?" I marched across the yard, bracing for bad news. "Are Dad and Ida okay?"

Amanda indulged me with a small smile and inclined her head, indicating I should follow her. She flipped the long dark braid back over her shoulder as we trudged up the entrance steps. I glanced behind me and saw CJ and Danica across the street. CJ nodded slowly, and I knew he'd been asked to keep an eye out too. Not only were they good neighbors, CJ's Navy SEAL training also gave him skills none of us could claim. The door to Ida's home opened, and we paraded inside.

Dad angled against one wall, worrying the carpet with the toe of his tasseled shoes. His eyes met mine and held me in safety. Ida paced back and forth across the living room. Her perfectly coiffed red hair pulled a smile from me. She wore makeup—rosy cheeks, mascara, eye shadow, and lipstick—and looked much more like herself. Lance settled his long frame in the wingback chair, twirling the ends of his thick moustache, tidying his head of mussed stark-white hair.

Maverick bustled next to me, wagging a thick tail with such ferocity, his whole body shook. My overzealous dog dropped in front of me and rolled onto his back. I knelt and rubbed his belly, waiting for an explanation.

"At nine o'clock this morning we found the blue panel van Rache, or rather Weber, has been using. The vehicle is registered to Columbia Home Health Care. We kept it under surveillance, but he must have caught on. He's missing," Amanda said. "Patrols are on the lookout, but I don't think he'll return. And although we didn't catch him in the act, he'll have to answer to his parole officer for leaving the jurisdiction and for certain items we found in the vehicle."

Lance cleared his throat. "Ida's slowly bringing her old self back around. She's always been one tough nut to crack."

"I'm right here. I can hear you. Don't think I'm cooking dinner for you, Lance Erickson."

"Wouldn't dream of it."

I could hear the sass in her voice returning, and my stomach relaxed, but only a bit. The man who had threatened Lance and Ida so many years ago was still out there, holding a grudge. And I could do nothing.

"We'll keep an eye out, of course, but you'll have to take precautions and stay vigilant, Ida. We don't know what Weber's ulterior motives are. You'll have to be careful."

Ida stamped her foot. "I will not be held prisoner. I've done nothing wrong." She glowered at Amanda.

An energetic voice called through the door to our apartment and broke the intense gaze between them. "Hey, where is everybody? What's going on?"

Ellen waltzed into Ida's living room, slipped out of her jacket, and scanned the faces, coming to an abrupt stop when she saw Amanda. Her eyes widened.

Amanda's eyes did the opposite, narrowing into slits. "Ellen, how did you manage to get past the officer covering the door."

"I waited until he twisted around to observe the crowd then walked right in, like I belonged here." She dropped her chin and mumbled, "I might have let him think I was Katie." I bristled. Her head snapped up and the petulance in her voice chafed. "I'm sorry. I didn't know what else to do. No one answered my texts."

Dad removed his phone from his inside pocket, opened it, and shook his head. Amanda dropped her jaw. Ida laughed. Maverick curled up on the rug in front of the fireplace. I stopped my eyes from rolling. Ellen knew I probably might not have answered if I *had* seen a message from her. My lids crashed together, and I imagined the quagmire created if I'd had the gumption to try to walk past the officer.

"What's with all the cops?" Ellen hung her coat over the back of a chair.

We gave Amanda the floor. "We were trying to catch Banning, whose real name is Gerhard Weber. It seems he's held a grudge against Ida—"

"And Lance," Ida said. "Don't forget Lance."

Another voice joined the throng. "Yes, let's not forget Lance." Ida lit up like a neon sign. Pete strode to my side and draped an arm over my shoulder. He grinned and planted a kiss on my forehead. The welcome presence of tall, dark, and handsome eased the rest of my frazzling nerves, and I breathed more easily.

Amanda rolled her shoulders, jettisoning another round of disbelief. "And how did you get past my officers?"

Pete didn't even look guilty. "Ambrose, Officer Wallace and I go back to kindergarten, and he worked with Dad for ... What was it, Dad? Seven or eight years? In addition, I'm often on site in the event of a death."

Lance considered and nodded. "Good man, Wallace."

"No one died here. You skated this time, Dr. Erickson, but next time follow protocol." Amanda pointed at Pete. "Call my office."

Ellen's persistent voice grated. "Why did Weber hold a grudge against Ida and ..." Her face flushed. "Pete's dad?"

Movement stopped and all eyes centered on Amanda. "Ida loved to act and—"

"Still do," Ida interjected. She nabbed a tube of lotion and squeezed a small amount in her palm, smoothing the white cream over her hands.

Amanda's glare silenced her, and she continued. "In an unsanctioned undercover investigation, Ida, the attorney who would become her future husband, Casimer Clemashevski, and a rookie cop by the name of Lance Erickson ..." Amanda tilted her head at the person named. "... found evidence to incarcerate Weber."

"What was he in for?" she asked.

Ellen cringed hearing the same word amplified by five different voices simultaneously. "Murder."

EIGHTEEN

"Banning? I mean, Weber? He doesn't look like a murderer." Ellen's face puckered. "I just saw him strolling through the dog park."

Amanda's laser sharp dark eyes drilled into Ellen. It felt like time stopped in the vacuum created when she flew out the front door speaking into the radio on her lapel with what sounded like an alert.

Commotion returned with a whoosh. Doors slammed. Excited voices punctuated the drone of the engines. The street in front of the house cleared. I hoped the one car remaining in our driveway indicated Amanda's orders included someone would continue to guard Ida. She wasn't out of the woods yet.

The uncertainty and tension showed on Ida's pinched face. She swayed. Fearful of a repeat of her earlier collapse and with a nod from his son, Lance made a quiet call.

Minutes later, the pulsing whine of an ambulance reached its peak and stopped in front of Ida's. Dad held the door open for the three EMTs who rushed in and diligently obeyed concise orders from Pete. They took vitals, secured Ida to a gurney, and whisked a mildly protesting bundle of subdued energy to her waiting transport.

Pete prepared to follow the ambulance, and a horrible thought occurred to me. "What do we do about the physician who wrote Ida's prescription, Dr. Riley?"

I'd never witnessed the fiery flare of anger in Pete's eyes, and I wouldn't ever want to be on its receiving end. It could have melted titanium. "We'll find him and see to it he never practices in Columbia again," he said through gritted teeth. "Or anywhere else." He whipped out his phone and the staccato of his clipped words followed him out the door.

The rest of us stared at each other, unsure of our next move.

Dad broke the stalemate. "Chief, where do you think Weber will go next?"

After a thoughtful pause, Lance said, "He's had forty years to fulminate. He won't give up easily. I can't imagine him leaving the area."

"You're on his list too."

"That I am, but now I'm prepared."

Thoughts covered the room like a heavy blanket. Dad disappeared into our apartment. Lance lowered himself into his favorite chair, relaxing his hands on the armrests. He stretched his long legs and crossed his ankles before letting his head drop back and his eyes close. Dad returned to the living room in measured steps, delivering a tray with glasses of ice water. Maverick flopped onto the hearth rug. I crawled next to him, plunging my toes under his torso. He arched closer when I rubbed behind his ear. Maverick almost purred.

An unusually timid voice crept into the church-like quiet. "Katie, I have news. Can we talk?"

My shoulders crawled. "Not right now, Ellen."

"Okay. Later."

Having her settle next to me, I felt the heat of ... What? Embarrassment? *Why was I being unreasonable?* I could've sworn Maverick raised his eyebrows, a bit disappointed, imploring me to be a better half-sister ... sister.

I took a breath and was about to acknowledge Ellen when my phone rang. Pete. I put it on speaker.

"I promised I'd call as soon as I had Ida situated in a room, safe and protected by one of Columbia's finest," said Pete. "She's bossing Ronnie Christianson around, and that's as it should be." It sounded like he smiled. "It'll take a while for her to feel like everything is back to normal, but she's well on her way. Good job, Katie."

"Redd too. She's been a blessing. Without her, Ida might still be taking those awful drugs, but how are they going to find those two degenerates?"

"Amanda sent a car to pick up Riley. He'd already vacated his offices, but she'll find them."

"Can Ida have visitors?" Lance said, rousing.

"Let's have her rest and see how she's doing tomorrow."

No sooner had I disconnected Pete's call and sucked in a fortifying breath when my phone hummed again.

"Hi, Jane." I shrugged. Dad yawned and left the room.

Ellen stood and dusted off her backside. She mouthed "later" and was out the door.

Dad gestured to join him in the kitchen. For the next few minutes, as I paced, Lance and Dad shot surreptitious glances between themselves while knocking cupboard doors, banging pans, and clanging utensils, chopping and boiling, pulling together a creamy mushroom soup and a fresh salad with tomatoes, onions, garlic, peppers, basil, and bacon. I didn't contribute to their conversation, nor Jane's. I couldn't get a word in edgewise, but I took a chance and dipped a spoon into the homemade salad dressing to taste. The robust spice had my eyes watering and deadened my palate, and I finally paid attention to Jane's words.

"After Drew requested a detailed description of the stolen articles, he discovered a tenuous thread tying them together. The burglaries might be related to the *Titanic*," Jane concluded.

I waited to see if she had more to say and asked, "And they're related to the *Titanic* how?"

She took a big breath. "An itinerant art instructor taught classes at a number of community centers and used the theme of 1912. A stolen acrylic was the student's abstract concept of items lost when the big ship went down, done in cubism ala Picasso—a shoe, dishes, wine bottles, books, jewelry, objects on a smaller scale. The artist called her work *Titanic* Treasures. The missing oil is an eight-by-twelve reproduction of a black-and-white photo of the iceberg thought to have caused the ship to sink. And when her crockery broke in the kiln, the easy-going potter renamed her sculpture Broken Dreams of April 14. Drew has requested reports of several new thefts with a similar theme, but until they are forwarded, he's mine. He should be home tomorrow.

"What's new with you?"

Where should I begin? Slightly afraid of the tongue-numbing peppery fragrance steaming from the hefty pot, I suggested, "Would you like to meet for supper?"

"I'll pick you up in fifteen minutes." She hung up before I could protest.

I scurried to feed Maverick and change clothes. Brushing my hair increased the static electricity and it swirled around my face. I tamed it as best I could and grabbed my purse, flying out the door and down the drive before Jane had time to honk her horn and scare the neighbors.

"I'm in the mood for fajitas. Sound good to you?"

My seatbelt clicked before I nodded. Fearful I might be tossed free during her lead-footed trip to the restaurant, I yanked on the webbed sash multiple times and held on to the dash as we rounded the last corner, barreling through the stop sign she considered 'merely a suggestion.'

Las Tapas had great food. We chose a booth, providing semi-private space for me to explain my day to Jane. Our waiter, Felipe—one of my bright math students, delivered crisp warm chips and slightly spicy red and green salsa to accompany our Golden Margaritas on the rocks.

"How're you doing, Teach?" he asked with a cheery voice.

"Felipe, this is Ms. Mackey. She's the—"

"I remember. She's the new history teacher and helps you monitor the extra curriculars." After an expansive bow, he whipped up, wearing a grin from ear to ear. "Welcome to Las Tapas, Ms. Mackey. I'm arranging my work schedule so I can join the science club next year. It sounds like you work *very* hard." His exaggerated wink led me to believe he knew precisely what went on in our meetings.

We had an agenda and lesson plans for each time we got together, but sometimes the needs of the group altered the objectives. It was good, however, to hear science club had positive reviews. "Thanks, Felipe. I hope it works out.

We'd love to have you."

"Are you going to attend the paper airplane contest Saturday?" He handed us each an unwieldy, oversized menu. "I can give you a preview of my engineering skills."

Jane squinted. "I missed the memo. What are you talking about?"

His eyes lit up. "It's the fourteenth year the industrial ed department is holding a paper airplane design contest to raise scholarship money. There's a one-dollar entry fee per airplane for students, teachers, parents, and even some siblings. After the free-will offering jar makes the rounds, they usually raise a few hundred dollars. It's a win-win."

"And you have an entry?"

He bounced back and forth, from heel to toe. "Six."

"What time is the air show?"

"Ten a.m. It's being held at Prada Park this year, in the industrial complex, next to Market Square." A bell rang and a family of five entered. An even more attentive façade replaced Felipe's congenial expression. All business, he asked, "Would you like the musicians to serenade you tonight? They'll be returning from their break in a few minutes, and I can send them your way."

"That would be great."

He flashed his charming smile and said, "What can I get you lovely ladies?" I hiccupped an embarrassed laugh, and he said as an aside. "I'm looking for a big tip. How's it working?"

Jane chuckled and said, "You've got it. We'll think of it as an investment in your education. Fajitas?" I nodded and licked my lips.

As Felipe shoved away from the table, my eyes wandered around the room. I turned to the host stand and caught the sheen of a balding pate attached by a scrawny neck to a pudgy body, seemingly stuffed into his crumpled tan suit, shouldering his way to the door.

Riley.

NINETEEN

I patted my pants pockets, my jacket pockets, and finally dug in my bag, searching for my phone. My fingers wrapped around it, but as I pulled it out, a server with a full tray of beverages clipped my elbow and sent the phone flying. It soared over Jane's shoulder on a trajectory for the floor in front of an exuberant group of fans cheering and stamping their feet for our Minnesota soccer team.

A long dexterous arm intercepted it, snatching it from the air and utter ruination. Felipe nodded his head as he handed it back to me, beaming.

"Thank you, thank you," I said as I swiveled around, hoping to glimpse the unscrupulous physician, but he'd vanished.

I scrolled through my short list of favorites and connected.

"West." Her harried voice made me second guess what I thought I saw. "Katie?"

"Amanda, I think Riley just left Las Tapas. I—"

"Stay put." She disconnected, and I stared at the phone in my hand.

"What was that all about, girlfriend?"

"I think I recognized the corrupt doctor who prescribed the medication Weber, um, Banning, was giving Ida. When Amanda checked, he'd emptied the office space he used as a clinic, and she thinks he's on the run."

"He hasn't gotten very far." Jane's phone pinged, and her eyes lit like heart-shaped sparklers.

"Go ahead. Take it. We can't do anything about Riley. Besides, Drew will wonder what you're up to if you don't answer."

In the middle of the table, Felipe set warm, foil wrapped tortillas next to a sizzling cast iron pan overloaded with caramelized onions, vivid red, yellow, and green sliced peppers, and slightly charred, garlic-scented, pulled chicken. He emptied his tray, lining up ramekins of sour cream, guacamole, and more delicious salsa.

He cocked his head and his black wavy hair slid over one eye. He tossed it back and said, "You aren't getting in trouble again, Ms. Wilk, are you?"

Was I? It took a moment, but I chuckled and shook my head as Jane returned her phone to her bag. A furrowed brow had replaced her elation.

"What, Jane?"

"Drew received an update and is investigating the theft of a twenty-fifth anniversary copy of the *Titanic* movie by James Cameron, a brass replica of a 1912 compass, a used *Titanic* puzzle with at least one piece missing, and a signed first edition of *A Night to Remember* by Walter Lord."

"I supposed the loss of the Lord book caused quite a stir. How much was it worth?"

"It could be worth a few thousand dollars to the right collector, but that's not what's most alarming." She took a breath and panned the room.

"What are you doing?"

"Scouring for eavesdroppers." She bent close and whispered, "Drew said he marked the seven thefts on a map, and they lined up." Her eyes shifted right and left, and she glanced around again. "Columbia is in the direct path of the burglar."

I jumped when Felipe appeared at the side of our table with a very concerned look on his face. "You haven't even taken a bite yet. Is everything to your liking? Is there anything wrong?"

Jane picked up her fork and shoveled the ingredients into the tortilla, filling it to capacity. Felipe waited until she took her first bite and murmured her approval before he eased away from our table.

I copied Jane and created a fat, succulent fajita. I carefully chewed my humongous bite and swallowed. "Is he worried the thief is on his way here to do some dastardly deed?" I twirled the ends of my invisible villainous moustache. "Heh, heh, heh."

Jane's food stopped on its third trip to her lips. "He's afraid they're already here, scoping out Columbia for the next heist. He'll be working the case, and I'm worried." She placed the fajita on her plate, took a sip of her margarita and slid that to the middle of the table. "I guess I'm not so hungry after all."

I waved one finger, and Felipe glided over from the next table. "Is there something wrong?"

"Everything is delicious, but could we get two boxes to-go, please?"

His eyes held big question marks, but working in the family business, he knew how to make every experience positive for their patrons. "Of course. Is there anything else I can do for you? An order of chips and queso? Dessert?"

"Felipe, you've already done more than enough." I glanced at my friend staring off into space. "We thank you and can't wait to finish our fabulous feast."

He boxed our meals and set them in a plastic tote, adding wipes, silverware, napkins, topped with four narrow white paper tubes.

"What do you have there?" I asked.

He answered as if I should have known all along. "Churros."

Jane wriggled her credit card out of its slot. "This meal's on me." It seemed as though she often paid for our lunches, but who was I to complain about a friend using her bottomless money card for our supper. Felipe tapped her card on his electronic reader. Jane added a tip and scribbled her signature.

Felipe's eyes sparkled, "Thanks," he said.

Jane was too distracted to notice, and resumed her introspection as we made our way to her car.

She dropped me off next to our garage and waved as she pulled away. I glanced through the kitchen window and locked eyes with my dog before he leaped from the kitchen table onto the floor. "Maverick."

If only every problem could be solved as easily.

TWENTY

Maverick kept me up until well after midnight, the last time I had a visual on my clock before I dozed. I dragged myself downstairs, a sleep deprived pain tapping away behind my eyes, and found Dad wide awake. He danced from one end of the kitchen to the other, frothing milk and delivering an artistically decorated latte in front of me, while slinging hash in the cast iron skillet and singing *Good Morning* from *Singin' in the Rain*.

Sipping the delicious hot caffeine-fueled beverage, the ache in my head receded. I self-consciously patted the hair standing up on my head into place with the tips of my fingers and adjusted the hem of my sweatshirt, my attempt to emulate a put together look. I had hoped some of my dad's morning effervescence might wear off on me. His depth of energy left me gasping, but Maverick seemed to be on par with me. He never lifted his head from his paws, letting his dark eyes follow Dad in disbelief.

He set a sizzling plate of crispy Yukon gold potatoes, onions, peppers, and melting cheese on the table in front of me, and my stomach rumbled.

Dad segued into *A Whole New World* while I sat and devoured the savory heap of food. Maverick quietly waited for my much more sedate morning ritual to begin.

When I grabbed my coat, he slowly rose to all fours and shook off his rest-mode. His leash snagged the hook, and while I wriggled it free, Maverick snatched one of my shoes and sidled away from me, playing keep-away.

"Get the big guy out for his walk but stay close. I've got this," Dad gestured to the table and the sink.

Maverick circled twice, just to make sure I noticed, and dropped the drool-slimed shoe at my feet. I silently protested as I crossed the slick laces.

Fully attired, Maverick and I began our quick loop around the neighborhood and ran into Danica. "Good morning, *Mrs.* Bluestone."

"Good morning, Katie." Danica's eyes glittered happily for a moment but quickly dimmed. "How's your Ida? I don't know her well yet, but CJ's intuition is second to none, and he says she's tops in his book."

"Mine too. She's in the hospital, but Pete thinks they've pinpointed the cause of most of her symptoms and, hopefully, she'll return to normal soon." I made a noise halfway between a sob and a laugh, and Danica lightly brushed my arm. "I'm sorry. I guess the reality of what could have happened finally struck me." I sniffed and shuddered, redirecting my thoughts. "I hope you are finding Columbia to your liking."

"I don't know if you're aware, but CJ is a very private person. However, everyone I've met has been very welcoming."

I almost laughed. The word 'private' didn't even come close. He'd much rather be in a room full of canaries, cats, and canines than humans.

"Have the police caught that awful man yet?"

I shook my head, swallowing hard. "They're still looking. My heart hopes he's gone somewhere far away, never to return, but my head repeatedly tells me Weber wouldn't skip town before taking his revenge."

"We'll keep an eye out." We almost finished our walk when Danica stopped and picked up my free hand. She encased it in her own. "How is the search for your mother progressing?"

At first, my tongue seemed too large for my mouth. I felt my face flush. Early on, I'd shared my concerns regarding Ellen with CJ and Danica. "I'm not exactly sure. Ellen is making the connections." A twinge of guilt added a heavy weight to my heart. I stammered. "I've been preoccupied with school." Danica gave a knowing smile and a nod to go on. "But she has a meeting on Tuesday, and then we should have more information."

"We hope it works out for you as it did for us, but you can never anticipate the emotions the answers you find may stir up. If you need anyone to talk to, I do understand." She patted my hand. "You are brave and will live up to the meaning of your name."

I blinked and stared as if I could read more in her face. "What do you mean?"

She flashed a bright smile. "Wilk means wolf."

We turned when Carlee appeared in the doorway of their home and waved. Danica's wistful eyes filled with love, and her face softened. "Have a good day, Katie." She released my hand and returned the wave to her daughter. CJ said finding Danica had been one of the best things ever to happen in his life, second only to finding their daughter.

I made an intention to show more enthusiasm for

Ellen's pursuit. With or without me, she would continue her quest, but she didn't need to do everything herself. I would be brave and try to help. A retinue of intense golden petals protruded over the edge of the walkway set off by a riot of purple lilacs. With new determination, I pounded the pavement the last few steps into our yard.

Energized by our walk and Danica's words of encouragement, I mentally prepared for a bustling day. Fridays in April hummed with excitement for weekends— no school, longer days, warmer weather, the sights, sounds, and smells of spring—and required active listening and thoughtful presentations to curtail distracted students' unintentional semi-subversive endeavors. I'd been warned. At this time of the year when they got antsy, the kids could get in all kinds of trouble. One more concern to add to my mounting worries.

"Dad, did you know Wilk meant wolf?" I knelt next to Maverick and scanned his face for familiar canine traits. I stuck out my hand to shake. He extended his paw and a lopsided grin. He had skills way beyond those of a wolf.

"Of course. And did you know your eyes twinkle with hearts after a call from Pete?" Dad gripped me in a one-armed hug. "Cuban stew for supper," he said with a crooked smile.

"That doesn't sound like one of Ida's recipes. Are you trying your own?" Before my dad's traumatic brain injury, he made sumptuous foods we couldn't find in any local restaurant. After he took a bullet, he cooked like me—unidentifiable lumps with extra char. Even though he was almost back to normal, I didn't want to show any trepidation, and I thought I'd pick up a take-and-bake pizza just in case.

TWENTY-ONE

Many of the students arriving late to my classes used the magnetic draw of the bright spring sunlight and temperatures soaring into the seventies as their excuse, ridding themselves of the last remnants of Seasonal Affective Disorder. With crystal cerulean skies, fresh fragrant greenery, softly whispering wind, and the delicate twittering of birds, being inside didn't cut it. After a truncated Friday lesson, most students finished their condensed assignments and looked hungrily at the doorway—the only escape from an interior room with no windows to the outside world. As much as I'd have liked, we couldn't wander the school or grounds without prior approval. Mutiny simmered in their eyes, and before my disgruntled students revolted, I related a short story of one of the earliest female cryptographers.

"Genevieve Young Hitt helped compile the first cryptography instruction manual before World War I, *Manual for the Solution of Military Cyphers*. In 1916, she and her husband intercepted and analyzed coded messages sent by the Mexican government. When the United States Army sent her husband overseas, she obtained formal instruction and offered her services to the Southern Department of the Army. As a female trailblazer in the profession of decryption in 1918, she received her first salary, $1000 a year, encrypting and deciphering official Army intelligence correspondence, maintaining control of the Army codebooks in the department, and breaking intercepted coded and enciphered messages. What do you think?"

The few carefully guarded comments quickly snowballed, and in the time remaining after the animated discussion about how much her salary would be worth today and obvious gender bias, I presented a puzzle and offered a gift card for a free ice cream cone to anyone who determined the solution.

"Annie, Bob, Cecil, Dick, and Esther are making predictions about the order in which they will place in their upcoming test. Annie says: Bob will be two places higher than Cecil. Bob says: I will be third. Cecil says: Dick will be first. Dick says: Bob will be second. Esther says: Cecil will be three places lower than Annie. After the test was completed, of these, only one prediction was correct, and that was made by the person who was first. There were no ties."

It was fortunate I maintained a huge stack of gift cards. Multiple students worked out the answer at the same time.

Jane and our mock trial team sauntered into my classroom after school for our last check in, to pick up costumes, and collect the information sheet for the regional contest. As she waited, Lorelei read the puzzle projected on the Smart Board and said, "Esther took first."

Brock squinted at her as if she were a specimen in a Ripley's Believe-It-Or-Not Museum.

"It's easy," she said to the blank faces surrounding her. "Bob's remark cannot be true because if it was true, he would have been first, so he's neither first nor third. Cecil's remark cannot be true. If true, Cecil would have to be first, so Dick is not first, and Bob cannot be second. That leaves Esther. Therefore—"

Brock's eyes grew round, and his mouth dropped open.

Lorelei touched his forearm. "Stay with me." Brock nodded slowly. "Therefore, Annie is second and Cecil is three places lower than Annie, fifth. We already—"

"Who's this *we* you're talking about?" said Brock, mystified.

She ignored him and continued. "We already determined Bob can't take third, so Bob is fourth, and only third place remains open to Dick."

Brock grabbed his head, rolled it from side to side, and moaned, "My brain is on fire. How do you do that?" Lorelei inhaled as if to answer. He stopped complaining and spewed the words in a rush, "Never mind, I don't really need to know."

Jane chuckled and handed out the documentation for our tournament, reiterating our early dismissal time for Tuesday and the competition schedule. In the absence of their usual dynamic tête-à-tête, I noted our team's restraint and tried to get them to lighten up by telling bad one-liners and true tales of my kitchen fiascos.

Their faces didn't give much away. "What's bothering you?" I asked.

The team looked to Lorelei. She shrugged. "Do you

realize this is for all the donuts?

"Donuts?" repeated Brock.

She sighed. "You know what I mean. This is the culmination of almost a year of hard work, ups and downs, and whether we go on to state or not, we have enjoyed the process. We are sorry if we've caused problems, but we've learned so much. We wanted to say thanks to you and Ms. Mackey. We couldn't have done it without you. And that's it."

Jane said, "All for one?" She threw her fist out.

We joined in a circle, chanting, "EsqChoir, EsqChoir, EsqChoir," After the third repetition, all hands flew to the ceiling. Jane had lightened the mood, and the students dispersed.

I picked up the extra papers. "What do you hear from Drew?"

"He'll be home tonight." She smiled as she lined up the desks. "He's made Columbia the center of operation for the thefts." Her smile seemed to fill her face, and she shuttled the chairs into place. With one final tap on the last chair back she said, "Maybe the four of us can get together for dinner tomorrow? I'll call you." She fluttered her hand and made a quick getaway.

On my drive home, my calls to Dad rolled over to voicemail. "Hi, Dad. Any news? Need me to pick anything up?" Besides, of course, the just-in-case-pizza.

I sniffed onions, garlic, sausage, and a hint of pepperoni. A real connoisseur probably could have differentiated the mushrooms, tomatoes, and the cheeses too, but the bouquet drew out one of Dad's favorite songs, "When the moon hits your eye like a big pizza pie, that's amore." My offkey singing filled the car, but the melody stopped as I neared home.

The dark and quiet house appeared uninhabited so Ida must not have been liberated from her hospital stay. Even our rear apartment lacked signs of life. I pulled into the driveway and scanned the windows to catch sight of wayward Maverick. Nothing moved. I sat in the car, trying out scenarios in my head and failing to find one to fit what I saw in front of me. Dad couldn't cook in the dark. Usually, I wouldn't notice the sounds the car door made, obscured by a welcoming bark instead, but the silence intensified the screech. I balanced my briefcase and the pizza box while I unlocked the back door and had the uneasy feeling I was being watched. I whipped around, expecting to see Dad and Maverick sneaking up the walk. Instead, I saw an empty yard.

I shoved inside, slammed the door behind me, and leaned against the wood. Disconcerted by the idea of being unjustifiably spooked, I flushed with heat, and my shirt stuck to my back. I flipped the switch, illuminating a vacant kitchen—no Dad, no Maverick, no fixings for Cuban Stew, and no note.

The refrigerator shelf accommodated the pizza box, and we'd still have room for more if Dad had other supper plans. I stood, cooling off in front of the open door, and contemplated the unforeseen set of circumstances. I dialed his phone.

The call went unanswered again, and my finger hovered over my list of favorites. Who would know the whereabouts of Dad and Maverick? Before I had time to press a button, I heard a soft rumble in the living room. The noise barely registered, but the lack of customary doggie sounds amplified the peculiarity. I froze. The hum triggered my imagination.

I hadn't heard anything new about Weber. He had to know he was a wanted man, but Lance didn't think he'd give up too easily. Could he be waiting in the dark?

"Maverick?" I whispered. "Dad," I hissed. My hand wrapped around the handle of the nearest defensive weapon at hand, probably the only one, and I crept to the living room doorway. Someone snorted.

TWENTY-TWO

The fading light cast long craggy shadows through the windows; skeletal tree limbs looking like giant fiendish fingers stretched out across the floor. My eyes locked onto a feathery lump raised above the back of the sofa at its center. I gazed at my side and gaped at the strainer clenched in my hand. I shook my head and wondered what good it would do.

With trepidation, I silently slid across the floor. As I closed the distance, the features coalesced in the gloaming. The figure exhaled and turned his exquisite face to the light.

"Pete, what are you doing here?" I squeaked.

His eyes flashed and he sat straight up. "Sorry. I must've dozed off. What ya got there?" He snickered.

The hand holding the strainer dropped to my side. "Nothing." I turned on the end table lamp and plopped onto the cushion next to him. "What are you doing here?" I repeated.

He yawned. "Ida's still laid up in the hospital, so Lance and Harry decided she needed visitors. I'd already made the rounds, so I told Harry I'd wait for you, and we'd grab a bite to eat." He lit up his watch face. "I've only been here about twenty minutes. I don't know what came over me."

"I do. You've been running yourself ragged. The hospital admin has only hired one replacement so far, right? You've got to take it easy when you can. I've got a pizza to bake and then home you go."

"Pizza sounds great." He took my free hand and held tight. "But I'm not leaving you alone until this guy, Weber, is back behind bars. Dad doesn't want anyone to be by themselves." One corner of his luscious mouth eased up into a smile and his eyebrows danced a little jig. "I'm sticking to you like rubber cement."

I did a double take, checking his lucidity status, and melted into his huge brown eyes. What I really wanted to say was, 'yes, please,' but instead I said, "I don't need a minder. Dad and Maverick will be home soon."

"I don't mind. But I have every intention of fulfilling my dad's orders or I'll be in serious trouble." He pushed off his knees to stand and offered me a hand. As I straightened, he added, "M'lady Katherine."

Significant snippets of my life circled me like a cyclone and alighted on the letter declaring me Lady Katherine Jean Wilk. In the letter, Charles' solicitor wrote he would keep me apprised and hoped I would visit soon. I sighed.

Pete's strong arms held me in place. I took a deep breath, and the fresh, heady scent of wood and citrus made my already shaky knees wobble. I held on tight. He hugged me to his chest. Leaning back a tiny bit, he searched my face. With his thumb, he caressed my cheek and raised my

chin. We locked eyes. He lowered his lips to mine. My arms
snaked around his neck and came together in a two-handed
grip on the strainer.

I closed my eyes and savored the warm lingering kiss
until clacking nails scraped across the kitchen floor, and a
cold wet nose nuzzled between us.

"Katie?" The voice reverberated around the big empty
house.

"Dad." I pulled back, smiling shyly. "We're in here."

Keys rattled on the countertop. "No stew tonight,
Katie." Dad emerged from the kitchen. "Did you two
already get something to eat?"

"I have a pizza in the fridge. I'm going to fix it as soon
as I've preheated the oven."

"Got enough for four?" Lance followed Dad into the
living room.

"I think we can accommodate you."

Pete draped his arm over my shoulder. "Any news
about Weber?"

"Nope. Nada. Nothing." Lance shook his head and
crossed his arms. His right hand came up, stroking the
grizzled whiskers on his chin. "I still don't think he'll give
up that easily. No one has seen anything of him, but he's
had too much time to fuel his anger."

I dragged Pete with me back into the kitchen and
preheated the oven. "Will pizza be enough, or will you
need something else?"

Dad dug in the grocery bag on the counter and removed
a pre-mixed salad and a bottle of wine. "All I have to do is
open and dress the greens. How does that sound?"

Maverick barked.

Dad stood still and stared at my dog. "That's why I

took him with me. He wouldn't stop barking, so he stayed at Erickson's. I can't read his mind but it's as if he is seeing some invisible scoundrel."

Maverick barked again. I called him to my side and rubbed behind his ear. "Good boy." He closed his eyes and stretched into the scratch. "How's Ida?"

Lance unscrewed the top on the wine bottle and emptied the contents into four glasses. As he resecured the top, his phone jingled, and he smirked when he read the screen. "Hi, you old thing."

I couldn't make out the individual words, but Lance held the receiver away from his ear and their intent came through loud and clear.

"She'll be released with Amanda's officer escort tomorrow," he said pocketing his phone and reaching for a glass. "She's acting like her ornery old self, but we'll need to be here for her. No one who's met Weber should be alone. I have no idea what his endgame is, but I don't want to find out after something happens."

When only the delicious vapors of our supper remained, I peeled the flyer detailing the various offerings from the box, folded it, and stored it with our growing stack of take-out menus from establishments around Columbia.

"Thanks for letting us crash your supper plans." Lance pushed away from the table. He picked up the plates and silverware and deposited them in the sink, then braced himself and shook his head. "We've got to be careful."

Pete said goodnight to his dad and acted like he was settling in here for the night. I gently guided him to the door. "As much as I'd appreciate your presence in our humble abode, you've got to be with Lance. Banning chose Ida and Lance as the objects of his venom, and if Casimer had been alive, I'm certain he'd have been on the list too. Ida's safe tonight. Dad and Maverick are here with me, but you should be with your dad."

"I suppose," he said, reluctantly. "But I'm off for the weekend. I'll bring Dad by to see Ida and your dad. Do you have plans for tomorrow?"

"Jane wants the four of us to go out for supper if it works out."

"I'm game. Since our schedules haven't meshed, Drew's almost a stranger."

"And Jane and I thought we'd attend the annual paper airplane contest tomorrow morning. One of my students invited us."

Lance snuck a quick peek at Pete. "Didn't you win one year? I think I still have that folded up paper in the family Bible."

Red mottling crawled up Pete's neck and onto his cheeks, and he bowed his head.

"Then we're definitely going." I prodded his elbow. "Do you want to join us? Relive old times. Inspect the new designs out there. Maybe we should see what we can come up with and enter a model against the competition. I heard there's an adult category."

"It's supposed to be a nice day. I suppose we could give it a try if Dad still has my winning design." I saw the boy he'd been in his hope-filled eyes.

"And I have a bunch of popup books and a booklet full of other flying prototypes we can study."

"Of course, you do." He laughed and wrapped an arm around my shoulder.

"It's for a good cause."

Or so I thought.

TWENTY-THREE

Cars parked at odd angles, on the grass, over the curb, front to back, and swelled out of the lot. Potential engineers and wood pulp architects crowded the yard, distracted and avidly scanning the preflight checklists provided by the Industrial Education Department.

Good thing we'd walked over. Maverick pranced happily, muscles rippling, and smiled as only a beautiful black Lab can, drawing bystanders like a magnet. He was in dog heaven surrounded by every sized person. Drew ran interference, instructing prospective dog-petters to ask permission and step to the dog's side when making contact, and wisely warning of potential slimy, slobbery kisses.

Jane and I had met Pete and Drew earlier, pored over schematics, scoured online resources, and read up on proper paper folding techniques to achieve the longest distance, one of the categories of the competition, as well as speed achieved, accuracy of flight, and overall aesthetics. It took all of fifteen minutes, and with the approval of our resident expert, we each had three unique designs to submit if we could make it through the slow moving, extra-long registration line before the competition began.

Having grown up in Columbia and returning to practice medicine in the ER, Pete greeted virtually every other person in the park by name, littles and bigs, right before they oohed and aahed over my dog.

"How's the bursitis, Mr. Slaveck?" Pete listened with such intensity, I had to tug him forward when the line moved.

He knelt on one knee and met a curly blonde preschooler eye-to-eye. "Is that your new puppy, Lyssa? He's a wild one, just like your brother." He mimed being shocked by a shrill bark, and Lyssa attempted to hide a giggle behind her tiny fingers.

Jane, Drew, and I received a few head nods, the only acknowledgments a teenage high school student might give his or her teacher in a crowd, until Felipe and his friend found us.

"Ms. Wilk. Ms. Mackey. You made it. Terrific. You're going to love it." He displayed a cardboard box and shuffled the contents. "And wait until you see my models. They're winners for certain." He noticed the manilla envelope anchored under my arm. "Are you competing?"

"We're going to try. For fun." Although deep down, if one of my planes could place, I wouldn't feel too awful.

His eyes skimmed the local crowd. Felipe straightened his spine, growing an inch. "You brought the big guns." He swallowed hard. "His design accuracy has never been challenged. Not even close. Maybe it was luck but more likely it was sheer determination and skill. Is he competing?"

I followed his gaze to Drew and Pete. "You mean Dr.

Erickson?" His face said I'd guessed correctly.

Felipe slowly turned his head, but his eyes stayed glued on my handsome hunk. "Yes. Dr. Erickson. They have photos of his winning design on the wall in the woodworking lab. Every year there are multiple attempts to copy it." Pulling his gaze away from his paper pilot idol, Felipe's eyes met mine. "We might as well go home." He blinked and his eyes gleamed.

"But you're throwing down the gauntlet, aren't you?"

His right shoulder rose to his ear and his dark eyes sparkled. "Thank goodness we're competing in different classifications. Have you taken a gander at those fantastic trophies?" A chuckle burbled from his cheery face. "Thirteen inches of shiny composite would look good on any desk, don't you think? Good luck, Ms. Wilk. May the best man, or woman, win."

As the surging stream of students headed over to the wide-open soccer field in the next block, lining up according to their assigned numbers, Felipe raised a hand with his victory symbol in full view.

We followed the rivulet of more mature creators and registered under the wire, with minutes to spare, four of twenty-two entries in the adult category. Familiar with the area, Maverick aimed for the geocache we'd found, and I redirected him behind the spectators.

Energetic high school students in black-and-white stripes herded the undulating scrum of grownups to the parking lot next to Market Square. Mr. Paul, an industrial arts teacher, stood next to the sculpture of grain and read a condensed welcome speech and instructions from his phone screen. The first three competitors in our category stepped up and took their places, holding a rainbow of colored pages, and crisply creasing the edges of their airplanes in nervous anticipation.

The chalk markings drawn on the asphalt in one-foot intervals resembled a compressed athletic field. We cheered the first hot pink test as it soared thirty feet in the air and chuckled as it crashed to the ground inches from the disappointed designer.

One of the student referees rushed in and made a show of pulling out a yellow tape measure and a protractor. "Distance, nine inches. Off course by forty-five degrees." He dutifully recorded the data on the clipboard in his hand, snickered, and said, "You hold the record to beat, Dad, for now."

The second attempt took a perpendicular turn and careened past the building, into a stand of trees, out of sight and off track. As the referees raced around the corner, a gleaming light flashed in my eyes. I thought I caught movement in a second story window. It could have been an optical illusion, so I shaded my eyes to make certain I hadn't imagined it. I saw it again, and I squeezed my eyes closed against the blinding flare.

"Did you see that?" Pete kept his eyes glued to his prospective opponents. I touched his arm. "Riley's office was on the second floor in the commerce building, right?"

"Yes, but Amanda said it'd been cleared out. He's long gone." His lips formed a gentle smile, concentrating on the competition and cognizant no one had come anywhere near his record so far.

Pete's attention locked onto the paper vessels, too preoccupied to notice me. "I'll be right back." I looped Maverick's leash around his wrist. "Keep my place in line," I said, more for my benefit, and headed to the entrance.

According to the Columbia Commerce directory, several of the establishments conducted business during reduced Saturday hours. I skated through the main door and hopped on the elevator in the company of an anxious, young couple. As our doors closed, the lift across from us opened and two men in dark business attire, engaged in urgent conversation, dashed through the atrium.

"It would be a great place to bathe a pet," the young man said, slinging one arm over her shoulder. He tossed back a lock of straight, dark hair and swiped at a dark smudge above his lip. I realized he'd been realigning the sparse hairs of what might have been a mustache.

"We don't have a dog or a cat." The woman made a big, slow circle with her head, and if I could have seen behind her huge sunglasses, I probably would have seen her eyes roll too.

"We could get one. Anyway, I'll use it to soak my stained work clothes and scrub my greasy hands."

"You don't even own a toolbox." She playfully shrugged off his arm. "What do you do to get your hands greasy? It'll just be something else for me to clean."

"I promise I'll take care of it," the young man cajoled.

"I've heard that before." She tucked strands of light-brown hair behind her ears.

"Our architect is highly sought after, you know. We're paying plenty for his services. Shouldn't we do what he suggests?"

Flustered, when the woman finally disentangled the pink frames from her hair, she put her hands on her hips, and turned to me. "What do you think of installing a sink in a garage?"

Although the idea actually appealed to me, the

indignant set of her jaw and the piercing glower in her blue eyes struck me momentarily mute, and the ding and the door splitting wide saved me from having to answer. They scurried out, continuing the discussion down the narrow hall.

"We probably can't afford the remodel now anyway," she said. "That jerk took off without so much as a 'how do' let alone paying my salary." She clomped down the hall in her heavy shoes, and their voices silenced once they stepped through one of the glass doors. I took a step to follow and noticed the elevator had bypassed the second floor. I stepped back and repeatedly pressed the button for floor two, but it wouldn't engage. I guess they programmed the elevator not to open on a floor without slated business hours. I exited and took the stairs.

My footfalls echoed in the empty stairwell as I jogged down the two flights. The shaft smelled faintly of paint and disinfectant, and the pristine steps didn't appear to be used much. I slowed as I closed in on the last few steps. A substantial stopper propped open the door to the suite on the second floor.

"Hello." I stepped into an off-white waiting room, sparsely adorned with two glaring crimson chairs, an end table, and a wall rack containing two magazines. My nose wrinkled when I glanced through the smudged fingerprints on the plexiglass partition secured atop a steel registration desk. "Anyone here?" I kept my voice carefree.

Sunlight streamed in the dusty plate glass windows, illuminating dust motes dancing in the air, and I squinted to adjust to the brightness. The mix of voices cheering for 'Ralphie' drifted in with a whiff of spring on a slight breeze from an open lower casement. I peeked through the window and scoped out Pete and his competition when I heard an angry squeak.

"Hello?" I edged around the desk and started down a long narrow hall. The knobs on the first three doors labeled 'Exam Room' wouldn't turn, but the door to the room at the end of the corridor stood slightly ajar. The hinges groaned under the weight of the heavy metal as I nudged the door with my foot.

A message blinking in blue and white from the computer on a counter caught my attention first. **I'm sorry**

I reached to scroll through more of the message and decided it would be wise to look but not touch. Proud of myself for not succumbing to the urge to know everything, I pulled back and knocked a yellow pencil from the counter. It clattered to the floor and rolled out of sight. I turned to search for it and pressed my hand against the creaking door. I bent to retrieve the pencil, and the door cleared another ninety degrees, knocking into a pair of blue clogs. As I stood, an uncontrolled terrified shriek cut right through me.

TWENTY-FOUR

J ust keep screaming and it'll come flying." I could hear Dad's words of wisdom as if he stood right next to me and immediately squelched the horrible sound issuing from my throat, as I came face to face with swaying stockinged feet extending beneath faded Disney scrubs. I knew I didn't want anything to come flying at me.

Remembering movies and television shows where someone is saved from asphyxiation by lightening the load, I grabbed the legs and heaved with all my might. He was a heavy man. I strained, glanced up, and stared into cold unblinking eyes dotted with tiny pinpricks of dark red. My heart hammered in my chest. Tears welled up in my eyes. I released the legs and backed out of the room, wiping my sweaty palms on the front of my jeans. With trembling fingers, I called Pete.

"Drew's up, and you're next."

"Pete." I inhaled, held my breath, and let it out slowly. "I found Weber. He's dead."

He knew me well enough to know fabricating stories

about corpses was not in my purview. "Where are you?"

"Second floor of the Columbia Commerce building."

"What are you doing there?" He tsked. "Never mind. Call Amanda. I'm on my way."

Amanda answered lightheartedly on the first ring. "What's shaking, Katie? I heard a rumor Pete's trying to replicate his paper airplane victory and relive the glory days of his youth."

I felt guilty putting a downer on her day. "Amanda, Weber's on the second floor of the Columbia Commerce building."

Her voice lowered to her most serious pitch. "Keep your eye on him if you can, but promise me you won't do anything to get him to run. We'll be right there." She hung up before I could assure her he wouldn't be disappearing again.

A dizzyingly rapid cardiac tempo thumped in my chest. Seconds loudly ticked away on the round industrial clock behind the desk until my dog swept into the office dragging Pete on the leash. Maverick panted, circled me, and sat. Pete swallowed me in a warm hug and rested his chin on my head. I inclined against his muscular chest, and I could feel the steadying thump of his heart.

I pulled back an inch when Maverick alerted. Of course, there was a dead body in the next room.

"What's with him?" Drew asked, stepping into the waiting area followed by Jane. I pinched my lips, biting down to keep it together and moved my forefinger a few millimeters to gesture into the corridor. Drew rattled the knobs as he passed. I hadn't checked as well as I might have. The first office on the left opened, and he peered inside, but the two remaining knobs didn't budge. Pete released me, one shoulder at a time, and went after Drew.

Jane sat primly on one of the red plastic chairs by the windows and tapped her fuchsia-painted nails on the hard surface next to her. I sighed and dropped into the seat. His job complete, Maverick relaxed between us.

"Oh, girlfriend. What am I going to do with you?" She smoothed Maverick's ear. He closed his eyes and leaned in for more.

We waited. When the sound of police sirens cut off outside and multiple car doors slammed, we eased back into our chairs. A herd of fast footfalls tromped up the steps and into the office. Amanda led; gun drawn. "Where is he?"

Pete stuck his head into the hall and called, "Amanda, Banning's, I mean Weber's body is back here. I've called for the ME van."

"Body? Weber? What did you do, Katie, and what on God's green earth possessed you to come up here?" She stared at me and shook her head.

"We were watching the industrial ed competition, and I thought I saw movement through the window. You said it had been vacated." My racing heart slowed. "As it turned out, I think I actually caught the shining reflection of something on Weber. I found him up here, and he was already dead."

Amanda holstered her weapon. "Oh, Katie." Her disappointed tone made me wince. We'd congregated over a dead body more than once. I suppose she wondered what she would do with me too.

"It doesn't look like he's been gone all that long." Pete said and disappeared back into the death room.

"Don't move. Either of you." Amanda shook her first two fingers at Jane and me. Maverick shifted from one paw to the other. She added a third finger and brandished all three, this time including Maverick. "None of you." I clutched his leash. He kind of had a mind of his own sometimes.

After Amanda disappeared with her two officers, Jane leaned toward me and whispered, "Weber's been planning his revenge for decades. Why would someone so single-minded do this instead?" Jane searched my not-very-good-poker face.

I shook my head and blinked. *Why, indeed?*

The chittering cacophony of unconcerned, hopeful voices continued to wend its way through the window. If I hadn't let my curiosity get the better of me, we could be outside in the sun with all the other Columbians, flying our airplane models, maybe collecting a prize. Instead, we practiced our 'hurry up and wait' strategies.

When the back room finally disgorged its occupants, Amanda spoke into her phone. "Dr. Erickson's here, and he's requested the wagon."

She pocketed her phone, and her dark eyes bored into me. "Katie, tell me again what you were doing up here?"

I scooted to the front of my seat and locked my hands on my jerky knees to keep both from moving uncontrollably. "One of the paper airplanes from the adult contest flew by the window. Something flashed in my eyes. I guess …" I faltered. Weber? "Something glossy caught the light just right. Maybe when he swayed." I shivered. "Anyway, something glinted. I saw movement, but the second floor had been abandoned."

Amanda opened and closed the drawers on the registration desk, searching, and not even finding a box of tissue or a paperclip. Strange to have the office cleared out so well in such a short time. It had only been a week since Ida's appointment with Dr. Riley. Didn't he have other patients? "You should have called instead of investigating on your own. You could've been hurt."

Inside I trembled but put on a sassy front. "Amanda, that's so thoughtful."

She cringed. "Riley's still missing—somewhere out there, so don't get any ideas."

"Moi?"

Amanda glowered.

"Amanda, do you think Riley was in on the plot with Weber? Do you think Ida was the object of his medical venture?" She glared at me. "And what do you think about the message on the screen? Any idea what it means?"

Jane turned sharply. She crossed her arms and legs. "What message? You never mentioned a message."

Amanda's eyes narrowed to small dark gashes. "Show me."

I swallowed. Had I imagined the letters on the computer screen? My fingers reached under Maverick's collar where I often found a bit of extra resolve. He yawned. I stood. I shimmied my fingers into the nitrile gloves Amanda handed me and bowed as she let me pass. I trudged to the rear room, keeping my eyes at the level of the desk, and frowned at the blank computer screen. I glanced at Amanda, seeking permission. She nodded, and I tapped life into the machine.

Confused, my head canted to the right as I tried to make sense of the prompt. "I didn't need a password before. I know what I saw. I read 'I'm sorry' on the screen in big white letters on a blue background. Honestly, I was going to scroll down." My head snapped to Amanda. "But I promise you won't find my fingerprints on the keyboard. I knew I should wait. I didn't want to compromise a crime scene if it was one."

"We'll bag it and let IT take a look at the device."

I meandered to the windows and craned my neck but could only see the edge of the field for the adult competition. Officer Rodgers ambled through the periphery of the crowd where Pete and I had stood, occasionally raising his eyes to this floor, searching. I hunted for what could have flashed the light in my face. The sun didn't penetrate far into this room and any reflection from Weber hanging in its recesses seemed impossible.

I pulled out my phone and turned its mirrorlike back to the sun. Manipulating the vectors, I altered the angle of reflection until Rodgers shaded his eyes.

Amanda's radio crackled with words unintelligible to me. Her eyes met mine. "What are you doing, Katie?"

I made a point of looking above Weber, down at Rodgers, and then at the phone in my hand. Understanding passed over Amanda's features.

"What's going on?" Pete said, eyes on the body, ducking to closely examine Weber's nails.

"Katie recreated the visual anomaly like the one she might have seen while on the grounds. Rodgers just saw the light, right, Katie?"

"While I wandered around the suite, I heard a strange sound behind the desk, and I went to check out the noise. The first three doors in the hall wouldn't open—oh, my fingerprints *will* be on all the doors, sorry. I stepped into this room." I shuddered. "The words on the screen didn't make a lot of sense, so I debated searching further and knocked a pencil to the floor." I spotted it easily and pointed. "And that's when I found ..."

TWENTY-FIVE

Why would Weber take the time to manipulate you, of all people, get you up here, leave a message, and commit suicide? Did you know him well?" Amanda asked.

"I just met him when he began taking care of Ida." I bit my bottom lip, keeping my wild ideas to myself. I watched as another conclusion dawned on Amanda coincidentally.

"You don't think he killed himself. Why?" The wheels rotated behind her intelligent eyes.

Putting the gripping thought into words sent a jolt through me. "I can't figure out what shined in my eyes and when I tried the first three doors, I'm sure they were locked tight, but later one of them opened for Drew. Do you think someone else could have been in this office?"

"Or maybe Drew was more determined. Weber knew we were onto him. His death has all the earmarks of suicide. But we'll investigate thoroughly." Amanda thumbed her radio. "We may be too late but lock the building down. Don't let anyone in or out."

A voice responded with a distant, "Ten four."

"If it was murder, we're already too late," I muttered, remembering the men I'd witnessed leaving the building when I entered, the first of countless others who left unobserved. I trooped into the waiting area, picked up Maverick's leash, and marched through the door. Jane tagged along.

Amanda's carefully modulated voice trailed behind. "I need you to stay until forensics completes its examination and we take your statement."

"I know." My shoulders caved, and I slumped onto the top step in the stairwell. Jane sandwiched Maverick between us, and together we massaged and scratched his silky black coat. Maverick leaned in. His tickling tongue gave me courage, and Jane's silent support strengthened me. "Amanda," I called over my shoulder. "Ida and Lance need to hear about Weber's death from you."

"You're right," she reluctantly admitted. Although I couldn't hear the words, I heard the short whisper of critical communication. When she finished, she directed us to the atrium on the first floor.

The anxious and curious business owners, receptionists, workers, and visitors on site in the four-story building on Saturday numbered about two dozen including Jane, Drew, Pete, and me. I recognized the young couple from my elevator ride, and their interview yielded interesting tidbits.

"What's going on?" she said. "We've never had to check out before."

"What's your name, ma'am? Do you come here often?" Officer Rodgers' youthful face concealed his expert interrogation skills, lulling his potential victims into a false sense of security.

"My name is Carolyn Hall and I work … worked on the second floor for the last two weeks."

"You worked for Dr. Riley? What did you do?"

"Receptionist." She turned the glasses in her hand to admire her manicure. "Girl Friday kind of stuff. He'd reopened his clinic after a five-year hiatus and started growing his patient pool. I had a *lot* to do. We had a half-dozen visits the first week alone." She tapped her sunglasses against her palm in a can-you-get-this-over-with gesture.

"Can you be more specific?" asked ever-patient Rodgers.

"I don't know," she wavered, as if she couldn't divulge confidential information but said firmly. "I did everything for the old Scrooge, and he and his partner closed the doors and took off without any notice. I don't owe them loyalty, but I won't tell you anything that can get me into trouble. We did have one weird, crazy busy day." Her chin jutted out and I turned my teacher ears on. "I had to work last Saturday, which wasn't in the schedule, and this old, skinny guy wearing ugly green aviator sunglasses and a bomber jacket came in. He filled out the paperwork, and while he went in to have labs drawn, a middle-aged lady with green eyes and crimson hair arrived, strutting in like royalty. I remember she peeled off twenty-dollar bills and paid upfront, like the sign said." Carolyn snickered. "I thought they'd make a colorful couple. He came out. She went in, and when her visit ended, she marched right out the door. The old guy tried to sneak out after her, but he hadn't paid yet, and I had to threaten police involvement. That same day we had my old piano teacher come by. Mrs. Clemashevski didn't even recognize me." She sounded melancholic. "You know, it must have been a fluke, but she has green eyes too."

Her partner pulled her protectively next to him, murmuring support. Rodgers addressed him. "And you, sir?

"Blake. Blake Hall."

"Have you been to Market Square before?"

"This was our second meeting with the architectural firm on the third floor. And I've been to my wife's office …" He looked to her for confirmation. "Once for lunch."

"Did you visit the second floor today?"

They exchanged confused looks and shook their heads. They answered a few more questions. Unfortunately, I couldn't overhear their address and phone numbers but not for lack of trying.

Even though he'd collected our contact information on more occasions than I'd care to count, we supplied the redundant data. Fifteen minutes after lining up to talk to Officers Rodgers and Wallace, providing the where, who, and why of our visit, Drew and Pete stayed to lend their expertise, and Jane, Maverick, and I began the return walk to her apartment.

Having completed the adult flying matchup, a small circle of onlookers remained, gawking at the door of the Columbia Commerce building. Most of the contestants scattered, some to observe the kids' tournament, others to complete tasks on a never-ending Saturday to-do list, and a select few closed in on the platform at the winners' circle. We waved at Felipe as we passed, and he gave us a thumbs up.

Curiosity nibbled at the back of my mind, and I could hardly contain it. "Who's sorry? Was the message from someone else? For someone else? If Banning or Weber or whatever his name was didn't commit suicide, could he have been killed? Although they'd be the most likely candidates, Ida's still in the hospital and Lance has been with her all morning, so at least they won't be suspects."

Jane chewed on her lip for a few steps and said, "Weber and Riley worked together. Maybe they argued. Or maybe Weber clashed with someone he met in jail, and they found him here."

"But why would any of them drag me into this disaster?"

"You could be accidental, collateral damage. Maybe the glare on the second floor came from sunlight glinting from outside." She added quietly, "Or maybe you know something you aren't aware of. Or Weber knew Amanda was closing in and committed suicide."

My head sagged to my chest. I envied Maverick's ability to parade down the sidewalk, tongue hanging out, ears flopping, without a care in the world.

My phone pulsed in my pocket. I read the screen and sighed. "Hello, Ellen."

"Katie, every genetic marker points to the woman as being our mother." I struggled to hear the rapid-fire words. "Sister Lawrence believes she can convince *Barb* ..." I could almost see the air quotes. "To meet with us." The pitch of her voice reached the stratosphere. "She said she's shared my emails and our photo, and Barb hasn't said no yet." Ellen's elation toned down. "But she doesn't want to have anything to do with Harry."

Why didn't Barb want to have anything to do with possibly the best person on earth? The hairs on my neck prickled. I thought I'd overcome some of the ache in my heart caused by the knowledge of my mother's disappearance, but Ellen's persistent dredging hurt anew. The events of the morning had rattled me, and I clamped my lips so I wouldn't say anything I might regret later.

"Katie, are you there?"

I mumbled an answer.

"I'm still meeting Sister Lawrence on the fourteenth and I know you can't be there, but if you have any message, anything you want me to tell her …"

"You're doing great, Ellen. If we don't touch base before then, I wish you the very best luck."

"That means so much to me. Thanks." She added, tentatively, "Sis."

I bristled again. "I'll talk to you later." Would I ever be as accepting as Dad wanted me to be?

I sullenly trudged the last few blocks with Jane. It seemed Maverick read my mood, and his cheerful demeanor dimmed.

"Would you like to join me for lunch? I don't think the boys will finish any time soon." Jane bounded up her walkway.

"No, thanks. I, ah, have to check on Dad." I fibbed, a bit, but I didn't want my rotten temperament to rub off on Jane, so I continued home.

Since moving in with Ida and me, Dad considered his conditioning a form of physical therapy and he worked out at the Y almost every morning. Today was no exception. He hadn't expected me to be home, so he'd be in no hurry to get back. I could use the quiet time to think happy thoughts of Pete or catalog my questions and answers about Ellen, Barb, and Weber.

I ran the tap to cool the water and filled a tumbler, but before I took my first sip, I heard an unexpected sound.

On high alert, my heart pounded immediately.

"Hello?" My voice cracked. I cleared my throat. "Who's there?" I caught Maverick in the corner of my eye, lying with his head between his paws, blinking unhurriedly. I determined my fear was unwarranted until I heard the creak of movement through my wood floor. I checked Maverick again. No reaction. He stayed rooted on his mat. I tiptoed to the door between apartments, silently turned the knob, and yanked the door open.

Ida stood on the other side of the door. She gasped and clutched her chest, and when she saw me, she feigned staggering. "Katie, you scared the bejeezus out of me. Lance told me you and Pete were tossing airplanes today. Why are you home so soon?"

"Why am I home so soon? Why are you home so soon? When were you released?"

"Lance brought me home after breakfast, about nine."

"Where's Lance? Did he stick around?"

"No. He wanted to clean up in his own home, and I can certainly understand his sentiment."

"You weren't in the hospital this morning at ten?" She shook her head from side-to-side. Their alibis went up in a puff of smoke. But then again, Amanda believed Weber killed himself.

Her hands morphed into fists she set on her hips. "What's this all about?"

"Did Amanda, Chief West, talk to you?"

Ida's forehead furrowed. "No. Why? What's happened?"

I raked my hand through my hair. "We found Weber."

Ida stood as tall as her almost-five-foot frame allowed and relaxed her arms, crossing them I front of her. "That's a relief. That man is nothing but trouble."

"He *was* nothing but trouble. Now he's dead."

Her sturdy demeanor collapsed. Her hand covered her mouth. "Oh, no."

"But Amanda called and talked to someone. Maybe she talked to Lance." Ida nodded, but her face began to pale, and her bottom lip quavered. "Let's get you sitting down. Why did they release you so soon?"

"You know I have the reputation as a force to be reckoned with. I ordered the nurse to help me pack up my things. She insisted I was leaving AMA, against medical advice, but what could she do. I signed all the paperwork. All I need is rest, and I can get that at home. My mind is clearer now than …" She trailed off and gazed over her shoulder into her living room. "Would you help me look for the family photo album? You know, the thick one. I can't find it."

TWENTY-SIX

The dozens of scrapbooks she'd pulled from the shelf teetered in tall stacks on the floor. I scanned the numbers on the homemade labels affixed to the spines like volume descriptions. Ida's fingers lightly brushed the worn leather covers of one pile. "It's the first, number one, the album with the photos of Sinead and Padraig that's missing."

I knew to which collection she referred. Not only had the album contained irreplaceable vintage snapshots, she'd also kept her heart's invaluable treasures together within its pages. Her husband, Casimer, died years ago, but she often reread his love letters, secured inside with a red ribbon. The priceless drawing of the *Titanic* she'd received from an art-student-turned-successful-movie-producer couldn't be reproduced; I'd helped resolve his homicide in September. And she had cherished the sepia-colored portraits of her ancestors, Padraig and Sinead. Padraig had gone down with the *Titanic*.

"When did you last see the album?"

She put her fingers to her forehead and pressed as if she could corral her flighty thoughts. Her eyes closed and she turned her head from side to side. "I don't know. It's always been on the first shelf, and now it's not." Her eyelids fluttered and she pulled her hand away from her head as if it was scorched. She gazed at me. "Do you think I lost it when I, ah, wasn't myself? Could I have destroyed it and not known?" Her head dropped back, and she mewled.

"You didn't destroy anything. It meant too much to you. It's got to be here somewhere. We'll find it."

She strode in front of her bookcases like a little general with her hands interlocked behind her back, carefully perusing the contents, occasionally sliding glass figurines, and realigning her collectibles. I opened cabinet doors and shuffled her belongings, lifting, reordering, and examining the deepest corners. We used the same investigative techniques in the dining room, kitchen, guest room, and office, but approaching her inner sanctum took more finesse.

She raised her head and marshaled her courage before turning the knob on her bedroom door. The way she acted, I worried it might be in utter disarray, and we'd have to comb through a jumble of clothes and through indistinct pathways amassed by a hoarder of some kind. But it was just as neat as the rest of the house, and each piece of her belongings occupied the perfect spot.

She fell backwards on to the bed. "Home." Her eyes slammed shut, and within seconds, the buzz of her dulcet snoring accompanied me to the brink of dozing as well. I surrendered to the gentle soft sounds, leaned against the door frame, and closed my eyes. As I reviewed my latest vision of her living room and pondered the album's whereabouts, Ida's doorbell dinged, dragging me back to reality. I couldn't disrupt her peaceful sleep, so I crept down the stairs and opened the front door.

"Is the missus in? I heard she got sprung." Redd's gaze swept the room. "Looks like a cyclone hit this place. What happened?"

"Spring cleaning." I hoped my nose wouldn't grow with the little lie and betray me. As I tidied the albums as best I could, clearing a path, I said, "Come in. Ida's resting but I'm sure she could use a pick-me-up. I'll get her."

Redd threw her cardinal jacket onto the hook and made a beeline to the piano. She straightened her matching coveralls, wriggled onto the padded bench cushion, and her fingers tooled over the ivories. The sprightly notes made me spiral the newel post where I came face-to-face with Ida. I bounced back and landed with a thud in a heap on the bottom step.

She laughed. "I saw you coming and prepared myself. Yoo-hoo, Redd." She shuffled around me and took her seat at the piano. The two broke into a four-handed Bach prelude. I exhaled. Ida was back.

When the last notes of the song faded, Redd said, "You are the most fun old lady to swing with, but ..." She flapped her hand back and forth at the mess. "What's going on here, Missus?"

Ida's eyes circled the room. "I misplaced one of my photo albums and Katie was helping me look for it. But I must have lost it during the last few days when I was indisposed."

"Indisposed? That's a good one. Missus, you were out of your ever-loving mind."

I waited for Ida to blow, but she accepted Redd's irreverence with a nod. "I suppose I was, at that. But no longer." She scowled. "Katie, we didn't check the trash."

"I'm on it." I jumped up and headed out back to dig in the can. I came up empty handed. The garbage truck had already made its rounds for the week.

Dreading the conversation with Ida, I trudged through my kitchen when a chorus of laughter drew me back to her living room. I stood in the doorway, admiring the tableau. Ida sat like a queen in her blue wingback chair. Ellen, who must have just shown up, sat cross-legged on the floor in front of her, drowning in an oversized Columbia cougar sweatshirt. Her knees peeked through the jagged tears in her jeans, and she pulled on the end of the ponytail snaked over her shoulder. Redd stood behind Ida and pointed at a brittle piece of paper clutched to Ida's heart. Ida wiped tears from her eyes.

Redd pulled Ida into a brusque hug. She saw me and dropped her arms, saying, "I've got a job to do today, Missus. I'd better be going. See ya."

"Are you free tomorrow? We could try the four-handed Puccini or Debussy." She clapped her hands. "And can you do lunch?"

"Yeah, sure. Sounds like a great time."

"About eleven?" I still read a bit of fragility but much more strength in Ida's words. "Ellen, can you come too?" Ida turned to Redd. "She's a fine pianist. I think I have the six-handed *Serenade* by Schubert. Ellen?"

"I guess so." Ellen nibbled on her bottom lip.

"Until tomorrow, Missus. Ellen. TTFN, Wilk."

As Redd skedaddled to her next appointment, Ida and Ellen turned to see me standing in the doorway. Ellen blushed and Ida's mouth gaped.

Ida called me over to sit next to her. "Look what Redd found between the pages of my family Bible. It's a miracle." She glowed as she extended a thin packet of envelopes. I tugged loose a shiny red ribbon, and the bundle fanned out on the table. "They're some of my letters from Casimer. I must have separated them from the album. I'll miss everything else, of course, and I'll surely keep looking, but these are the best part.

"Now, before I forget, tell me everything."

She nodded at my recitation of the half-day's proceedings, but I don't think she heard much. She relaxed and burrowed into her couch. Her eyes closed, and although Ida was back, the week's long ordeal had taken its toll, and she needed recovery time. I pulled a quilt over her and tucked it under her chin.

I shushed Ellen and led her out of Ida's apartment.

"Did you require something, Ellen?"

She lifted her chin and attempted to deny a need but slumped and said, "Ida's important to you and Harry, and I wanted to see for myself how well she's doing." She gave me a half smile. "She's one tough cookie. I want to be just like her. I came for inspiration." She cleared her throat.

"And," I prompted.

"I know you can't come with me, but could we get together at my place when you get back?"

"I don't know what time that'll be." Her face fell. "But if you don't care when I show up—"

She threw her arms around me and squeezed. "Any time will be great. Thanks." She backed up shyly and pointed.

Maverick dangled his leash in a not too subtle hint at

walking. Ellen declined my invitation to join us. She left, and we headed out in an attempt to clear my head. Could Weber have taken Ida's items in an attempt to further confuse her? He had opportunity. If he had, where would he have hidden them? Could they be returned? Or had Ida been burglarized by another thief altogether? I found it peculiar her missing items had a link to the *Titanic* and mentally filed a reminder to inform Drew.

At the two-mile turnaround mark, my phone buzzed.

"Hi, Jane."

"Drew called. We're doing dinner together at Thai Fyre. Can you be ready by six?" Before my laugh exploded, Jane said, "Yeah, I know. It'll take you fifteen minutes to get ready, but really girlfriend. You could pay a bit more attention to your wardrobe. No slight intended."

"None taken."

"I think you should wear your light blue shirt, the one with the pearl-like pattern on the cuffs and collar."

I grinned. "I think I can do that." I needed all the advice I could get.

TWENTY-SEVEN

The food at Thai Fyre was good but the company and conversation were sensational—until I brought up Weber, that is.

"Girlfriend, Amanda told you to leave the investigating in more skillful hands," Jane said with her eyes glued to the handsome guy at her side.

"I'm just wondering. Weber waited forty years for payback. If Weber didn't commit suicide ..." I eyed my beau, picturing him wearing his county coroner hat.

"Not for me to say," said Pete, raising his hands in surrender.

"Then who would have wanted him dead and why?"

Drew nursed a tonic with lime. "Any outlandish theories you'd like to share?"

"Riley's at the top of my list. I wonder how he got together with Weber."

"I've read up on the case. Before his conviction, Weber worked for Riley's uncle as a nurse," Pete said. "Riley took over the practice, but he's had issues, and has had to meet with the medical board more than once. I wouldn't be surprised if he was practicing without a license."

"Riley partnered with Weber and wrote a prescription Ida didn't need. If he was unscrupulous enough to consent to be part of the plan, he could have killed Weber. If his conscience checked in, and they fought, it could've ended in disaster. If Amanda hadn't discovered Weber's true identity, Ida could be …" My heart leaped to my throat.

"That's a lot of ifs." Jane grabbed my arm in a reassuring squeeze. "Ida will be fine."

Drew fiddled with his tie, his tell for deep thought, and turned on blinking lights marking the centers of the white daisies.

Pete threw his hand up in an exaggerated attempt to protect his eyes from the glare. "And I thought you'd matured."

"Too much, huh?" The lights stopped flickering. "What about one of his cronies from prison?" His head snapped to his right and his eyes directed our attention to the Halls seated at a table for two at the perimeter of the room. He lowered his voice. "Or that Hall girl, Riley's Jack-of-all-trades? She wasn't happy with Riley or his partner."

"I think the clinic was a sham, intended solely for Weber's use." I slowly sipped my drink and swallowed, carefully crafting my words. "When Riley had done his dastardly deed, he and Weber packed up and left Carolyn without a job. I don't think they paid her either. She'd have a reason to be angry."

I felt my face heat up under the stares from three pairs of eyes. "She might have mentioned it when we rode the elevator together on their way to see the architect. She didn't believe they had money to spend on a garage sink."

I watched the Halls. They ate silently, shoveling food for sustenance. If they communicated, it would have been telepathically. Her fork stopped on its way to her mouth and Carolyn's forehead crinkled, and I glanced at Jane before she caught me staring.

The elephant in the room, the one none of us wanted to bring to the table, still plodded through the alibis Ida and Lance did not have, and our ideas dried up.

"Drew, tell us about your case," I said, abruptly.

He leaned back in his chair and flipped the switch on his tie again. "We're investigating a series of home break-ins. The thieves have stolen nearly a dozen items with a link to the *Titanic*. We can trace the earliest thefts to the Moorhead area. Unfortunately, the trail leads here. I'm just waiting for someone to report a loss."

I tapped the tabletop. "Ida lost a photo album."

He smiled indulgently. My pronouncement didn't get the reaction I'd hoped for.

"And?" Pete prompted, hoping my aside meant more. "What did she lose?"

"Photos of her ancestors."

"She's had a rough couple of weeks. She could've misplaced them," Drew said.

"She thought so too."

"Forgetfulness was one of her biggest complaints, wasn't it?" Drew sat back with an I-told-you-so pose and twiddled his fingers beneath his tie, glancing across the room. Pete leaned forward and patted my hand.

I hadn't given them the connection. "Well, her great-great-something went down with the *Titanic*."

Drew froze and stared at me. His chair flopped forward.

"And she's missing the pencil drawing Robert Bruckner

gave her when he was still a high school art student."

Jane and Pete spoke at the same time. "The *Titanic.*"

Drew held up his credit card and motioned for the server to bring the check. "And his final movie production was—"

"*Titanic: One Story.*" They said together in barely a whisper.

I bobbed my head in a 'so there.'

"Let's go see Ida," said Drew, scribbling his name on the bottom line of one large bill.

We moved so quickly I almost missed the glittering stars filling the night with hope. I clambered into Pete's truck, not waiting for his gentlemanly assist, and drank in the calming pinpoints of distant but ever-present balls of fire. Pete shook his head, but when Drew peeled out of the lot, Pete readily followed, albeit more coolly, and in minutes we'd pulled into my driveway.

Dad casually flipped his solitaire cards and eyed us curiously as we barreled through the kitchen in search of my landlady. We found her cuddled with Maverick on her couch, reading the latest Jennifer J. Morgan novel under a bright lamp. She raised a finger in a sign of the number one and put her finger to her lips. We waited.

She might have been finished reading for a while, lording her control over us, but finally raised her eyebrows from the riveting text and glanced up. She gently closed the tome as if it were a prayer book. Her hand laid atop the cover when she asked, "What can I do for you?"

Jane, Pete, and I took a step back from Drew. He took a deep breath. "I am here in a semi-professional capacity."

She nodded and tilted her head. "Semi-professional what?"

"Ah," Drew stuttered, disconcerted by her feebleness.

For a moment, I thought she'd slid back into her drug-induced fog, but her emerald eyes had an impish gleam.

"Gotcha. You're here as an officer of the law. What did I do now?"

"I'm investigating a series of burglaries."

"I know I haven't stolen anything." One corner of her mouth turned up. "Not this week anyway."

"Katie told me you lost a photo album."

Ida's accusing eyes cut my way as she nodded. "Giving away my secrets?"

"And the items may have a connection to the *Titanic.*"

Ida slowly set the book on the end table. "Where's this going?"

"Is it possible it was stolen? Could someone have taken the items?"

"Do you have someone particular in mind, Drew, dear?"

"There have been a number of items stolen from the Moorhead area to Columbia and I'm exploring the possibilities. The *Titanic* has come up in each of these thefts." He retrieved a notebook and flipped to the pages marked with a green tab. "Have you had your windows washed?"

She shook her head.

"Or maintenance work completed? Painting done? Carpets cleaned? Water mitigated?"

"None of those things."

"Who have you had in the house?

"Banning. I mean Gerhard Weber has been here since …" She trailed off, closed her eyes, and sighed. When she opened them, she said, "Since he assisted my cousin in Fargo."

Drew sat in the chair opposite Ida. He loosened his

tie. "Can you give me a detailed description of what's missing?" He pulled a pen from the elastic band holding the pages together.

"I can do better than that. I took a movie of everything I own for insurance." She picked up her phone from the end table and scrolled through the items, forwarding the relevant ones.

"Do you have any idea where Weber lived? Who he hung out with?"

She shook her head, and tears filled her eyes. "I knew nothing about him."

"I'll connect with Amanda. When she searched Weber's lair, she might have found some, all, or none of the loot, not knowing its significance. I don't know if he was in on the burglaries, but we won't discount that theory yet. Amanda's tech wizards may be able to track his movements, if they found any of his devices. I'll check with her." He flipped the notebook closed. "Assuming his death was not a suicide, be careful."

"We'll never get them back, will we." Ida shrank back onto the couch.

Pete pulled the colorful quilt up to her chin. "Never say never, Ida."

TWENTY-EIGHT

One week earlier, we worried Ida might have serious memory issues, but after Mass she informed her friends over coffee and pastries, her deficits were all behind her. She turned her back to the table and wiggled. Her laugh pealed like bells. The miraculous recovery astounded us. Saturday, she had trouble moving from the couch. Sunday, she, Ellen, and Redd played lively piano music for about an hour, and when her winning dance partner came to visit, she lambasted him with jibes of being too slow and plodding. We knew her recuperation neared completion when she reprimanded Cash for plopping ice from the refrigerator dispenser into a full glass and sprinkling sticky lemonade down the front of the door.

She waltzed around her kitchen. "Can't you read, you old coot? Why do you think I stuck that label there? It reads, 'Ice In Empty Glass Only.'" Perspiration from the physical exertion made her face glow, and she dabbed daintily with an embroidered handkerchief.

Cash answered with contrite words, but the mischievous gleam in his eyes told me he knew exactly what he was doing. He left with a promise to return daily and get her back in competitive form.

Pete and Lance invited us for grilled steaks to keep Ida from overdoing her first day back in the kitchen. Jane and Drew brought baked potatoes with multiple flavors of cheese, sour cream, butter, salt, pepper, and a sweet chili sauce from Thai Fyre. I helped Dad pull Ida's Jumbo Chocolate Crinkle Cookies out of the freezer. Ellen showed up with a container of veggies and dip. And Ida sat like a queen surveying her realm until Amanda made an appearance.

"You're just in time, Chief," Lance said, transferring the grilled beef to a serving platter. "What's new?" He corrected the angle of the tray, balancing the meat and drippings.

She ran the rim of her cap through her fingers. "Thanks, I'd love to stay, but there's no rest for the wicked." Her lips curled up in a smile and fell as she examined the binding in her hands. "We're investigating Weber's death as a suicide. There's little evidence to tell us why, but in case we're wrong, I need you, Ida, and you, Lance, to remain ultra-cautious."

Maverick lumbered to Ida's side and pushed her hand with his nose. She blinked, concentrated on Amanda's words, and ran her hand over the ridges on his head. He budged closer. She startled when he let out a bark, gave an embarrassed grin, and rubbed with more vigor. I knelt on Maverick's other side and scratched above his tail.

Amanda continued, "We have no reason to believe you're in danger, but we know Weber had ill intentions toward you. Until we tie up loose ends, and find Riley, you should be on guard. We've kept the number of those in the know to a minimum and—"

We turned in unison at the sound of a throat clearing. "Hi, all." Redd blushed. "I had a job down the block and saw Katie's car among all the others and worried something else might've happened to the missus."

Ida welcomed her. "Except for this ..." Maverick dropped his head into Ida's lap, demanding she continue scratching the sweet spot behind his ear. "I'm bored silly," said Ida, patting the narrow bench next to her. "Join us."

"I heard that bit about being on guard." Redd's admission came with an embarrassed grin. "Is it problematic I know as well?"

"It's not secret information," Amanda said. "Anyone spending time with Ida should be made aware. We're looking for Dr. Riley. If he's still in the area, we'll find him." Before I could ask if she'd considered anyone other than the corrupt doctor, she left us with uncomfortable, unanswered questions.

Lance easily overrode Ida's complaints of "I don't need a babysitter," and while he organized a week's worth of chaperones for her, the eight of us devoured every morsel of food. It was probably a good thing Amanda hadn't stayed.

In the easy company, the sun set and the stars popped on to the clink of silverware scraping across the Erickson stoneware. Maverick awaited the few remaining crumbs I brushed off the table as Ellen pulled me to the side. "I'm nervous for Tuesday. What if Sister Lawrence decides I'm not good enough? What if she can't persuade Barb to meet me ever?"

"Ellen, you've done everything you can. What will be, will be."

She knelt next to Maverick who offered a paw to shake. They both gazed at me with puppy dog eyes, and Ellen said, "Do you want to go for a walk?"

Maverick heard the word walk and bounded to standing. Dad's hopeful expression slathered guilty icing on the sister-cake. I capitulated. No reneging now or I'd pay the price one way *and* the other. "We can make a short loop." I attached Maverick's leash and checked my pocket for doggie bags. Dad smiled when I said, "We'll be back shortly."

I appreciated the silence of the first few blocks but forced myself to make conversation at the same time Ellen spoke.

"I wish you could come with me—"

"Give me a call as soon as you've finished—"

After sorting the ownership of the words, she smiled. "My meeting is scheduled smack dab in the middle of your mock trial meet."

"Leave a text message. I won't be on my phone every minute, and I can't answer a call, but I'll check often. I promise."

We passed another block, and while observing my fabulous furry friend, I contemplated my good fortune. We settled into an easy gait until Maverick picked up his pace and pulled, and I staggered behind him. I followed his intent and caught a slight figure in a royal-blue Columbia sweatshirt darting across the street. From beneath the hood, dark unhappy eyes met mine. He wouldn't have been the first to misinterpret my pet's bark. "Quiet, Maverick." Maverick checked my resolve and complied.

I lifted a hand to send an apologetic wave, but before we connected, Ellen quietly said. "Katie, I'm glad I found you."

I didn't even wait a beat. "Me too," I said. I meant it. And I forgot about the figure.

By the time we returned, only Dad, Ida, Lance, and Pete remained. Ellen picked up the Monday and Wednesday morning shifts with Ida. After profuse thanks to the Ericksons for the generous invitation, she bid us good night.

Dad escorted Ida to our chariot while Pete convinced Lance to share the next few nights spending quality time, catching up on ancestral stories, and cooking family favorites together. Rather than reject Pete's lightly disguised solicitousness, Lance accepted the request.

Maverick's second wind caught me by surprise. He pulled away. My best recourse had always been to ignore his antics and wait him out, let him get close enough to nab his collar, but Monday would begin a convoluted week and I wanted time to wind down. My impatience only invigorated him.

"Maverick, here." He bowed and stretched, springing right and left. "Here," I repeated with as much authority as I could muster the fifth time he leapt away when I extended my hand. Pete snuck behind him and caught him in a bear hug. He picked up the squirming bundle of solid muscle, carried him to the clip at the end of the leash, nuzzled in Maverick's neck, and stood him upright. "Good dog." His hug moved to me.

"Thank you," I sighed. I fit perfectly under his chin where I rested until Dad tooted the horn. I gained strength from Pete's hug and reluctantly pulled away. "Well, good night then."

My knees caved at the sight of his smile. "Good night, Katie." He planted a light smooch on my forehead.

In a smitten daze, I turned and started toward the car, but when Maverick yanked me off my feet, I released the leash again, and Pete caught my elbow. Maverick zoomed out of reach and stopped a few feet inside the dark, woodsy area behind the house. Neighborhood barks answered his agitated woofs.

"Maverick, what is it?" I approached slowly, holding out my hand. I wanted to know what caused his anxiety. He didn't play keep away, but barked until I tromped in front of him onto a narrow path between the trees. I stooped to acknowledge whatever he found and knelt next to a pair of pink sunglasses.

TWENTY-NINE

Over morning coffee, Dad and I discussed Maverick's discovery.

"Lance will look into it, Katie. He has a meeting with Amanda today, and they know what they're doing. Do not get in their way."

"The sunglasses resembled the ones Carolyn Hall wore Saturday," I said, feigning nonchalance and sipping my aromatic brew.

"You made that perfectly clear, Darlin'. That's why Lance used a napkin to grab the frames by the edge. He heard you. But the glasses could've been dropped by anyone. The path begins in the waterfowl protection park and extends for five miles, running along the tree line at the edge of the yards along the creek. And Maverick can't be the only pooch who moves items from one place to another. Even if they do belong to Hall, she has every right to be there. She only lives three houses down the block toward the high school."

I lowered my head. In Maverick's excited state, and to make sure I'd paid attention, he'd dropped onto his belly and was ready to roll the glasses to me using his nose, but Lance rescued them from further contamination and dog saliva. I tentatively raised my head. "It wasn't only me. Pete remembered the glasses too. If she's a suspect, maybe she was spying on us or Amanda."

Dad shook his head. "I know you mean well, but let it go, Katie."

"Hall had reason to be upset with Weber and Riley, especially if they let her go without any warning and without paying her. She and her husband have a building project—"

"Do not get yourself worked up. They'll investigate if there is anything there. Go to school. Take good care of your students. Leave the police work to—"

"The police. I know." I bit back a sassy retort and smiled. I jumped up and collected my jacket and briefcase. "I will, Dad."

I rustled Maverick's ears. "Good boy." Then I planted a kiss on Dad's head. "You too." Before turning to leave, I inhaled his light spicy scent laden with bergamot, jasmine, vanilla, and lemon—Brut. "Today is going to be a busy day."

And it was.

Members of the math department volunteered alternate days to help students taking the AP calculus exam, and I'd reserved my shift a month prior. We didn't spend an inordinate amount of time covering the advanced placement test sample questions during our math classes because three-quarters of our students had not chosen to take the exam. That meant clusters of earnest students armed with urgent questions bombarded me, beginning twenty minutes before the first bell, between classes, and long after the last bell.

When I finally had time to breathe, I had to respond to a long list of text messages and missed calls. Ellen sent more than half, so I saved those interactions for last.

Lance's voicemail included a warning for continued vigilance. Weber's parole officer didn't know he'd flown the coop. He'd continued to check in, and they had no knowledge of his association with Riley.

Lance's second text noted Carolyn Hall's full cooperation with Amanda. She'd lost her sunglasses and would be happy to have them returned. Amanda asked about the job, her boss, and her house project. Although she tried not to show dissatisfaction with Riley and his partner, she couldn't wait to tell all she could. Hall admitted she'd been required to drop off two or three files of legal papers from Dr. Riley at another location for Weber. Although she didn't have any idea where Riley had gone, she offered to lead Amanda to Weber's alternate local accommodations.

Amanda texted a short note saying they'd searched Weber's digs and found one small item of interest, but the place was deserted and trashed. Riley was in the wind, and we still needed to be cautious.

Among the remaining messages, I found a text from Ida with a list of groceries for me to pick up, the ingredients of which sounded vaguely like beef stew. Dad's voicemail reiterated his warning not to be involved. Drew called twice. He never left a voicemail and didn't respond when I tried to reach him. Then I read Pete's message and couldn't wait to get home. He said he had a lucky talisman for tomorrow's meet, and maybe I'd get a charmed hug or two.

I dialed Ellen's number. She didn't answer either. I read the message written in her own style of shorthand.

Sisla frwdd Eml frm Barb. Cn u undrstnd?

She attached a blurry photo of the gobbledygook—a mishmash of letters—to her message. My eagerness to see Pete superseded my usual curiosity to decipher a puzzle, and I made my trek home.

I felt certain I would not be in Riley's crosshairs but kept my eyes peeled on my drive to the grocery store and on to Maple Street where the line-up of vehicles gave the illusion of a party at Ida's. I scooted past Redd's car, Pete's royal-blue truck, Jane's green Ford Edge, and a police cruiser parked in front, and I shimmied my car onto the cement slab next to the garage. As I grabbed my homework and Ida's grocery bag of provisions, I heard Maverick barking from within.

Juggling a handful, I teetered when Dad unexpectedly threw open the door, but he caught me. "What an entrance."

"What's going on, Dad?"

"Amanda found liquid and powder diphenhydramine, so Weber had been overdosing Ida in every possible way. We don't know what he'd planned, but we can guess."

"How is she?"

"Crabby. Angry. But she and Redd have a small concert planned and that will center her emotionally. Amanda is here because she needed to question both Ida and Lance again and dismiss them as suspects. She's covering her bases in case Weber had planned to commit suicide and throw the blame on them."

"That backfired. But I think someone else could have been in that room."

"The minutes make all the difference. That unknown person could have assisted with the suicide, or committed murder, or happened upon the body and used you to bring the crime to light. Amanda's working to find Riley, but although Carolyn Hall has been helpful, she's not quite off the hook, either. It appears she and her husband secured a loan based on the combination of their projected incomes. They scrapped their dream home plans and are not pleased."

"And the glasses belonged to her." The words came out as a whisper.

Dad nodded.

Pete came through the adjoining door beaming. "Hydrangeas." He held out a glass vase. "Symbolizing good luck and fortune. They also represent happiness and enlightenment."

"Thank you. They're beautiful. They're sure to help us win."

"I hope so, but win or lose, have a great day tomorrow. What time do you compete?"

"After the students report for roll call, we'll load the bus. Our first head-to-head is scheduled for ten. The university has them scheduled for a campus tour during their bye time at eleven, followed by a cafeteria lunch. The rest of the afternoon is full. I know the kids are nervous, but they're so ready."

Amanda stuck her head in the doorway. "The concert's starting. Are you coming?"

For the next half hour, Ida and Redd played short solos and duets, rocking and swaying on the bench, pounding and tapping on the keys to raucous applause.

At the conclusion of the short evening, Amanda thanked Ida for the invitation, but before she said goodnight, she pulled up a photo on her phone and showed it to her.

Ida frowned and shook her head, but said, "It looks familiar, but it isn't mine. Did you find it among Weber's belongings?"

Curious, I slid closer and peeked over Amanda's shoulder. I caught her hand before she swiped it away. "Is it an oil painting? About this size?" I held my hands in a twelve by eight-inch rectangle.

Amanda's jaw clenched and she gave a tight nod.

"Drew's been following a string of thefts linked to the *Titanic*."

Amanda almost blew out a puff of air and her shoulders relaxed. "This is definitely not the *Titanic*."

"But it could be an amateur rendering of the iceberg blamed for sinking the big ship."

"Maybe we can bring one of the investigations to a satisfactory conclusion." Amanda sighed and texted Drew. When her focus locked into the furious pace of the texts flying back and forth, Lance steered her past Pete and me and through the furniture maze into the night.

We turned to Redd's anxious voice behind us. "Missus, what's wrong?"

Ida slumped at the piano. Pete rushed to her side and took her hand. "Ida?"

"I'd prayed she'd find my photo album with the other stolen items." She sniffed and sat up tall. "I'm just sad, not sick. It would have been more evidence Weber took it. How much spitefulness can one man entertain? If it's not with the painting, I can only hope Riley has it."

Sleep eluded me. I fiddled with my phone, caught in a search of surnames. Wilk did indeed mean wolf. If only I could live up to the admirable characteristics listed for the beautiful animal: bravery, courage, and loyalty. Erickson came from the Scandinavian name for 'son of Eric.' The Irish name Mackey translated to virile. (Wait until Jane found out.) Kidd didn't stray far from its Anglo-Saxon derivative for young goat, and I snickered. I continued my search and discovered, to my horror, the German word *rache* translated to revenge. Weber planned far in advance.

THIRTY

My students mounted the steps to the bus in a quiet anticipatory drone. The driver cranked the steering wheel and the bus lurched forward once, then rolled into a gentle thrumming along the highway. Jane's eyes closed and her head fell back against the seat. During the hour ride, I occasionally heard a few whispers as my students either pored over scripts or unobtrusively encouraged each other.

I pulled up Ellen's peculiar communication on my phone and zoomed in. The text suggested Barb had encoded the message like a crypto quip. Although I didn't have time to unravel it entirely, I noted a few clues I thought might help. I suggested she skim the arrangement of letters for recurrences: the most often used letter—E, the most repeated word—the, or single-letter words—I and A, and make the substitutions. Before the puzzle enticed me too deeply into its clutches, the bus came to a grinding halt. I hit send, packed up, and we launched into competition day.

If you didn't know our team, you might not have noticed the tension building in the set of their jaws or the straightening of their shoulders.

The trial opened the day with, "Good morning, Your Honor. My name is Lorelei Calder. I represent the plaintiff, Maggie Murphy." Our team visibly relaxed. The first round rolled out easily and came to a successful resolution.

I could tell my kids didn't want to halt their momentum, but being troopers, they didn't let their disappointment show much. The college freshman guide began our tour outside the fine arts building. She read her script and marched us briskly past the athletic complex, upper class apartments, dorms, chapel, science and math areas, lecture facilities, administration building, the student center, slowing to circle the newly constructed library, and stopping at the dining hall. She handed out brochures, stickers, and a ticket for lunch, and, without bothering to take questions or comments, disappeared.

My seniors tossed the information they thought worthless, but my underclassmen stashed the swag with stars in their eyes, dreaming of the possibilities this school could provide. After scarfing down a passable lunch, they provided each other with silent support.

The mild commendations they received for a job well done throughout the remaining sessions brought easy smiles, and they reveled in kudos from their opponents, going into the fifth and final trial pleased with the work they'd done.

Jane and I observed the last case of our competition. The opposition performed better than any other team we'd met, and their remarkable costumes lent an extra layer of credibility to their enactment, but our team rose to the challenge.

Our kids stayed in character throughout the serious subject matter of a *Titanic* lawsuit, but Jane never stopped smiling, and I mirrored her grin as they completed their case.

After she summarized the evidence and reiterated the important supporting legal issues, Lorelei proclaimed with practiced precision, "The preponderance of the evidence demonstrates you can only come to one decision. We have concluded our case in chief and ask that you find for the plaintiff, Maggie Murphy. Thank you, Your Honor." She swept the suit back vents beneath her and sat primly. She interlaced her fingers on the table in front of her and focused her attention on the end judge—the one who rolled her eyes when our Molly Brown dumbfounded the opposing attorney for a full ten seconds by adopting the gruff personality depicted by Kathy Bates in the 1997 *Titanic* movie.

Lorelei's challenger lumbered to his feet, delineated his case, and said, "Defense rests, Judge."

I straightened the front of my blazer and tamped down my pride. At least my kids had addressed the bench correctly, with proper etiquette and deference due, as Dorene had taught them.

Without acknowledgement of any sort, the judges gathered their score sheets and notes, rose, and exited through the door behind them to the chamber set aside to provide a quiet, uninterrupted place to deliberate. With the duel completed, Brock swiveled in his seat and scooted forward. He tapped Lorelei on the shoulder, nodded to her in admiration, and supplied her with a solid crash of knuckles. Her rigid back softened.

The smattering of mild, polite applause for a truly masterful performance by both teams quickly erupted into hoots and hollers after parents, friends, and teammates deemed an appropriate time had passed for their dignified courtroom decorum. Whistles and foot stomping accompanied the ovation. The teams congratulated each other and beamed at their audience. They clasped hands in a long line, and bowed as one, just like actors on stage after a tremendous performance.

Jane and I stood off to one side or I might not have seen the short, gray-haired man standing in the doorway. He clapped as if he'd been told he had to, without any enthusiasm, so he wouldn't stand out, but standout he did. His black Polo shirt stretched over his bulky frame, accentuating the muscles of his shoulders. He stopped clapping and rubbed the scruff of his thick neck, but his pale eyes widened when he caught me staring. Before I could look away, abashed, he bolted.

"Did you see that guy?" I asked Jane, slightly unnerved.

She could hardly see over her plump smiling cheeks. "Huh? Who? Where?" she followed my gaze but there was nothing to see.

Maybe I'd imagined his watchfulness. Maybe he was a dad who only had a few minutes to enjoy the celebration before he had to return to work? Maybe he'd come from another section in the state to scope out the competition? Maybe. But I had the strange sensation he'd run from *me*.

Jane and I shook hands, accepting and dispensing equal compliments. Dorene Dvorak waited patiently for the adulation to die away, her expression grave. My students wished the opposing team good luck in every endeavor, no matter what the outcome of the tournament and gravitated to Dorene. They slowly encircled her, surreptitiously glancing around the room, suspicious of her mood.

After she'd caught the eye of every one of my students, Jane, and me, she puckered her lips and peeked down at a note in her hand. Her shoulders rose to her ears. She ducked her head and squealed in glee. "You were awesome. It's true. It really doesn't matter who won, you gave your best performance ever, and I couldn't be any prouder. Thank you for this amazing opportunity." She put out her arms, encompassing her protégés in a heartfelt group huddle. They pulled away, and one at a time, threw their right hands together in the middle of the circle.

"EsqChoir," they chanted, pumping their fists three times and flinging high at the end of the cheer.

"Now we wait," she said.

Wild imaginings of Ellen's meeting exacerbated the agonizing wait time. Had Sister Lawrence provided more contact information for Barb? Did Barb show up as well? Would there be a future meeting? I examined my phone, but Ellen had not checked in. I chewed on my lower lip and decided to place a call when the voice from the overhead speaker requested we report to the largest lecture hall to reveal the day's results.

Too late now to make any difference, we either had netted a state berth or would return to everyday school life having amassed a wealth of knowledge, new skills, and friends from around the state. Our team filled two rows on the left side of the auditorium, wriggling and squirming, sweating through the congratulatory oration, the obligatory restatement of the objectives of the mock trial program, and an invitation for underclassmen to schedule a return to campus for an official visit.

The interminable speakers elevated the suspense like ominous music playing behind the scenes of a thrilling movie; however, my restless students sat still when the heels of our head judge shambled across the stage, and he took his place behind the lectern.

"Students, teachers, family members, friends ..." he began in a tone like the reader of a funeral eulogy. The somberness deadened our levity. "This competition was brutal."

My phone's screen lit up. I couldn't change where I was, and everyone who counted knew what was going on in my life today. The caller would have to wait.

Dorene's fingers gripped the armrests more and more tightly as Columbia's EsqChoir made it through each pronouncement of teams ranking from last to third. With great pomp and circumstance, the judge called the final two teams on stage where they stood to listen to his drawn-out monologue until an older voice from the audience yelled, "Give it up already."

He huffed, and the entire audience leaned toward the stage. My phone buzzed again but I couldn't tear my eyes away from my team.

"We have an unusual finish. The team from Columbia, EsqChoir, won their trial against the team from St. Cloud—"

My elated team's struggle to keep their feet on the ground without making the team from St. Cloud feel bad was cut short by the sound of the judge's gavel. "Order, order in the—" He searched for the word and struck the gavel again. "Order, please."

THIRTY-ONE

The timbre of the evening's quiet ride home differed from the morning's miles.

"How could we win the trial but lose the competition?" Jane whispered none too quietly, rolling her eyes in disbelief.

"They tally the individual case scores for the final total. We came close but just didn't make it. The head judge lauded our kids as great attorneys and witnesses though. He wished he could give out two first places, but the numbers were clear. Hey," I said and gently nudged her side. "We did much better than anyone expected. We're bringing a trophy home."

"Second place." She crossed her arms, wilted against the seat, and closed her eyes. Nothing I said would help, especially when I didn't want to accept the outcome myself. Our team had won every challenge but hadn't had to work as hard for the first two cases, and the accumulation of creativity points had suffered. So close and yet so far.

My phone buzzed for the umpteenth time, and

although I was in no mood to take the call, I accepted it without bothering to read the screen.

"Katie, I'm in trouble."

I strained to hear Ellen's soft words. "What trouble could you be in? What happened?"

"You're never going to believe it, but ... They're here. I've got to go." She ended the call.

My heart rate picked up and I said, "Ellen. Ellen?" even though I knew she no longer listened. My phone buzzed again, and I punched the button to accept the call.

"Ellen, it's not funny. You've got to stop with the drama." All the vehemence and anxiety I'd tried to squelch built up and detonated. "You can't just—"

"Excuse me," came an unfamiliar female voice. "I'm not Ellen."

I slowed my ragged breathing. "I'm sorry. I thought this was a prank call."

"You may well still think that, but I assure you it's not." She chuckled. "This is Kerstin Edwards. I'm with the Minnesota State High School League Mock Trial committee and I'm calling to let you know your team secured one of two wild card spots at the state meet. We'll email the registration paperwork. Please have it back by Friday. Questions?"

Gob smacked, my mouth gaped, and no words came out.

"Ms. Wilk? Are you there?"

I cleared my throat. "We're on our bus ride home, and it's a bit noisy," I lied. I muted the call and lightly elbowed Jane. "Listen to this." She groaned and curled away, pointedly ignoring me. Unmuting I said, "I'm not certain I heard you correctly. Could you repeat what you said, please?"

"I suppose." She sighed like a winter wind. I put my phone tight to my ear as she said it again.

"Is this a joke?" I asked, skepticism crawling up my arms like a million tiny ants.

"I would never joke about the state competition," Ms. Edwards answered. "I hope to hear from you soon."

I thanked her and stared at the phone in my hand. "Could it be for real?" I said quietly.

I pulled up the MSHSL website and searched for some kind of confirmation. Scrolling through the long list of committee member names, my forefinger landed on Kerstin Edwards. Her job titles included state mock trial tournament chairperson which lent credence to the caller.

I spun around and knelt on the seat, watching my kids. Phone screens mesmerized a few faces. Outside lights pulsed through the windows as we passed through the headlights of oncoming vehicles and flashed on the others, scowling or feigning sleep, the best way to hide dejection.

"Hey, people." I said brightly, waving. Probably assuming I merely wanted to make them feel better, my team ignored me. "I have great news. I just got off the phone with a rep from the state high school league and—"

Our driver hollered, "Sit down."

The bus swerved around a tight corner, flinging me into the aisle, and I clung to the seat back to avoid clattering to the floor. A few more pairs of eyes followed my unceremonious tossing. I was so close to the floor I could hear the wheels beneath the bus churning pebbles into the undercarriage.

When I could breathe, I settled on the slippery vinyl seats, faced the rear of the bus, and began again. "Drop your sullen faces." Jane shuffled back and forth into a sitting position. "I have some important news." One of Brock's big brown eyes opened. His bottom lip protruded as if I'd interrupted his beauty sleep, and the eye closed.

"We made it to state." I announced and waited for any type of response. My anticipatory grin morphed into confusion. "For real," I added. Galen gave me a look of compassion. I flopped next to Jane. "Honestly, we wrangled one of two wild card spots from the contenders around the state. We made it, but I don't think anyone cares."

Jane flicked her hair back, and I saw the earbuds. She couldn't hear me. I'd been talking to myself, but before I could get her attention, Lorelei let loose an earsplitting whistle from the rear of the bus. In a panic, I twisted so quickly I wrenched my back. She held up her phone and yelled at the top of her voice, "We made it."

Her strident words pierced the sound cancelling accoutrements and listening devices flew from almost every pair of ears. No wonder they'd looked at me with pity, not accepting what they thought might have been my pointless words of consolation.

"We're at the bottom of the list of state competitors," she said and added perfunctorily, "but we're there." Lorelei was one of their trusted own, and our team didn't need more corroboration. Their delayed reaction filled the bus with noisy chatter and laughter, hand slaps and fist bumps. Lorelei reclined with a satisfied grin and a scheming glint in her blue eyes.

Jane bounced on the seat, applauded above her head, rotated her shoulders, and danced a little jig. "Why didn't you tell me?"

"I tried." I pointed to the earbuds resting on her palm.

"The story I'm listening to has an important message, but ..." Her words drifted off. Her eyes glinted, and she announced, "I knew it."

She laid her hand on my wrist and wobbled my arm. She clenched her free fingers in a fist around her earbuds and squeezed with a tiny bit of merriment. My phone glowed with the first of a nonstop series of congratulatory texts from friends, parents, and colleagues.

News traveled fast. Carlee told CJ and Danica who called Dad and Ida, who in turn informed Pete. He'd already heard from ZaZa but mentioned Drew received an alert from the principal's admin.

When Drew's smiling face filled Jane's screen, she reinserted her earbuds and limited her besotted interchange to her fiancé. My phone rang again, and I answered with a chuckle. "How do?" Nothing and no one, not even Ellen, would put a damper on my mood.

Except perhaps a nun.

THIRTY-TWO

"To whom am I speaking?" came the haughty, terse greeting.

My nose turned up at the unfriendly tone, and I carefully answered. "Katie Wilk. May I help you?"

"What is all that howling? I can scarcely hear you."

I cupped the mouthpiece with my hand, trying to block some of the rollicking noise. "I'm on a school bus full of boisterous kids." Ecstatic students, I thought, and I was ready and willing to join in their revelry.

"My name is Sister Lawrence Evercrest. I've waited for Ellen Griep for hours. I am facilitating the meeting between her and her mother, but she hasn't answered any of my calls or texts. Where is she?"

I faltered. "Hours? I have no idea where she is. I know she'd planned to see you, Sister."

"This is the backup number she gave me, and you're the relative, correct?" Sister Lawrence went on without waiting for my answer. "Having a neutral person at these gatherings provides a buffer between parties, but I can't find Barb either. Did they decide to cut me out of the middle?" She sounded miffed. "Not that they couldn't, of course."

"I don't think so. Ellen said she'd be meeting you today at three, and perhaps Barb, if she decided to tag along. But I'm not sure she even had contact information for … Barb."

"Well," she huffed. "When you see Ms. Griep, please tell her if she wants to see me, she'll need to reschedule, and I don't know how soon I'll be able to fit her into my *very* full calendar." The call ended.

I supposed Ellen could have chickened out; I might have. But she'd been so focused and wishful, she'd have told me. And why her weirdly whispered call earlier? I started to compose a text, but first I'd have to deal with an enthusiastic Lorelei and an ecstatic Carlee who plopped down on the seat behind us.

"Ms. Wilk, we held out small hope." Lorelei held up two fingers with a miniscule space between them.

Carlee hooted. "We never really considered what would happen if we won, but what happens next? When is the state meet? Where do we go?"

Jane helped me sort through the paperwork in my briefcase which contained many of the answers they wanted but also raised new questions and before we knew it, we'd concluded our trip. Columbia High School loomed in the windshield.

"We have two and a half weeks until the state competition, and it's been a very long day." The excited but dazed looks on the happy faces confirmed my diagnosis. "Let's take a break, regroup, and review the information and judges' critiques on Thursday. I'll let Ms. Dvorak know."

The bus came to a jarring halt in front of the school. I caught myself and twirled around before I could skid onto the floor. After a smattering of small gasps, I stood and took a tiny bow. My response and subsequent performance received raucous applause. The students filtered off the bus and out to their respective rides. Jane accompanied me, dragging one of the plastic tubs to my classroom, sharing some of her news.

"The painting of the iceberg Amanda found had the artist's signature on the back, so it appears Weber was in on the *Titanic* heists. Riley has become more than a person of interest to Drew as it's unlikely Weber operated alone. It also provides another motive for suicide. Drew hadn't exactly kept his team's investigation a secret." She tossed her container on top of mine in the cupboard. "While Drew and I talked, my phone exploded with congrats texts. Did you get any good messages?" she asked, winking suggestively.

I grinned. "Nothing like that, but I had a strange conversation." I stared at the reflection on my phone's screen as if it might have an answer for me. "Ellen scheduled a meeting with a Sister Lawrence Evercrest today at three." Jane nodded, knowingly. "The nun waited at the restaurant for hours and Ellen never showed."

Jane cocked her head. "I realize Ellen might not have her ducks in a row in perpetuity." She startled. "Sorry. I guess Drew is rubbing off on me." She shuddered and tittered. "But that meeting was important to her."

I nodded.

"Who waits hours for someone they don't know? Ellen

has never come across as rude. I wonder what happened. I hope Sister Lawrence at least had a chance to eat."

Instead of texting I pressed the call button. In answer to Ellen's chipper message, I left a voicemail. I shrugged and glanced at Jane. "It's late. We both need some down time. Thanks for helping … all season. You're the best." I grabbed her in a hug.

"You are too, girlfriend." When she pulled free, she tossed her silky blond locks. "Byeeee."

Before I locked up and turned out the lights, I checked my email. Every once in a while, bombarded by too many communications, I'd miss one or two earlier messages. Sure enough. I scrolled through the long list of unwanted and unnecessary notices and found an unread blind carbon copy thread between Sister Lawrence and Ellen and also Ellen and another party.

Sister Lawrence's message said Ellen's inquiries about Barbara would be resolved. I sat back in the chair and mumbled to myself. "Huh, I wonder which questions have been asked?" I continued to scroll. Sister Lawrence contacted Ellen a half dozen times after three thirty and in each email, she sounded more annoyed. I couldn't blame her. But her slightly snide, unkind insinuations about Barb made me uneasy: reappearing mother, ex-druggie, street person, college dropout. I winced and closed the email.

Ellen had included me on another thread begun earlier in the day, and I read an exchange begun as introductions between Ellen and Barb. Successive messages hinted at the urgency and significance of full disclosure. I found the original message Ellen had asked me to translate, a hodgepodge of random letters in a variety of arrangements. It still didn't make any sense. At first glance, the indiscriminate convolution of characters meant nothing.

I studied the text. The most commonly used word in English is 'the,' so, just as I'd instructed Ellen to do, I searched for letter groupings and found the triplet '5y3' replicated often and the keys fit the same finger configuration as 'the.'

I settled my fingers correctly on the keyboard, then shifted them so when I typed the letters 'the' I pressed the keys '5y3.' I typed 'Aurora,' 'I,' 'a,' and 'family,' and found repetitions of my random choices in her email. Barb must have done her typing blindfolded or in the dark and her fingers, although following the normal path, hadn't been oriented accurately.

I slid my hand back into the correct position on the keyboard and typed the first five letters: '3oo3h.' When I checked the printing on the screen, my eyebrows arched to my hairline. It read 'ellen.' I laboriously copied the characters, hunting and pecking the letters and numbers from Barb's page as they should have been beneath my fingertips, not bothering to look at the typed text. When I finished, I gasped. I scrolled to the beginning of the note.

'Ellen, I know Sister Lawrence contacted you. I have so much to tell you, but I'll be gone when you receive this email. I'm sorry for the deception. I'm not your mother.'

'You have the right to know, Aurora finally kicked her drug addiction and had decided to try to get her daughter back.'

Daughter, singular.

'Blinded by his promises to love and care for me and protect our unconventional household, I believed Ozzie. He said all the right words. I wasn't like Aurora. I wasn't hooked on drugs. We controlled our futures. We could get out of Chicago when we were ready, but he hadn't adequately prepared Aurora to leave. She didn't have all the necessary skills.'

'I was new to the game. It was my fault. Six years ago, she went so far as to order a DNA test to help her find her family. I spilled the beans to Ozzie, and he was livid. He didn't like the idea of losing one of his girls. I should have known.'

'I realize now, he was just a handler. I couldn't have done anything to stop him. He killed her.'

I wiped tears from my face.

'I have no doubt, but I couldn't go to the police; he had friends in high places, very high places. I didn't have anywhere to turn, so I ran. I took Aurora's jewelry and what little money she had left and got out of there. I used it to start fresh. She wouldn't be needing anything any longer, and I knew she would've supported my escape. Her spit sample ended up in my belongings, and I submitted it but attached my name to the results. I always planned on telling her family, you. I held on to the information to remind me of her goals and set my own.'

'Right before the grand opening of my tutoring business, I saw that ugly, vile, little man scoping out my shop, and I thought Ozzie had found me. I took what I could and disappeared again, having assumed the name of one of my favorite old-time actresses, Barbara Hale. I eventually ended up at the convent. It afforded me more safety than I deserved. But Ozzie found me again.'

'I'll leave my journal with Sister Lawrence for you. I hope it answers any other questions you might have. Don't bother looking; you won't find me.'

I didn't know how high my hopes had risen until they were dashed. I had guardedly dreamed of a reunion and the possibility of getting to know my mother. But Barb had transformed the dream into a nightmare. Dad was right. He would have known if my mother was still alive.

I printed the page. When I sat down to log off the machine, I brushed the track pad. Ellen's final reply screamed at me.

'HOW COULD YOU EVER DO SUCH A THING? I'M COMING FOR YOU.'

THIRTY-THREE

I drove past our dark house onto the parking pad next to the garage, so I hadn't anticipated the back door being yanked out of my grasp. I lost my balance and stumbled inside beneath a congratulations banner as the lights flickered on and blinded me. Ida beamed. Dad popped the cork on a bottle of Ida's favorite bubbly. Maverick's wagging tail could have knocked me into next week. I unloaded my briefcase, hung my jacket, and accepted a generous pour, clinking glasses with two of my favorite people. I slurped greedily and wrinkled my nose at the fizzing tickle.

Dad read my face. "I know that look. What's up?"

I set my glass down. "It's Ellen."

He sighed with relief. "Is that all?"

"That isn't enough? She never showed up to meet the nun who found her on the ancestry site. She isn't answering my calls and texts." I flattened my palms on the table and braced myself. "I'm getting worried."

Dad set his glass next to mine. "And?"

Ida patted my hand. "Ellen's caused you a bit of anxiety before today. What's new?"

"Sit down, Dad. I have something more to tell you." He cocked his head and pulled out a seat. "The woman communicating with Ellen is not Aurora. Aurora—" I choked up. "My mother is dead."

"I thought so," he said in a hushed voice. "Has Ellen been made aware?" I shrugged, and he retrieved his phone, punched the keys, and pulled the device to his ear. The ringing continued until he disconnected. His forehead formed a deep V. "And you don't know where she might be?"

I shook my head.

"We need to worry about the living," Dad said. "We can worry about the dead later."

Words of argument and explanation coalescing in my mind jerked to a halt when I heard the familiar, but muffled, "Dragnet" ring tone. "It's Ellen," I said. I batted at my pockets, dug in my purse, and fumbled, finally opening my briefcase. The sound stopped. I called back immediately, but got a busy signal. Heat crept up my neck and I punched redial. She didn't pick up. *What kind of game was she playing?*

My phone rang again, a classic violin riff, and I stabbed at the screen, sounding exasperated even to my ears. "Hi, Pete. What's up?"

"Ellen called me."

"What does she want now?" I sniffed decisively.

"Katie, is your dad with you?"

"Yes." I slid onto the chair at the table. "And Ida. I'm putting you on speaker." After Ida and Dad greeted Pete, I said, "What's wrong?"

"She's been arrested."

"She who? She Ellen?"

"Yes. I'm afraid so."

"At least she's somewhere safe." My head dropped into my hands. I scrubbed my cheeks and dragged my hands over my face and through my hair. "What's she done now?"

"They're holding her on suspicion of—"

Pounding on our door drowned out Pete's words. "Hey," a voice called. "What's going on in there. I've been knocking at the front for the past fifteen minutes. Let me in. I've got critical information." Dad unlatched the door and admitted an animated Redd, speaking so quickly I couldn't understand her. She flinched at Maverick, and I tucked my hand around his collar and directed him closer to me.

"Sorry, Pete. What did you say?" I took a sip of my effervescent beverage.

"They've arrested Ellen for second degree murder."

And I spewed it all over the table. I had no suitable retort. "Where? Why? What?" I asked rapid fire, grabbing a white flour-sack towel, embroidered with orange and yellow roses, and dabbed at the dribbles.

"When you didn't pick up, she got me on the rebound. She's lucky they let her make two phone calls. I was her last chance."

"Where is she?" Dad said. "What does she need?"

"She's being held in the Theisen County Jail. And I think she needs an attorney."

Dad, Ida, and I exchanged glances and said simultaneously, "Dorene." Dad concentrated on his phone and stepped into the living room.

Redd set her fists on her hips. "That's what I was gonna tell ya. It's all over the news." She hollered at the phone on the table, "Hey, Doc."

Pete stammered, "Hello, Redd."

"Thanks for the update." Seldom so laconic, it dawned on me. "You're on call. I'm sorry. We'll take it from here and talk when you're not busy."

His weary yawn culminated in a grunt. "Keep me posted."

Conspiratorial whispers masked my grateful sigh. "What are you up to?" I asked.

Ida said, "I don't mean to sound callous, but I seem to concentrate and think better when I'm playing classical music, and Redd is going to help."

"Go," I said. "We can use any help you can give." They excused themselves and shuffled through the adjoining door, starting their harmonic diversion immediately.

Dad reentered the kitchen. "I left a message with that enchanting …" He gestured over his shoulder. "… musical backdrop, requesting Dorene's help in a new case and a call back. I don't know what else we can do."

On top of being a great role model and coach for my students, Dorene practiced criminal law—a partner in Casimer's former law firm—and she'd been instrumental in successfully defending the wrongly accused in too many cases to count.

Dad swirled the light golden beverage in his glass and set in on the counter. "We don't even know who she allegedly killed." He raised his dark eyes to mine. "I'm not blood, but I wonder if they'd allow her sister a chance to visit."

No, no, no. My head pounded, but my lips said, "Of course, Dad. I'll run up there after school tomorrow."

"We can go tonight—right now. It'll take thirty

minutes." His hopeful expression paralleled Maverick's puppy dog face, and laden with double the guilt, I picked up my keys and purse.

"No time like the present, but I've got to be quick. I need to get back and be ready for tomorrow." I guided him into the backyard.

After he buckled his belt, I said, "Ellen included me on an email thread. This is the last correspondence." I handed him the copy of the email. He perused the page, folded it, and returned it. I slipped it into my back pocket. He nodded forward and, at first, said nothing.

Lost in deep thought, the only words heard during half the trip were spoken by the slightly mechanical voice of our GPS, giving directions to the address Dad had entered. He adjusted his seat. "I have a few things I've kept that belonged to your mother." His voice grew soft and pensive. "I knew she was gone." We pulled into the lot and sat, taking in the colossal two-story building and massive task in front of us.

Dad cleared his throat. "Visiting hours are over in ..." He glanced at his wrist. "Thirty-seven minutes. Dorene cleared the way, and I've already submitted the paperwork. You're authorized, but I'm not." He leaned over and threw his arms around me. Before he released the squeeze, he sniffled, and I quickly wiped a smudge of mascara from below my eyes.

The car door banged and echoed through the night. The scuffing of my shoes reverberated around the empty parking lot. When I tripped and caught myself, I glanced at Dad. He gave me a thumbs up. I pressed the key fob, an audible indicator he should stay in the car. I silently repeated 'my sister' over and over as I marched in the front door and presented myself in front of the registration desk.

"Excuse me." The officer never looked up from her writing. I cleared my throat. "My name is Katie Wilk. I'm here to see my sister."

She checked a list then used the pen to point at the door which had begun to buzz. I pulled on the handle. A solid hulk of an officer with dishwater blond hair and penetrating hazel eyes pivoted on his heels. With my eyes glued to the light brown fabric stretched across his wide shoulders, I traipsed down the corridor which seemed to grow longer with every step I took. He turned the knob on a metal door with a small square window set in the top half and motioned me inside.

THIRTY-FOUR

Ellen sat behind a clear partition, pale faced, red eyed, disheveled, and having shrunk three sizes. Fine tendrils of hair escaped a ponytail and stuck to her forehead. Tears had washed lines through the grime and down her cheeks.

"Katie," she cried. She fidgeted in the pea-green plastic chair and surged forward when I took the seat opposite her. "I didn't do it."

The door opened a crack, and a hard voice said, "Back away."

If I could've deferred to my baser instinct, I'd have found a way through the glass and given her a reassuring hug. Instead, I braced my fingers against the divider and waited for her to match each, transmitting as much positive energy as I could. "I know."

The hope in her eyes dulled when I pulled a notebook out of my bag instead of a magic solution to her dilemma. I intended to take a deep breath before asking any questions but had to utilize every ounce of my limited acting ability to not hold my breath at the pungent odor of stale humanity in the room. "Dad called Dorene Dvorak. She's a great attorney. She arranged for me to visit, and she'll be in touch tomorrow. What happened, Ellen?"

"I parked my Cruze in the lot across from the restaurant where I was supposed to meet Sister Lawrence. Can you find it and get it back?" She sighed. "I love that car. The blue matches my eyes."

"Focus, Ellen," I said curtly.

She covered her face with her hands, then dragged them down her cheeks. "When I got back to the lot, I thought my car was stolen, but I found it one row over." She tilted her head, and her eyebrows came together in a question. "My headlight was busted, and the dent on the fender will need real body work. I was flabbergasted. I don't know how that happened, and I guess I locked my keys in the car; I saw them on the floor. But before I could call my insurance hotline, two sheriff's vehicles pulled into the lot, blocking me in. Four officers jumped out and barricaded themselves behind the car doors with guns drawn, just like on TV cop shows. They told me to drop my bag and raise my hands. The witnesses said my car was used to run someone down."

"Did someone see you?"

"No one could have seen me. I wasn't there," she said, offended I might think she could have hit someone. "I might have raised my voice at the restaurant, yelling about how inconsiderate people are. I tried leaving so many messages, but they came back undelivered. I was so frustrated, and when they asked me to leave—"

"They asked you to leave?"

She had the sense to look sheepish. "The manager

wanted me gone before they got busy. He said I was too loud. It was all horrible. And I don't even know a Joette Falsch."

I cocked my head, confused. "Who's Joette Falsch?"

"She's the woman who was hit by my car." She clawed at the back of her hand.

It took me a moment to process her story. "If you were in the restaurant, why didn't you see Sister Lawrence?"

"I *was* inside. I waited ninety minutes. I figured she'd ghosted me, so I left." She used the same tone of voice Sister Lawrence used to indicate she'd been inconvenienced.

"She told me she waited hours."

Ellen swung her head back and forth, thoughtfully. "Not possible. I left a little after four thirty, and by that time I knew I was being followed. I tried to tell the sheriff, but he ignored my words and cuffed me."

"Wait. What? You were being followed by whom?"

"I didn't know him. The hostess seated this guy across the restaurant. It wasn't busy. We were the only two patrons in the place, and the only things between us were two big, plastic ferns and some empty tables."

I closed my eyes and attempted to shake loose an explanation. "Ellen, Sister Lawrence waited for you. She called me to ask why you hadn't shown."

"I was there the whole time, except when I took my laptop out to my car." She looked down at her hands. "And I might have played a game or two on my phone, but I went right back in." She rushed her words. "I'd have seen her for sure. She never came into Little Italy."

I muttered. "You were supposed to meet her at Italia Fabulosa, Ellen."

"Oh." She blinked back the crystal pools filling her

eyes, and her chin quivered. "I'm hopeless."

I cringed. "Tell me what made you think you were being followed?"

She swiped at her eyes and sat straighter. "I've read up on what to watch for when you're a woman alone. I had time to kill, so when the hostess seated this skinny guy wearing a leather jacket and sunglasses at a table …" She tilted her head. "Who does that? Who wears sunglasses inside a building. I couldn't see where he was looking." She chewed on her lower lip.

"Ellen," I admonished. "Did you speak to him?"

"Who would believe anything he had to say. I used my powers of observation, checking on him out of the corner of my eye. He nursed one beverage with a little pink umbrella the entire time I was there, and he gave me the willies. When Sister Lawrence didn't show …" Her eyes shifted to the floor, as if remembering she'd incorrectly chosen the wrong restaurant. "I left, and he followed."

"It could've been a coincidence."

Her face squinched. "Yeah. Right." She shuddered. "But he …"

"But what?"

The heavy door clunked opened again. "You have ten minutes."

"I caught a glimpse of a guy again over the head of the sheriff as I was being hauled away, wrapped in the same jacket and glasses. He watched the whole thing."

Did I believe her? Of course. Who could possibly think her capable of hit-and-run.

Ellen tapped the tabletop. She'd been talking and waited for a comment from me.

"Say again, please." I concentrated to catch up.

"The trick you provided to disentangle that mixed up message worked, and I could make sense of most of it." Her almost-smile faded. "Mom's dead." She searched my face. I had no reaction left to give. "You knew?"

"I decrypted the email on the thread."

She nodded and gritted her teeth so hard the edges of her jaw turned white. "I don't know who that woman thinks she is, but I could just strangle her."

I sucked in a quick breath and said quietly, "I don't think you're in the right place to be using that hyperbole."

"What?" She glanced up, at first confused, then her blue eyes paled and grew round. "I didn't mean it, but she made me so mad I could spit tacks. Maybe you could talk to Sister Lawrence. Tell her I'm sorry. Maybe she'll know more about Barb." She drummed her fingers. "I hope your friend Dorene can perform miracles because the way everyone here is acting, I'm going to need one."

The deep voice called in through the narrow crack in the door. "Time's up."

"Ellen, you've got a good head on your shoulders." I hadn't meant to, but I clipped the last two words. "Use it."

She stood, nodding, as another officer herded her out the door at the back of the room.

The bear of a man escorted me to the exit at a wordless, plodding pace. The officer rammed his arm against the panic bar and held the door. I slipped into the night and lumbered toward my car.

Garish shadows danced across Dad's face as he thumbed through varied screens on his phone. He startled when I touched the handle, and the locks snapped free. I slunk into the seat and stared at the tall brick edifice in front of us, worrying how Ellen would get any sleep.

"How's she doing?"

"I'm not sure she entirely understands the gravity of the situation." I told him what she'd said.

"She's young and idealistic. Trusting. Like someone else I know." Dad smiled and held up his phone for me to see, and I hoped we'd soon have the opportunity to remedy the indistinct picture depicting a smiling Ellen and a surly me.

I started the car and pulled from the lot. "I'd like to talk to Sister Lawrence."

He tapped the clock on the dashboard. "It's not too late."

"Her contact information is on my phone. In the zipper pocket on the outside of my bag."

He fished it out and held up the locked screen. It took a second for him to recall the code—my birthdate—and enter it. When he found the information he needed, he raised the phone in victory. "Got it. I'll connect you."

After three rings a fatigued voice answered. "What do you want?"

I stammered and gripped the steering wheel. "This is Katie Wilk."

"I know who this is. I can read my screen."

"I'm sorry. Is this Sister Lawrence? Maybe I should call back at a better time."

"I don't think you should ever call back. Haven't you and your family done enough?"

I inhaled sharply. "You've heard about Ellen's difficulty."

"Difficulty? She killed a woman."

"She didn't do it."

"That's what they all say." In the quiet, I heard Sister Lawrence sniffle. Her voice was softer, stricken. "I'm sorry. I've been given very distressing news."

"My dad and I are not too far, and we'll only take a moment of your time. May we stop?"

After a longer pause, she said. "I suppose."

We found the address and pulled in front of a wooden sign illuminated by three bright spotlights. The block lettering read, 'All are welcome.' Shining solar lights, planted a foot apart, lit the front of the neat, symmetric, white, two-story colonial style house with black shutters and trim. It glowed like a beacon on the street of family homes in the small community.

I took three deep breaths. "Well, I—"

"Not without me. Let's go." Dad exited the car and tramped to the front door. I ran to catch up, and as I pulled alongside, the door creaked opened. I took hold of Dad's elbow, and we entered.

Soft light from a lamp on a small table against the wall cast an elongated shadow of the dour woman, standing erect, but otherwise looking every bit as intimidating as she did in her photo at the piano.

"Sister Lawrence?" I said.

"Who were you expecting?"

"I'm Katie—"

"You look exactly like your photo." She crossed her arms and tapped her foot.

"We're sorry for the inconvenience we've caused. What can you tell us about Barb?"

"Other than she's dead?"

THIRTY-FIVE

Y ou didn't know." A harrumph came from deep within the woman. "That's rich. Daughter finds mother and kills her after ... What was it? More than a dozen years? Ellen ran her down."

"That's wrong. The victim was Joette Falsch," I countered. Sister Lawrence puckered her lips. My jaw dropped. I should have put it together sooner. The hit-and-run changed everything. "Ellen didn't do it." This time I had the strength and conviction to defend her. "That woman, Barb or Joette or whoever, wasn't our mother."

"Of course she was." But I'd planted the seed, and Sister Lawrence sounded less certain though looked even more austere, if possible.

"She truly wasn't. She emailed Ellen, explaining how she appropriated our mother's DNA and attached her name to the sample."

"It seems Barb couldn't be trusted." Sister Lawrence

tapped her forefinger against her lips. Her demeanor changed and her laser eyes bore into me. "Joette, bah." She clipped her words. Suffused in red, her face radiated heat. "I don't blame your sister one bit."

It appeared Joette had fabricated stories for Sister Lawrence as well.

I shook my head. "Ellen had nothing to gain from the death. Now she can't even get answers."

"Revenge?" One of Sister's eyebrows rose. I remained still, and when neither Dad nor I reacted, Sister Lawrence said, "Come this way."

The heavy wooden double doors opened to a cavernous room. Sister Lawrence switched on the top globe of the table lamp on the credenza, sending its dim rays onto a ratty yellow velour couch, a tufted avocado green chair, two mismatched scratched end-tables, and a well-worn rocking chair. In contrast, the lustrous high-gloss black grand piano at the back of the room should have been the centerpiece on a glorious stage.

She sat straight-backed on the edge of the piano bench. I sank into the rocker, maneuvering my backside to avoid the jab of the sharp springs. Dad lowered himself onto the couch, maintaining balance by draping his arm over the back of the sofa and hanging on. Sister pointed to an envelope positioned at the center of the nicked coffee table on top of a short stack of books.

Someone had scribbled 'Ellen' on the front in red pencil. I leaned forward and seized it before she changed her mind.

"She had all the proper identification under the name Joette Falsch, but I knew the dead woman as Barbara Hale. The first police officer on the scene recognized her—she'd tutored his son—and he reported the accident to me. It seems whatever plans she had died with her." She crossed her arms. "I suppose you'll want the journal too. It details her last few years. I don't need it any longer."

"You've read it?"

"Of course." She snorted. "She left everything behind and entrusted her story to me." Sister Lawrence reached into a deep pocket and held up an envelope with her name filling the front in the same messy red scrawl. Vacillating between cynical and contrite, she said, "The Welcome Residence is …" A vein pulsed in her forehead. "Was a halfway house of sorts. Barb came seeking anonymity and a place to begin anew. I presumed the name could be an alias, but I should've dug deeper. I had such high hopes for her." She drew in a long breath. "What questions do you have for me?"

Dad sat forward and planted his elbows on his knees. "We don't believe Ellen was driving the car when it killed, um, Barb, but the police believe she had a motive to run her down."

"Ellen came to talk to you but waited at Little Italy, instead of Italia Fabulosa, so you couldn't connect." I watched her carefully. I'd skip mentioning the unobserved time Ellen spent returning her laptop to her car and playing games. "How did you find Ellen in the first place?"

"I've retired from performing." She glanced wistfully at the beautiful piano and ran the knobby fingers of her left hand lightly over the corner of the instrument. She stretched to straighten the deformed appendage and winced with pain. Her chin rose and she said haughtily, "I started recording the history of our convent. We've had illustrious sisters and oblates, and I wanted the world to realize the vast menagerie of hard-working lovers of mankind, bluebloods, intellectuals, scientists, and artists who gave over their lives and came together, devoting themselves to serving our community, helping the poor, teaching, or providing health care. Those who wished submitted DNA samples in order to reconnect with family or provide ancestral statistics.

"Barb came at an opportune time. She knew her way around the ancestry site, using the results of the DNA sample she'd submitted for the purpose of demonstration and helped me immensely. Barb had searched for relations, but she'd resigned herself to a solitary life until you and your sister emerged as a match. At first, she seemed pleased. I really thought she was your mother, and I hoped she'd concluded the wayward chapters of her life and owned up to at least one of her past mistakes, but that didn't happen." A hint of anger played on her face. "Her journal details her shady origins and the continuation of her impulsive lifestyle." She took a few breaths to settle down and shook her head in disgust. "I thought David was so good for her."

"David? Who's David?" I asked.

"David Koskiniemi owned the tutoring service where she worked. I thought someday they'd get together. He thought so too. I do not appreciate deception in any form," she said indignantly. "Her extracurricular activity sullied our impeccable reputation and sabotaged the work we've been doing." She spat the words. "Barb's death derailed the project, my project, and I can't let her tarnish our good name." Sister Lawrence inhaled sharply and bowed her head. "I'm sorry. I'm having a difficult time processing everything I'm learning. "

I wondered what had infuriated Sister Lawrence. Was she angry enough to kill Barb? I understood why someone would want to use Ellen's car and shift blame, but how would Sister Lawrence have been able to pull that off?

As if she could read my mind, she volunteered, "From three until five, I sat in a booth at Italia Fabulosa. I had tea and called you. If there's nothing further, I have a funeral to prepare."

"One last question, if I may," said Dad. "Who was Joette?"

"Perhaps the police will be able to tell you. I don't know. I worked next to her for the last five years and can't be certain anything I believed was true. Here's your next read, mostly fiction, I surmise." She lifted the linen covered book from the table and placed in in Dad's hands, and we headed out.

The door closed behind us, and Dad threw me for a loop, saying, "I'm ravenous."

I crinkled my brow. "Want a burger?"

He shook his head. "I'd like to eat a good, solid, sit-down meal. It's been a while since Ida's been able to provide her great cooking."

"Dad? What do you have up your sleeve?"

He pulled up both sleeves. "As you can see, nothing." He lowered the cuffs and checked his phone. "How about we check out Italia Fabulosa? It's six blocks away."

I was too tired to be wary and capitulated to his whims. We took the first open parking spot I found on the street. "Why are we here?" I asked, pocketing my key fob.

"Lobster ravioli for me, and I wouldn't be averse to leftover lasagna alla Bolognese."

My mouth watered and my stomach grumbled in response to the air, redolent with basil, tomatoes, onions, garlic, and wine, pouring over us as we entered. Even as late as we were, the place was hopping, and the hostess seated us at one of the few remaining tables in front of the plate glass window.

"Would you like something to drink?" our tall, blond, blue-eyed server asked. "May I suggest the Pear Martini? It's our signature cocktail."

We requested two. While I read the mouthwatering menu, searching for something equally satisfying to lasagna, Dad scanned the restaurant.

Our agile waiter successfully dodged patrons and servers alike, weaving through the busy tables, returning with a two-tone beverage—a maraschino cherry floating in a vivid narrow red layer topped with a delicate pale-yellow liquid.

"This cocktail is beautiful. How do you make it?" I asked.

He mimed zipping his lips on the secret as he stepped away and returned shortly with a bowl of mixed greens dotted with small chunks of cheese, black olives, and croutons, smothered in a berry vinaigrette, and a linen napkin covering an aggregate of bread stuffs. He dutifully recorded our order, but before he could retreat to the kitchen, Dad took an appreciative sip of the drink and said, "Do you know Sister Lawrence Evercrest."

Our server shot Dad a dubious eye roll. "Everyone knows Sister Larry. She started the Welcome Residence fifteen years ago and has been here ever since. She's put her heart and soul into that place and our little community. Why do you want to know?"

"She recommended this restaurant and gave it rave reviews."

"She's quite the promoter for us, always telling someone new to come in for lunch or dinner. She's here Monday through Friday unless she has a church meeting, in which case …" He leaned in and whispered conspiratorially, "She usually shows up for a cup of tea." He used finger quotes when he said tea, winked, and bobbed his head. I nodded back as if I understood.

"Did she come today? Is she here now?" I made a show of craning my neck over the crowd.

"Did we miss her?" asked Dad.

"Yes, sorry. She was here for a few hours." He sorely confounded our efforts to find a hole in her alibi. "She's always writing in her notebook, but today she acted like she might've been expecting someone. Was she waiting for you?"

"I don't think so. She didn't know we'd be here," I said with ease, and I wasn't lying.

The pleasant waiter secured his pen in the breast pocket of his white linen shirt and smirked, reminiscing. "Sister Larry comes in everyday at the same time, three-thirty on the dot."

My drink stopped on the way to my lips, sloshed over the edge and onto my fingers. "Today too?"

"For sure today. I had a barber's appointment at three o'clock and we walked in together a touch after three-thirty." He closed his eyes and clasped his hands over his heart. "Adore that lady. She gave up everything to follow her heart's desire and make Welcome Residence a success. It's too bad the bishop pulled the plug. One of the occupants was up to no good, using it as her private bordello."

Dad and I exchanged looks. We didn't know what the loss of thirty minutes meant other than Sister Lawrence had lied.

THIRTY-SIX

The speed limit sign reflected in my headlights, and I lifted my foot off the gas pedal, willing my nerves to settle down.

"So what if Sister Lawrence didn't get to the restaurant at exactly three o'clock?" Dad's stern look kept me in line. He had limitless experience poking holes in my theories. I'd grown up having to justify my paltry excuses and accept responsibility when warranted. He'd give me a new perspective and help me scrutinize the possibilities. "Just because she was late doesn't mean she ran Barb down."

"The name was Joette Falsch."

"Okay, but if you'd question every person who couldn't account for their whereabouts from two to five today, you'd be flooded with suspects. Even me. What possible motive would she have had?"

I squared my shoulders. "She lied. The history she was writing was important to her, and she made it a point to tell us she was going to exclude that *woman*. And having to pull the plug on her life's work might definitely have fueled her anger."

Dad shook his head. "You don't need to go there. We don't know for certain if Joette caused the Welcome Residence to close. We have to read the journal." With the voice of reason, he added, "The hit-and-run could've been an accident."

"Maybe, but if we don't prove a suitable alternative, accident or not, the sheriff is going to believe Ellen did it, and you know they'll stop searching for the real hit-and-run driver."

He yawned, loudly, and it sounded painful. "Who or what else do you have?"

"Do you think Joette planned to leave because she didn't want to face Ellen." *And me.* "Maybe her friend, David, didn't entertain the thought of her leaving. They could have had different expectations for the relationship. Or her life before might've caught up with her. That guy, Ozzie found her once. Maybe he found her again?"

Dad's head dropped back against the seat, and within seconds he was snoring. Rest was a balm. "What do I do next, Dad?" I whispered. "I look into it."

I concentrated on the road and kept my meandering thoughts in check until the North Maple Street sign came into view. I jostled Dad as we turned, hoping to rouse him enough to be able to walk into the house but not enough to fully wake him.

I parked, and he mumbled, "Leave me be."

"Not happening. I'll get you inside and you can flop down anywhere you want." I opened the passenger door. Over his objections, I pulled him to standing, and arm-in-arm we stepped onto the pavement. Movement in the shadows startled me, and we nearly toppled. That woke him up.

A familiar figure swayed and hummed under the large oak. "Ida?" I said.

She moved tentatively into the yard light, brushing small pieces of bark from her hands, but recoiled when Dad stepped toward her. He backed up, and his brow furrowed.

"Do I know you?" she said.

Understanding replaced his confusion. "I'm Harry. What's your name?"

She shivered and hid her face, glancing at her stockinged feet. "I'm … I'm lost," she said without a hint of teasing. Her hair stuck out in every direction, and she tried, unsuccessfully, to pat it into place. Even the last few weeks, I'd rarely seen her without lipstick let alone mascara, eye shadow, and blush, but she didn't wear a lick of makeup.

"This is Katie." Dad gestured for me to go to Ida's aid. "She's going to get you a cup of tea, and I'm going to call my friend, Pete."

"Are you cold?" I removed my blazer and threw it over her shoulders. My words were thick. "We're here now. You'll be alright." I guided her inside and settled her into a chair at our table.

"You have a nice kitchen, but it's small."

I put water on and sifted through the bags. "What kind of tea would you like?"

"Do I like tea?" She lifted her head and swiveled it around the room, alighting on the over-sized ceramic range. "My mother has a stove like that, I think."

Maverick roused from his mat and waddled to Ida, sticking his nose into her side. She giggled and said, "Good dog." She carefully placed her hand on his head, gently ran it down his back, waited a beat, and repeated the process. "Is he yours?"

She didn't remember him, but Maverick knew her. I sucked in air to keep from crying. I thought stopping all the weird meds Rache/Weber prescribed had halted the progress of her malady. I set a small plate in front of her. "Biscotti? Chocolate, sea-salt caramel, or lemon?"

She chose the sea-salt caramel and bit daintily, catching the crumbs in her palm. She said something under her breath while I brewed the tea.

"What did you say?"

"Limone and cioccolati," she said, indicating the two flavors remaining on the plate. "Is that right?"

"I think so." I wanted to add, 'but only someone familiar with a kitchen would know that.' She took a sip from the cup of tea and sighed. I said, "Is there anything you need?"

"My memory." Her green eyes glistened. She didn't often cry, and I didn't know how I'd be able to stand it. She stared at the teacup and her mood altered, and she growled, "I won't tolerate being like this. What am I going to do?"

She cocked her head and swiped her eyes at the sound of a knock on the door.

Dad entered first. "Hello again. Look who I found."

When she figured out Dad was talking to her, she turned to study the man who'd accompanied him. She'd known him for his entire life, and yet there was no hint of recognition, but I'd never been happier to see Pete.

He bent at the waist and said with his dashing smile, "Hello, pretty lady."

"Who are you calling a pretty lady?"

"You." He lowered his chin and grinned as Ida blushed. "Would you like to ride in an ambulance? They only allow one patron at a time, and this is your lucky day. I think they'll take you." He extended his elbow. She looked to me for confirmation, and I nodded. She grabbed his arm, and he hauled her to standing.

"You look like a nice boy." She gushed like an infatuated schoolgirl and stepped regally out my rear door.

"Dad, what's going on? Weber's gone. How could it still be happening?"

"Pete's carefully weaning Ida of the drug, and her confusion may be symptomatic of residual poison, but Ida's definitely relapsed." Dad shoved his hands into his pockets and grunted, disgusted. "The substance can be delivered in so many different forms, Pete believes Weber sabotaged whatever he could get his hands on. Amanda is sending a crew and under the direction of Pete's pharmacist friend, Matt Lannie, they'll check or chuck everything."

"You mean diphenhy …"

"Diphenhydramine. While he was here, Weber had free reign. Redd was right. She did see him fooling with the medication, adding the drug to the turmeric capsules, and probably Ida's sugar and flour, hand cream, soaps, vitamins, and anything else."

"Where did he get it? Was Riley in on it? Is he still a threat to Ida? How's Lance?"

"Whoa. One hurdle at a time."

I jumped when the siren whooped outside. "She'll be okay, won't she?"

Dad exhaled with deliberation and said, "Yes. Of course. We're talking about Ida, and Pete's on the case."

Our back door opened, and a man covered from head to toe in a white HAZMAT suit shoved his safety glasses onto his head and said, "Folks, I'm Matt Lannie. I'm going to have to ask you to leave while we sweep the premises. Pete didn't think the perpetrator had access to your half the house, but just to be on the safe side, we'd like you to find someplace else to stay while we remove any possible remnants of the pharmaceutical."

My tired eyes flashed wide. "Can we pack a bag?"

"Yes, but be quick about it. The drug can be anywhere. It comes in powder, liquid, or cream form—"

"Cream? Ida slathers lotion on her hands all the time. She uses it to smooth and soothe after she plays her piano. I think there's a tube on the music stand."

"She's quite the accomplished musician. The sooner we take care of the contamination the better. We'll start upstairs at Ida's. Pete hired a team to clean both apartments when we finish. But you know Ida. It'll be difficult for her. We'll record what we discard for insurance and for her piece of mind."

My stomach clenched. "What are you hunting for, Dr. Lannie?"

"Call me Matt." He settled the protective lenses back on his face. "We'll toss any open toiletries, cosmetics, toothpaste, soaps, things the guy could've exposed to the chemical, as well as unsealed food stuffs, and cleansers, that sort of thing. We're not taking any chances and eliminating every possible tainted item in Ida's home. The cleaning crew will polish the surfaces, wash and vacuum the floors, and change out all the filters, clean the vents, and the fireplace. We'll leave no speck of dust unturned."

"Thanks, Matt. Will Ida be okay?"

"You caught her right away. She didn't have time to wallow in her predicament. And Pete's the best. He said she'll be right as rain in no time. She'll have some withdrawal, but he's watching her."

Three days' worth of outfits, walking gear, a plastic bag of dog food, two pairs of shoes, and a toothbrush left plenty of room for my toiletries. I debated bringing my makeup and toothpaste with me and lost. With the possibility, however slim, of being tainted, I tossed it all. I clomped down the stairs and met Dad by the back door.

He hefted his small backpack and asked, "Ready?"

I shook myself and clipped the leash to Maverick's collar. "Where are we going?"

THIRTY-SEVEN

Dad plucked a number of disinfectant wipes from an industrial-sized plastic box on the counter near our back door and thoroughly scrubbed his hands. "You're dropping me off at Lance's, and you and Maverick are staying with Jane. It's all arranged." As a precaution, I followed his lead, fished two wipes, and tossed the used disposable cloths in a large, heavy-duty garbage container.

We hauled our suitcases down the steps, evading the swarm of PPE clad purgers buzzing around the house, flitting in and out the front door, hauling bags and boxes of refuse. Matt supervised the separation of the meds and sorted the hazardous articles destined for assorted colored waste containers.

We threw our luggage in the rear seat, and I started the car. I bounced from the driveway and onto the lawn, squeezing past the pileup of vehicles. Dad ducked his head to keep the bright third-floor turret in his sight. "Every nook and cranny is under scrutiny. They won't miss anything this time around," he said. "I hope."

When we were out of sight, he sat back in the seat and exhaled, releasing his tension. "Whatever possesses someone to want to hurt another? I can't understand it." My breath caught—this comment from the victim of a gunshot to the head.

The porchlight blinked on when I parked in front of Lance's modest ranch-style home. Dad reached over and pulled me into a tight embrace. "I love you, Katie. Give Jane a hug from me too." He snatched his pack and strode up the walk. The door opened before he reached the buzzer, and Lance put up his hand.

After I returned the greeting, Maverick slithered over the seatback and nestled next to me. "I suppose I should reprimand you, but you know exactly what I need, don't you, boy." He sat tall, watching the passing scenery until we parked in front of Jane's rental. He slathered dog saliva up my cheek, and when I opened my door, he leaped over me, wagging his tail in anticipation of seeing her. Bright lights gleaming from each of Jane's windows blinded me, and I hoped we wouldn't cause a city-wide power brown-out with the combined electrical utilities consumed at Ida's, Lance's, and here.

My suitcase snagged on the seatbelt, and as I stooped to slide the bag loose, I gulped. The corner of Joette's journal appeared under the driver's seat. I clamped two fingers on the cover, dragged it over the top of my suitcase, and secured it under my arm.

"What's going on, girlfriend?" Jane said, pulling the door wide. "Your dad said you needed a place to hang your leash tonight." She knelt in front of Maverick and ruffled his ears. "What a good boy you are."

I purposely gave her an enigmatic smile. "Good news or bad news first."

"Good. Always."

"Ida relapsed—"

"That's the good news?" Jane slapped her hand over her mouth.

I said in a rush, "But Pete said she should be fine. The bad news is Dr. Lannie has to scour Ida's house for any remnant of the pharmaceutical Weber used to make her believe she had dementia. They are tearing it apart and cleaning it up. Weber didn't like Maverick, so I'm fairly sure he didn't plant any of that poison in our apartment. We had to leave, and Dad pawned me off on you. I hope it's okay."

She left finger indentations in my arms with the fierce hug she gave me.

"I'm ready for you both." Jane yawned. "Your room is the first one on the right. We'd best call it a night. *You* need your beauty sleep." She reached for my suitcase, wearing a smug smile.

"You don't need to do that," I said, and as I rolled it out of her reach, the journal slipped out of my grasp and hurtled to the floor. Jane picked it up, and a slim leather folio of photos skidded from under the back cover.

We both went to pick up the booklet, looked deep into each other's eyes, and giggled. "It's all yours," I said.

Jane squeezed the upper corner between her thumb and forefinger and flipped the first few pages. She stopped on one and turned it toward me, making the face visible. "I recognize this guy from somewhere."

I scrutinized the photo, squinting past the suit coat, tie, and horn-rimmed glasses. "He stood in the doorway after our last trial." My head tilted, remembering the exhilarated chaos after our final case. "But you said you didn't see him."

"Not there, but he left as we walked into Thai Fyre

Saturday night. Why would Barb have his photograph? Who is this guy?"

She slipped the picture from its plastic guard. I always turned photos over to see what information, if any, the historian might have recorded, and so did Jane.

"Who's David Koskiniemi?"

"According to Sister Lawrence, he is, *was* a good friend of Barb's."

She picked up on my word change. "He's not a good friend of Barb's now. Oooh, tell me more."

My bottom lip protruded, wishing I could retract my statement. I slithered to the floor, and Maverick, with a cold nose to my cheek, persuaded me to continue. "She's dead." Jane drew back, but before she could ask anything, I went on. "She was the victim of a hit-and-run."

"Are you sure this guy is, er, was a friend?" Jane flopped beside me. "Could he have done it? He has shifty eyes. She tapped the photo, and her wild imagining had me shaking my head.

"They've arrested Ellen."

"Ellen?" Her mouth dropped open.

I hung my head. "Dad and I visited her tonight—"

"After our meet?" She checked her wall clock. "How did you manage to find the time? Never mind, I don't want to know. But where's Ellen? How is she? What do you need? Tell me everything." She popped up and marched to the kitchen.

Bracing against the wall, I hauled myself upright. I trailed her, feeling like a lost soul. She stood in front of her impressive wine rack, studying the bottles and extracting a Caymus Cabernet Sauvignon. She always served nice wine. When her dad visited, he stocked up on what he liked, and I benefitted from his palate. It helped he had a deep pocketbook. She used a pneumatic opener, sniffed the cork, and poured a taste. She swirled, and the ruby red liquid left enticing thick legs dripping down the sides of the big crystal bowl. She sipped and purred, and I accepted my own glass.

I sat at her table while she stuck her head in the fridge, rooting around for something to accompany the wine. She nabbed a wedge of Jarlsberg and a brick of cheddar. Although I had no need for food, my mouth watered as she deftly sliced the ambrosial cheeses with a wire cutter, overlapping the slices on a narrow white tray. She tossed a small chunk to Maverick. "Crackers?" she asked.

"No. I—"

She plopped onto the seat and took a swig. "Did Ellen do it? That's one way to get rid of a poor excuse for a mother."

"She wasn't our mother." Remembering the printed copy, I wiggled the email out of my pocket for her to read. Jane's eyes narrowed as I tried to relay my abridged explanation and theorization.

She jabbed her finger at the photo of David. "We have to figure out how he fits into this."

"I'm not sure he does. Let's take a look at the rest of the photos."

Jane tapped on a handsome woman in one. "Is this Barb?"

I shrugged. "I guess so."

The thin folio held a few dozen snaps of the same woman, several with David, one with a table full of young children pouring over a stack of books, and a few landscape stills. The last two took my breath away.

THIRTY-EIGHT

The worn crackling plastic pages fell open as if viewed more often than the rest. The photo on the left showed three people on a city street.

Following the previous images of the same female, this much earlier shot had the younger likeness standing with an arm wrapped around another woman as they posed for the camera. Her long dark braid hung over one shoulder. Her white teeth gleamed through scarlet-colored lips. She stood provocatively in a risqué black dress as if having dared the photographer to take the picture, and by the surprise in her face, couldn't believe the photographer had done so.

"These two could be sisters," said Jane.

On anyone else, the platinum blond hair color of the second woman would have come from a bottle, but the lustrous waves spilled from a loose topknot with a natural sheen. The familiar ears showed off hoops dangling beneath the casual updo. The eyebrows, nose, full lips, and cheekbones resembled a more mature, fuller version of Ellen, and I found the Wilk cowlick in the curls near her forehead, but she forced a smile, and the hooded eyes were difficult to read.

"Ellen looks like her." Jane tapped one figure in the photo and watched me. "Is that your mom?"

I might have even seen a bit of myself there and slowly traced the outline of a face I thought could belong to my mother. As if I'd touched a livewire, I jerked my finger back when it came full circle and landed on the third image. The chiseled man in the background inclined against an older model car. He scowled, and I shuddered. One could lose the sense of up and down, right and wrong, looking into those bottomless black eyes. He watched the two women possessively, his strong muscles tense and ready to spring. Where had I seen eyes like that before?

"This one has to be Barb, doesn't it?"

I screwed up my face. "It sure seems that way, but I don't know." I glanced at the clock, noting the late hour. "I'll have to show Dad tomorrow. He'll be able to tell us more, though he never met Barb either."

Jane removed the photo from the plastic sheathe and read the back. "It doesn't identify Barb. The names written on the back are Joette, Aurora ..." She stopped reading and stared at me.

I inspected the photo again, checking it from every angle. "This must be my mother. Dad always said he was a lousy photographer, so I've only seen a handful of blurry pics. She ..." I summoned my courage. "My mother preferred to be the one behind the lens." I tried to drown out the sound of blood pounding in my ears.

Jane nodded as if understanding. "She was beautiful."

She continued to read, "And Ozzie."

I grabbed her hand and tightened my grip. She winced, but I couldn't help it. "This is Ozzie? In Barb's email, she said this man murdered Aurora, my mother." I scrutinized the photo and gulped air. Maverick brushed against my leg. "I've seen him before." I rubbed my forehead, trying to recall where. "I've got to tell Amanda. Barb's hit-and-run case isn't in her jurisdiction, but she needs to know what happened to Ellen. Do you think she'll help?"

"You have good instincts. Send her a copy of the photos and share your suspicions. She listens. Let her do her job."

I texted, but Amanda didn't respond; she probably slept at night whenever she could. I tried to make my body relax even though my heart thudded in my chest.

Jane returned the picture and slid the folio between us. She hooked her blond locks behind her ear, and we leaned over to peer at the last image—a chubby baby with plump pursed lips clapping pudgy dimpled hands and big round eyes gazing at the camera. "You can almost hear this one coo." Jane said with a smile. I nodded.

She withdrew the photo and turned it over. My heart flip-flopped. The chronicler had drawn hearts in the shape of an E. "It has to be Ellen." I failed at sounding anything like upbeat. Jane reinserted the picture.

Joette stole my mother's DNA, her money, and a photo she'd kept of her younger daughter. I swigged my wine and examined the photo of Ozzie again. Some of the warm liquid went down the wrong pipe, and I sputtered. If I avoided the eyes, he had an ordinary face, one lost in any crowd, nothing unusual, but as I studied it, I remembered where I'd seen him before.

My hands started to shake, and the wine splashed from inside the glass, over the rim, and onto my fingers. I trembled. Maverick sat in front of me, trying to calm me as he laid his head in my lap, the same way he did for Ida when her agitation spilled over. "Jane, this guy's in Columbia."

"Here? How sure are you?"

I buried my face in my hands and rubbed my temples, clearing my mind of extraneous thoughts so I could remember better. When I came up for air, I said, "Seventy-five percent. Ellen and I ran into him one evening walking Maverick. Why would he be here? What could he be looking for? If he's the murderer, he has to be found." I texted Amanda again, with my additional concerns. Still no response.

When exhausted, I yawned like my dad—loudly and noisily—and I couldn't contain it any longer. Jane stilled and her eyebrows knitted together. "C'mon, girlfriend. You've done what you can. Let's get some sleep. Remember we have classes tomorrow, and I don't know about you, but my carriage turned into a pumpkin at midnight."

I followed her to the second floor. Before she released me from a firm hug, she whispered in my ear, "We'll figure this out."

Maverick jumped on the bed and curled in a ball, asleep before I could even brush my teeth. I tossed and turned for what felt like hours. Every time I closed my eyes, I either saw Ozzie hovering at the back of the photo behind Aurora and Joette, or David standing in the doorway clapping but ready to bolt.

Dim light from the streetlamps filtered through the blinds, and I finally dropped off, but it seemed the alarm went off as soon as my eyes closed. I stretched and moaned, then grabbed my phone from the nightstand and sent a copy of the photo from the folio to Dad. I waited for a few minutes, but either he wasn't awake or wasn't sure what to say. I dragged myself out of bed and released Maverick to the outside before feeding him his bowlful of nuggets. Getting ready for the day took concentrated effort.

I picked at the waffles studded with fresh strawberries and drenched in maple syrup Jane placed on the table. She funneled her energy into flitting around the kitchen. Mine came out as knee jerks, bouncing up and down. We didn't exchange many words, but before we left for school, she squeezed my arm. "It'll be okay. You'll see."

Maverick punctuated her statement with a gentle woof. "You be good, Mav. Dad will stop by and let you out. I'll be by later."

I drove to school on autopilot. Jane pulled up and parked next to me. We walked into the building together, and before she veered off to her classroom, she said, "Let me know when you hear something."

I nodded and plodded slowly to the math department where Lorelei, Carlee, Brock, and Galen hovered around my desk.

At the sound of my footsteps, they turned as one. They glanced back and forth until Brock said, "Lorelei, you've got to tell her now."

She breathed deeply and said, "I guess we need to talk."

THIRTY-NINE

W e need to talk' always sounds ominous," I replied. "Don't think I'm going to change my mind about taking the day off. We all need a break." Brock not-so-secretly prompted Lorelei with a light jab, and she batted at his hand. "What's up?"

"The state tournament is going to be held the weekend before the advanced placement exams begin." Lorelei forced a half-hearted smile. "Some of us—"

"Not me," Brock said dismissively.

"A few of the more serious members of our team are concerned about the slate of tests scheduled for Monday and don't think they can give one hundred percent to both proceedings, so they've decided to forego our mock trial."

"No problem. We have two excellent understudies, and we've interchanged roles enough we shouldn't have to worry." The rules allowed for six extra students, but between attrition and activities, our number of spares had dwindled.

"We have *two* great backups." Lorelei corrected and lowered her head. I waited for the hammer to fall.

"And three seniors are taking the Monday AP Chinese exam." said Brock, mimicking shock. "Sheesh. What sane person even does that?"

"Our friends have taken four years of Chinese. They've earned the chance to get college credit," said Lorelei. "And the likelihood of our winning is infinitesimal."

Brock lifted his hands and rolled his eyes in mock disbelief. When he finished his exaggerated tirade, given entirely for show, he nodded and said, "Go on. Tell her the best part."

All three students eyed Lorelei as she raised her chin and glued on the hint of a smile. "Prom is the same Saturday evening."

"Oh." Sadly, I deflated. "And you really don't want to miss prom. I get it."

Four mouths gaped for a second but immediately couldn't talk fast enough or loud enough. I held up my hand and stopped the blustering.

Galen cleared his throat and swung his finger in a circle at the four of them. "We want to compete at the state mock trial, but we can't force anyone to skip their last prom or whatever. We figure if all goes according to the schedule posted online, in all likelihood, we'll be back in time to make most of the dance anyway."

"Brenna's mom doesn't want her to miss the flowers and vehicle, the dinner, the glitz and glam getting dressed up, and taking photos at the last big high school hurrah, and it's the same for Allie and Ashley," said Carlee. "More than half of our team have another shot at prom next year."

I searched Brock's face. He'd been able to balance his practice schedules, but as a senior, this would be his final season pitching for the Columbia High School Cougar baseball team. "What about sports?"

"We don't have any golfers on the team. There isn't a track meet or softball game scheduled, and the only possible conflict I could have would be a makeup game, and I'll just be too sore to pitch." He massaged his formerly injured shoulder and moaned, effectively displaying discomfort until the grimace morphed into a grin.

"We don't want to pressure anyone, but we're wondering if you have any ideas for possible stand-ins," Lorelei said.

I pointedly gazed at each in turn. "Truly? We don't have to go. Have you spoken to our other team members? Are they good with this?"

"Yup. We only need one more body. It has to be a quick learner, but Allie promised to provide some fast acting lessons."

I felt the walls of the rooms loom close. As our strongest acting asset, Allie believably played any part we threw at her. She'd be missed.

Brock flipped a lock of black hair from his forehead. "What'll it be, Ms. Wilk? Are you in?"

I prayed I mirrored their hopeful expressions. "I'm in, and I can say with complete honesty, I believe we will find an adequate replacement. You give it some thought, and I'll talk to Ms. Mackey. If we can find more than one, it would be even better."

They'd already begun tossing around names of friends, listing their positive and negative attributes, as they left my room. I picked up the in-school line and called Jane while scrolling through my emails.

"Hello, Jane Mackey." The signature graphic on one of my messages caught my eye, and I didn't answer Jane immediately. "Hello?" she repeated.

"Sorry, Jane. I was distracted."

She went on alert. "Is everyone okay?"

"I haven't heard anything new, but our state entry email invite arrived and sidetracked me."

"That's great news." When I didn't respond she added, "Isn't it?"

"Yes and no. Three of our students will not be participating at the state mock trial. We'll be one competitor short, but the rest of the team would still like to go so we need to find a fill-in fast." I couldn't hear any sound. I pulled the ancient receiver away and shook it to make sure we were still connected. "Jane? Are you there?"

"Yes." The word came out in three syllables. "How are we going to do that?"

"We have until Friday to turn in our registration materials. Any ideas?"

"I'll think about it. It's good we haven't scheduled a practice for today, but we'll probably need tomorrow's rehearsal for everyone. I'll meet you in your room after school and see if we've been able to drum up any potential candidates."

She suggested including a plea in the morning announcements, sending a message to the public speaking instructor for suggestions, and approaching the theater arts classes as well. I concurred and began drafting the communications.

"I'll take the government and history departments, as well," she said. "I may have some takers."

By noon we had five students query the requirements,

but two thought it sounded like too much work, and one vowed he could work any lighting needed for effects but wouldn't speak in front of an audience for a million dollars. I gave the remaining, promising candidates a packet, including the case and a transcript of a sample trial for them to peruse if they had time, and texted Jane the results of our fishing expedition.

After the final bell, Jane flew into my room. "I thought you had two hopefuls. Where are they?" she asked with wide eyes.

I glanced at the clock. "Give them a few minutes."

Ten minutes later, she still paced the room. "Have you heard anything from Amanda?"

"No. And I'm a little surprised, but I know she's busy." I pulled my phone out of my purse and searched the screen. "That's funny. I don't have a signal." I pressed some buttons under settings and shook my head.

Jane dug in her bag and found her phone. "Neither do I. I wonder what's going on?"

A laughing voice said from the doorway, "Teachers are always the last to know." Felipe grinned. "A gopher chewed into the fiber optic line. They had to turn off most of the local service to be able to reconnect everything correctly. It should be back on shortly."

The young woman he accompanied smiled shyly while she returned the mock trial information bundle to Jane.

"Not for you?" The girl shook her head, gave a pleading look to Felipe, and exited.

"Hey, is this for real? You're looking for an actor?" said Felipe.

Jane nodded emphatically. "Are you interested?" He shrugged. "It's the same Saturday as prom and we only have ten days to prepare, but we have great students to guide you. Do you know Allie Vomacka?"

"Yeah, I do. She's impressive. We did Sidney Michaels' *Dylan* together. I played Dylan Thomas, and she was Caitlin, the wife. From Act I." He lifted his head and cleared his throat. With his fist clenched at his chest, he leveled his gaze and recited, "Baa, baa black sheep refers, of course, to me, who am the black sheep of my family, mankind," and completed the entire monologue Thomas used to demystify his life story.

Stunned, Jane and I gawked at Felipe. He bowed with a flourish. When we could finally blink back our astonishment, Jane said, "I never knew the specific meaning of that verse before."

"Hey, that's exactly what the character, Brinnin, says in the next line." Felipe grinned. "Good job."

I gave Jane a high five. "That was brilliant, Felipe. Are you up for mock trial?"

He nodded.

"I know you have a job at your family's restaurant. Do you think you can work around the schedule for the next two weeks.?"

Before he could answer, our phones connected to the server, lighting up and dinging annoyingly.

FORTY

Jane provided Felipe the relevant materials while I concentrated on my phone, searching the long list of messages. I had replies from Amanda, Dad, Ida, Pete, and even an earlier one from Jane, but none of them shed any new light on Ellen's difficulty.

I almost cried listening to Dad's clinical comment on voicemail. "Aurora is standing on the right. We need to see Sister Lawrence again. Won't that be fun?"

Ida texted a smiley face emoji. I texted back.

How are you feeling?

Ready to get out of the hospital but Pete's keeping me locked up for one more night at least.

After reprimanding me for getting involved, Amanda texted she'd keep watch on the proceedings involving Ellen. She added:

Found Riley. He's been in Cancun. Hadn't heard about Weber's death but wouldn't rule out suicide with a plan to frame someone. That fits. Said Weber was high strung and

single-minded in his quest. Riley will be facing charges of his own, and he's next on Drew's list to question about the *Titanic* thefts. Won't be practicing medicine again.

Why did he help Weber?

Blackmail. Weber knew about Riley self-medicating. He was afraid he'd lose his license.

She included a smiley face much like the hand drawn cartoons in Ellen's April Fool's jokes. I returned another question mark. A little more information would go a long way in figuring out what happened over the course of the last few weeks. I started typing a more probing question but deleted it. I didn't want to push my luck.

Pete's message stream grew from playful to worried. If I didn't respond quickly, he sounded as if he'd sic the dogs on me, or worse—Amanda.

Sorry for not replying. No connection at school today. Your messages just came through. Everything is the same.

Glad you're okay. Matt said the house is ready for occupancy.

Leaving a thumbs up emoji, I slid my phone in the pocket of my purse and remembered, belatedly, how much had changed. Pete only had skeletal information about Ellen's arrest. He wouldn't have the foggiest notion about Barb, Joette, Ozzie, David, Sister Lawrence, or Aurora. What a difference a few hours could make. Before I could send him the latest, I remembered he'd been executing the most important task of all—taking care of Ida.

Jane said, "Anything new?"

"We've been given the green light to go home. I'll pick up Maverick when we finish here. But I've heard nothing about Ellen. It's so aggravating." I crafted a text to Dorene and received a terse response.

Attorney—client confidentiality.

I stared at the message. *Nice way to put me in my place.*

Jane yawned, covering her mouth politely. "I'm going home to unwind and stockpile some rest tonight. I want to get ahead of what's coming over the next long days. You should too. On my way, I'll pick something up for dinner. Join me before you head home. Coming?"

"I have a slew of emails to clean up before I can relax enough to even try to sleep. I'll leave shortly."

She glanced at the time. "Maverick will be fed, and I'll have pizza in the oven. Don't stay long." She disappeared around the corner.

I sat at my desk, opened each message, and skimmed it, before sliding it to the appropriate file, mostly the trash bin. However, one of the flagged emails, with details for the state mock trial event, appeared to originate with a Koskiniemi.

I poured over the generic email invitation. It listed the benefits to students taking part in the mock trial program from enhancing critical thinking skills to observing the law in action as a possible career opportunity. I opened the attachments which included copies of our score sheets from the qualifying meet, featured publicity scripts, timeline for competition day, and a plethora of registration materials. David Koskiniemi electronically signed the message as secretary of the state mock trial committee. I shook my head. There couldn't be two of them.

He included an address and phone number beneath his name. I punched in the number.

A light, refreshing female voice said, "K-Twelve Tutorful -Tutors, for any stage at every age. How can I help you?"

"May I speak to David, please?"

"I'll see if he is available. One moment."

An entire piece of semi-classical, elevator-type Muzak concluded with a glissando and drifted away as a deep male voice came on the line. "This is David. How can I help you?"

"I coach one of the teams going to the state mock trial tournament, and I wanted to thank you for the complete information."

"Congratulations. Great job. It's tough to make the top sixteen. Is there a question I can answer?

"I'm Katie Wilk." He waited. "I'm with the team from Columbia."

The voice lost some of its cordiality. "What do you want?"

"I honestly did want to thank you, but I also was wondering how you know Barbara Hale."

"You're the one who looks like her friend." More confirmation, but I hadn't realized I resembled my mother as much as Ellen. His objection reached through the phone and zapped my eagerness. "I'm sorry I ran out, but the likeness is uncanny. She told me about the communications and her deception. Barb said Aurora died years ago, but she always wanted to connect with the real family and explain the circumstances of Aurora's death. I'm sorry for your loss."

"And I'm sorry for yours. Do you know any of the story she wanted to tell us?"

"No. Barb was an enigma."

"Sister Lawrence said you were probably Barb's closest friend."

"I like to think so. I've known her for years."

"Did you regard her as something more than a friend?"

He said, a little leery. "I never would have hurt her."

"I know. I saw you at the competition, miles away at the time she died." He hadn't hung up on me yet, so I forged ahead. "Did Barb ever talk to you about Ozzie?"

"Just to say if she ever saw the man again, one of them would have to die. He made her former life miserable. At least this time the sheriff caught the hit-and-run driver. I hope she rots."

"Could I come talk to you? See if I can learn anything that will help—"

"Help who? Barb's killer? Barb had a tough life and now an equally tough death. I don't think so."

"Do you and Barb visit Thai Fyre often?"

He didn't answer immediately. I waited.

"Barb might have gone there. She liked spicey food."

"Did you ever go with her?"

Again, he didn't answer instantly. Maybe he was making up an answer.

"Did you follow her there?" I paused. "Why was Joette leaving?"

"Who?"

"That's Barb's real name." He didn't answer. "You didn't know."

A very hard voice said, "Don't call here again," and he disconnected.

When Dorene taught the kids how to put together their case, she started with a diagram. I pulled the cover off the marker and began assembling the knowns, scribbling over the entire white board.

The center oval contained Joette's name and connected to Ellen, Ozzie, Aurora, Sister Lawrence, and David. By the time I'd drawn the links supported with probable causes, tangential relationships, and a cursory timeline, I had a big knot on the board. My eyelids grew heavy. I thought I would close them for a second and be reinvigorated. A picture of Weber's strange footwear began to coalesce in my mind until my head met the desktop and the thoughts scattered.

I texted Jane.

I'm on my way

Pizza in the oven

After erasing the tangled web from the white board and my thoughts, I grabbed my gear, checking the lock on my way out. I leisurely drove through the familiar neighborhoods, content to have a moment to appreciate the spring sunlight streaming through the buds on the trees. Mother Nature rolled out a carpet of green for the children squealing and scampering from parents, playing games. A bright red cardinal swooped in and alighted on the expanding lilac shrub in front of Jane's. I stopped my car and with intention, lowered my shoulders, closed my eyes, and breathed in and out to a count of eight.

The warm pizza, fresh from the oven, hit the spot, and the smooches from my dog helped to further uncomplicate my mind.

I didn't cook, but I cleaned up and as I put away the stoneware dish, Jane said, "You've got to see this."

She pushed the button on her phone and a Viennese waltz began to play. She bowed and of course, Maverick bowed in response. I clapped, and Jane said. "You ain't seen nothin' yet."

She rhythmically counted, "One, two, three, one, two, three," and then began taking steps on one and two, stopping with her feet together on three.

"You think you can dance?" I giggled. She knew how to dance, and well. We'd taken lessons. Pete and I knew the fundamentals, but she and Drew could have rivaled any professional dance couple, even Ida and Cash.

"Shush," she said. She waved her hand to the right, and repeated, "One, two, three," and Maverick joined her. He took two steps and stopped, two more and stopped. On the fifth pass, he gave up, breaking concentration and circling Jane. He wiggled his tail with such ferocity he almost knocked her down. On top of the treats she'd already given him, she ruffled his ears, and buried him in praise.

My mouth hung open. Jane brought me out of my stupor when she lifted my jaw. I said, "You taught him to dance."

Her smile was so broad, she could barely see out the slits remaining above her cheeks. "He's learning."

FORTY-ONE

Dad and the Scrabble board joined Lance at the hospital during what remained of the visiting hours, and at home in the quiet I began to organize my next few days. I filled in the hourly increments on my daily calendar with before-school help, lesson plans and standards for the first three hours, lunch, more lesson plans for remaining classes, mock trial rehearsal, supper, walking Maverick, and prep time.

The printer output tray overflowed with score sheets, event schedules, and registration materials for the state mock trial meet. Maverick had a keen sense of timing. He woofed as soon as I closed my computer laptop lid, and if I understood his communication correctly, he needed a walk.

We routinely ventured into the waterfowl protection area Maverick loved to explore, even after finding a body in September. Maverick ignored my occasional pangs of squeamishness, and swung his entire back half to and fro, contentedly bouncing from paw to paw in anticipation of good exercise, heavenly wild scents, and maybe greeting a new friend or two. My thoughts usually elsewhere, I'd never before noticed the wooden post with the painted arrow pointing to a narrower branch of the trail to negotiate.

With another hour before sunset, we took the path less travelled and that, as Robert Frost wrote, "made all the difference."

Tramping in the crisp fresh air brought everything into focus and allowed me to process some of the clues. Ellen needed my help; I began with the premise she didn't kill anyone. I arranged my thoughts, starting with what happened most recently and working backward. In the first scenario, I assumed the victim was the woman living life as Barb instead of Joette. Ellen's car had been used in the hit-and-run. She said she was not behind the wheel so someone else had run down Barb. I had a limitless suspect pool if Ellen's rattrap had been taken for a joyride, and the death was accidental. If Barb had been the target all along, then Ellen's angry diatribes on her email added weight to the sheriff's suspicions. She could've intentionally ditched the keys to divert suspicion. Although Ellen was on site and angry, she wasn't alone in her fury.

Sister Lawrence lied about where she was at the time of death, and there was an outside chance she had the time to hurt Barb, but would she have used Ellen's car? Could she have even known which car to use? She hadn't held Barb in high regard and wouldn't have included her in the coveted convent history, believing Barb would cast aspersions on the accomplishments of the other contributors, but would that be reason enough to kill her? Or did she harbor a grudge against the woman whose actions might have shut down Welcome Residence?

David and Barb had a relationship. Had he followed her to Thai Fyre? Did she meet someone else there? He hadn't realized she was leaving and might've had his feelings hurt, but he was too far away at the time of her death to be a viable suspect; I was his witness. Would someone else have committed murder for him?

In the second set of circumstances, Ozzie would have known the woman as Joette. The man in the photo looked strong and formidable, and perfectly willing to steal a car and run someone down. If he killed my mother, he could've killed Joette too. Did Barb or Joette have any other enemies? I cringed at the possibility she had other pseudonyms as well.

My head started to throb. I'd hit a dead end for answers, but Maverick and I had found a new area to investigate.

I hadn't heeded my surroundings and wandered through the relatively sparse Minnesota spring foliage beginning to show signs of filling in. Tiny, fragile April buds, moored to the tips of the spindly twigs and branches, waited to unfurl and wave as May greenery. The lived-in details in many of the yards drew my attention: big and small toys, droning lawn mowers, the loamy scent of freshly turned garden dirt, clanking tools, colorful flowers, empty swings squeaking in the breeze, a twitchy pet rabbit in its hutch, and even an abandoned tree house. I'd needed the peaceful walk but was surprised when Lance Erickson's home came into view and decided 'as the dog trots' might not have been as quick 'as the crow flies' but was much faster than meandering by car on the paved roads.

After another hundred feet or so, the path divided. Rather than continue along the tree line, I headed out of the woods and ended up face-to-face with Carolyn Hall. I should have thought meeting her was a possibility. She paused a moment and looked up from raking. With a huge smile, she said, "Glorious day, isn't it?" Her eyes widened at the sight of my dog, and I went on the offensive, but my unease melted away when she said, "Aren't you a handsome devil?"

I didn't know what to say, and before I could string the correct words together in a sentence, I was further stunned by exquisite jazz piano music wafting out the open window at the side of the house.

Carolyn said proudly, "That's my husband, Blake.

"He's fabulous."

She nodded and narrowed her eyes as recognition dawned. "I know you." I stepped back. "You never did weigh in with your opinion on the garage sink. I'll introduce myself formally. I'm Carolyn Hall." She removed her worn leather garden gloves and stuck out her hand.

"Katie Wilk." We shook hands.

"This must be the wonderful pooch who found my sunglasses." She reached out her hand. "May I?" I nodded, and while she smoothed his glossy coat, she continued. "You don't know how happy I was when Chief West brought them by. They're ancient and all I have left to remember my grandma. I didn't even realize I'd lost them. I haven't been out on the path since, well, since the day my employer, Dr. Riley, closed his office."

She sounded sincere, but I was confused. She'd been wearing the sunglasses in the elevator when we first met. "Glad to be of service," I said.

The light in her eyes dimmed a bit. "Boy, did I ever luck out. You were there when they found Riley's partner's body, right? I never liked the guy, and he made Dr. Riley nervous. When I delivered paperwork, he didn't engage in small talk, and he had disgraceful social skills. I guess he couldn't handle life in the real world."

"What do you mean?"

"Blake calls him a recid … a criminal most likely to return to bad behaviors."

"A recidivist?"

"Yes. The guy had only been out of prison three weeks. Blake believed the real world puzzled him, and he didn't want to be locked up again. Of course, the good doctor hasn't much more to brag about." Carolyn's eyes took on a faraway, dreamy look. "Blake knows everything." She laughed. "Except where I lost my glasses."

While I had the opening, I asked, "How's job hunting going?"

"Terrific. This week Blake was hired as the community college jazz director, and I begin my new job as an administrative assistant for the director of the history center. It's so cool, and I learned from my mistakes. This time I received my signing bonus up front. And I think I'm going to agree to a sink in the garage."

"I should be getting home. It was nice seeing you."

"Come by again some time and keep that boy safe. He's a miracle worker."

I left her to her chores. Maverick led, returning the way we'd come, weaving and happily bobbing down the narrow lane. As we whizzed past a dark Erickson home—Lance must have been enjoying the game of Scrabble—I reached for my phone to call Pete but remembered plugging it into the charger on the kitchen counter at home. Upon entering the refuge, I urged haste.

Maverick, however, stubbornly sauntered unhurriedly for three steps along the quiet wildlife footpath and turned to look over his shoulder. After repeating the action a fourth time, I followed his gaze. A lone figure in dark clothing hugged the tree line, slinking from tree to tree. Using the emergency backup treat in my pocket, I persuaded Maverick to pick up the pace and when I checked again, our distance apart remained the same. My thoughts rolled like waves on a windy day. Who followed us and why? How could I make us safe? Which way should we go?

As the sun set, the lengthening shadows made running dangerous, but having walked Maverick here daily, I knew the path as well as I knew the wrinkles on Ida's face. Around the next bend, we'd take a sharp right as the trail turned back on itself. If we hurried, we could get to the picnic area without being seen. I prayed for some last-minute walkers or joggers.

Maverick yanked the leash the last few yards and dragged me through the, unfortunately, deserted tables. He stopped us next to the community firepit. I wasted a few precious seconds, searching for a hiding place when inspiration in the form of a four-footed friend struck. "You're a genius."

The loping individual wearing a dark hoodie under a leather jacket came to an abrupt halt when faced with a growling, rippling, black Labrador retriever and an angry woman brandishing a thick fireplace log, screaming, "Stop where you are."

FORTY-TWO

The man in Joette's folio, identified as Ozzie, held up both hands. "Don't swing," he said. His almost-smile sent goose bumps up and down my arms.

"Why are you following me? What do you want?" I roared and continued to sling the wood, crouching closer to Maverick, but the momentum caused by the shifting weight knocked me off balance, and I teetered.

He reached out, and I screamed. "Stay back." He might've killed before—twice.

"Whoa. Easy." He patted the air with the tips of his fingers. "May I reach into my pocket for my identification?"

I prayed his ID was all he had in his pocket. I lifted the log and nodded. "No funny business."

He straightened one arm above his head and gingerly reached into his jeans, pinching two fingers together and extracting a dark wallet. He flipped one side and it opened to reveal an official looking card with the name Agent Z Oswald.

I squinted, peering at the serious photo. "How do I know it's real? You can buy anything online nowadays."

"BCA Agent Thomas Blaise was right about you."

I stood straight. My head came up, and my hand fell to my side. Thomas Blaise was a friend and his name equated with safety, not harm. Maverick wagged his tail and edged close enough to the man to get a hearty scratch. "Traitor," I whispered.

The man pocketed his ID. "Call me Ozzie." Capitulating, the heavy piece of timber thudded to the ground.

"As you know, being an agent doesn't discount the possibility I'm a bad egg, but if you contact your friend, he'll tell you I'm a straight shooter, which is what he said about you."

I wasn't entirely convinced. "Why were you following us? What are you doing?"

"Could we have this conversation over a cup of coffee with your dad?"

"What conversation? Why should we talk to you? How do you know about my dad?"

"I was a friend of your mother."

The hairs on the nape of my neck bristled. Joette's words replayed in the recesses of my mind. "What do you know about my mother?" I asked warily.

When he stepped forward, I retreated, and he stopped. Maverick stood in rapt attention at my left side, swinging his head between the two of us. I sent a disappointed telepathic message his way, *You're usually a much better judge of character.*

"Your mother reached out to the BCA—Bureau of Criminal Apprehension. I ended up as her contact." He kept his distance. "I'd like to tell you and your dad the story together. And, although the threat has been neutralized, I don't know if it's safe to chat here."

"What are you talking about? What threat?" My strident voice sounded unfamiliar.

"If your dad has not returned yet, I'll wait." I started to shake my head, but he said, "Call Chief West. I reported to her, letting her know I was here. She did a thorough check and was satisfied." He snorted. "She's one tough cookie, but she'll vouch for me."

I reached again for my phone, and, unfortunately, it hadn't magically appeared. Instead, to hide the fact I didn't carry it, I maneuvered to my pocket and pulled out a doggie bag. I didn't want to lose my advantage, so I nodded, shifting my eyes and fixing them on the exit out of the park. He followed at a discreet distance. I walked tough, head up and gripping the leash as though I wasn't scared out of my mind, but patently aware of the terrible things that could've happened in the woods when we'd been alone.

The big Queen Anne loomed in front of us, and with the lights glowing in the back half, someone had to be home. We entered the back yard, and Ozzie said, "I'll wait here."

Dad sat at the kitchen table, nursing a pale brown beverage from a teacup. I unhooked Maverick's leash. He sauntered to his mat and hunkered down.

As I unplugged my phone from the charger, I said, "Everything okay, Dad?"

"Just spent." He took a sip from the cup and brightened. "Ida should be home tomorrow."

"Dad, there's someone outside who wants to talk to us," I said cautiously. "He said he was Mom's friend."

Dad slowly turned his head and raised his eyebrows before nodding. I opened the door and waved to him. Ozzie materialized from the gloom and tossed a tree limb onto Dad's growing spring brush pile accumulating next to the house. "Be careful. This tree needs a good pruning."

Dad cast unblinking eyes on Ozzie, watching him remove his boots. "You're a friend of AJ?"

"Yes, sir." Ozzie stood and thrust out his hand. He held it forward. He looked more benign and a lot less malevolent in the kitchen light, and I saw compassion in his eyes.

Dad reluctantly accepted the gesture, looking Ozzie up and down. "In what capacity did you know Aurora Jeanne?"

Ozzie looked at his feet, and I was almost afraid to hear the words he had to tell us. He gazed at Dad and his eyes filled with pity. "She made some poor choices in her past and wanted to get out of her crazy life, but the things she could tell us would've been helpful securing convictions against those with more serious crimes. She brought it all to the BCA, for which we were truly grateful. But she paid the ultimate price. We're sure the madam wanted her silenced."

Neither Dad nor I anticipated a story with those elements. "Wait. What?" Dad said.

"Are you sure she wasn't running away from you?" I grumbled.

"Is that the story Joette told? Aurora was a smart and beautiful woman. Joette didn't want to relinquish her assets. She thought Aurora would be better off if she made the move from accountant to call girl, but Aurora understood the business. She wanted out, and she came to us. If it means anything, I think Joette only meant to frighten Aurora, but things went bad."

"What do you mean? Why should we believe you?"

He bit the inside of his cheek, considering what to say. "I have nothing to gain." He waited until Dad gave a sign to go ahead. "An ancestry DNA kit was part of Aurora's reentry package, helping her heal the rifts in her life. She had almost succeeded with her quest. How Joette found out, I have no idea. Joette and Aurora argued in front of witnesses. Aurora shook off Joette and stumbled in front of an oncoming car. Nothing could be done. I'm sorry."

If I didn't know Ellen, Joette's death would certainly look like payback. "I saw the picture of you, Joette, and Aurora."

"I got caught in the background of that one— Joette's proof positive she was being watched. Aurora's gut reaction gave something away, but I never knew I'd been compromised. Immediately after Aurora died, Joette vanished. There were clues. I tried to find her. I got close to Joette a few times. When the results of the DNA test became public and recently showed up online, linking to her daughters, I hoped I'd been wrong about Aurora, that I'd made a mistake, but I knew Aurora was gone. It had been Joette all along."

Both stories fit the facts, and I didn't know who to believe. In either case, my mother was dead. "You did a lousy job protecting her."

He flushed.

"Did you kill Joette?"

"What? No."

With one eye on Dad, and the other on my keypad, I punched in the number to Blaise's phone. It rang once.

"I thought I might hear from you," Thomas said. "If you're calling about Oswald, he's real, and if you send me a picture, I'll verify—" I snapped a candid and texted it. "Yup. That's Ozzie. Anything else I can do?"

"Thanks, no, Agent Blaise." I disconnected the call.

"Did I pass?" I nodded but kept my eyes trained on him. He tried to look understanding. "It was probably sheer coincidence that led Ellen to Joette. I understand the anger Ellen had to deal with, discovering the link to a woman who might have been your mother only to have had the possibility ripped away."

"Ellen did not kill her." The intensity I focused on Ozzie would have sizzled a lesser man. Ellen's description of the man she thought trailed her to Little Italy came back to me in a rush. I squinted. "You followed Ellen to the restaurant. Why?"

"Ellen requested a meet on the family chat board. I wanted to warn her and, maybe, see who answered."

"If you were in the restaurant the entire time, you couldn't have killed Joette, and you know Ellen didn't do it either. You're her alibi."

He lowered his eyes. "I can't account for her the entire hour and a half. She left her table for about thirty minutes." By the commiserative tone in his voice, I could tell he was not unwilling but unable to provide her with an alibi. "Too close to the time of the accident."

The logistics didn't work. "If you followed her in, why didn't you follow her out of the restaurant?"

"I knew she'd be back. After I told her about Joette, she raced out of the restaurant with her computer but left her purse."

"You told her what you told us?" My mouth went

dry. He nodded and bowed his head. "And you told the sheriff?" I pictured a rattled Ellen, carrying her computer protectively, hurriedly stowing it in her car, dropping her keys. "But Ellen didn't know what Joette looked like." He looked up with mournful eyes and turned his phone screen for me to see. "This is a picture of Joette, and you showed it to Ellen?"

The legs of Dad's chair screeched, and he stood to pace.

I was angry. "When Ellen returned, did she *look* like she'd just run someone down?" Ozzie glanced away. I fumed. "You've almost sealed her fate, but we know she didn't do it. You *are* going to help us find the real killer."

FORTY-THREE

Maverick hauled himself to standing and barked, seconds prior to the faint sound of a doorbell ringing in Ida's flat. I glared at Ozzie. "I'm answering that, and you're not to move."

Dad's glower would have stopped a Labrador puppy on her way to a bowlful of kibble, and Ozzie nodded slowly. Maverick parked himself at Ozzie's feet, pestering him for attention.

I stepped through the pristine kitchen, past her grand piano, and into the welcoming living room. Everything reminded me of Ida, and I missed her terribly. Frustrated, I tore open the door as Redd reached for the bell.

"Hey, Katie. Is the missus in? I promised to play duets again today and wasn't able to meet up." She narrowed her eyes. "She's all right, isn't she?"

"Ida's in the hospital again."

"What happened now?"

"Pete said she was exposed to more of the diphen-hydramine."

Redd made a horrible face. "She was fine when I left."

"Come on in. You may have been the last one to see her before it caught up with her. She had so much of the drug in her system, it wouldn't have taken much to activate the symptoms again. It might have been the hand lotion she'd been using."

"Oh, man. I sure hope she'll be okay."

"She should be fine. They're keeping her one more night, and she'll be safe there. Dr. Lannie, the pharmacist, analyzed everything in her home the drug could have contaminated."

Redd stopped in her tracks and searched the room, glancing suspiciously for any telltale signs of the chemical.

"It's clear now."

She blew out a puff of air and resumed walking. "I haven't seen anything more about it in the news, but did you figure out what happened with Ellen?"

"Her car was used to kill a woman in a hit-and-run."

"That's awful. Who was the woman?"

"Her assumed identity was Barbara Hale. Ellen had been researching her ancestry and matched Hale's DNA with a ninety percent probability of belonging to her mother—our mother."

"What reason did Ellen have to run down her mother?

"Turns out they weren't even related."

Redd stumbled and caught herself. "I'm sorry." She resumed following me, and we stepped through the adjoining door. "Who was she then?"

"The woman, Joette Falsch, submitted our mother's DNA test and claimed it as her own. According to one of their agents, Falsch had been in the crosshairs of the BCA for a number of years."

Redd asked, "The who?"

"Bureau of Criminal Apprehension. I know Ellen didn't kill her."

Dad hadn't moved and stared into his cup. Redd hustled to his side. "You okay, Harry? Is there anything—"

Ozzie cleared his throat, and Redd stood quickly. "I didn't know you had company."

"Redd, this is—" Ozzie coughed. I remembered he lived some of his life in the shady undercover world and continued prudently. "Z Oswald. Ozzie, meet Redd Starr, piano tuner par excellence."

Ozzie bowed his head, and cocked it, searching Redd's face. "Have we met?"

Redd similarly cocked her head from across the room. "I don't think so, but I'm pleased to make your acquaintance," she said.

Maverick stepped toward Redd, and Redd's back went rigid. "Maverick, down," I cued and he dropped to his tummy.

"Since the missus is not here, and I can see you're busy, I should be off," said Redd.

"Check back tomorrow. I'm sure Ida would love to noodle away on the piano," I said.

She made a beeline to the exit. I caught the door before it slammed shut and saw Drew and Jane strolling up the sidewalk, exchanging pleasantries with a retreating Redd.

"Pete's kept us in the loop. Is there anything we can do?"

"Come on in. We can use all the help we can get."

Drew held the door for Jane and me. "Ida will be okay. It'll take a while, but Pete's watching out for her. Let's see what we can do about Ellen." The door clicked and he turned. His eyes met Ozzie's, and he came to an abrupt halt. "What are you doing here, Oswald?"

"I could ask the same of you, Andrew," Ozzie said begrudgingly. "I'm on a case."

"I live here in Columbia," Drew muttered, his hand still gripping the doorknob.

Jane assessed the uncomfortable sizzle between them. "Fellas, I don't know what's going on, but from what I gather, you know each other, and I assume you're on the same side." She nudged her fiancé. "Drew."

"We're closing in on the perp for a series of burglaries including one in Columbia."

Ozzie relaxed. "The *Titanic* trouble. I'm intrigued. But how did you follow the trail here?" he said, with a hint of admiration.

"You've heard about that." Drew resisted smiling. "Old fashioned map work. The first losses occurred six weeks ago, but we discovered the connection to the *Titanic* only three weeks ago and mapped the locations of the burglaries in a trajectory toward Columbia."

"And only one item carries a value over a few hundred dollars. They rest are all petty thefts."

The two men pulled out chairs and sat on either side of Dad, cagily sharing as little as possible.

Jane and I rested against the counter. She whispered, "While they're talking shop, tell me what's going on."

"There is so much that doesn't make sense about the hit-and-run of Joette Falsch, alias Barbara Hale."

"Do you believe Ellen?"

I backed away so I could see all of Jane's face. "Of course." She nodded. A bit more convinced myself, I relaxed and added as I shoved away from the counter. "Yes, I believe Ellen."

"Your deductions have been successful before. Tell me what you're thinking." She glanced at the men and indicated with a nod we should leave them to their conversation.

Maverick joined us in the living room. I rustled his ears. "The latest is that Ellen has no alibi for the time of death. She knew Aurora had died." I took a deep breath. "And Ozzie said he told Ellen about the toxic relationship between Joette and her mother. She knew."

Jane's beautiful brown eyes widened, and I barreled ahead.

"I'm convinced Sister Lawrence had a motive. She and Joette had a falling out. I think she planned to include Joette's transformation from life on the streets to local work and tutoring with David, but she found out Joette's devious behavior had continued on the Welcome Residence premises, and although the diocese was closing the safe place down, I can't honestly see Sister Lawrence committing murder. Everybody loves her.

"I thought Ozzie might have had reason to kill Joette, but it turns out he spent the entire time in question at the restaurant where Ellen waited, and he has witnesses. Joette's story checked all the right boxes, but now that I've met him, his story is equally plausible. And he is exactly who he says he is."

"An agent of the BCA. Anyone else?"

"Even after five years, David Koskiniemi really didn't know Joette; not her name, her history, how she used him, nor her future plans, but he was at the section mock trial meet. I saw him. He couldn't have killed her." I sighed. "But there are little things I can't quite put my finger on."

Drew called from the kitchen, "Hey, Babe. Are you ready?"

"Be right there." Jane's hand rested reassuringly on my arm. "Amanda's very good at her job. She'll keep her finger on the pulse of the law in Theisen County Sheriff's office.

Drew's finishing up with his case and he'll help. Maybe Ozzie too."

"You're right, girlfriend."

Ozzie stood next to Drew as he prepared to leave. "Sorry I went off on you. I thought you were moving in on my investigation. It's been a long time but with the latest development, I think I'll be able to close the case." He extended his hand. Drew shook it, and he and Jane said goodnight.

He turned to Dad as he tied the laces on his boots. "I'm glad we met. Harry, I think your daughter is a lot like her mother."

What a loaded remark.

Maverick wanted to go out, so we followed Ozzie. At the bottom of the stairs, he gave me the side-eye. "You don't entirely trust me yet, do you?"

I shrugged. I knew something was bothering me, but I couldn't put my finger on it.

"If you ever need help—"

I gave him my best teacher *you've got to be kidding* look, and he grunted.

"Your dad has my number," he said and faded into the evening. If I was lucky, I'd never need to see him again.

As if reacting to his sixth sense, Maverick raced up the steps, pulled down on the door handle, and budged his way inside. I chased him, only to find him sprawled on the floor next to Dad who was staring at his phone.

"Dad?"

He looked at me, blinked, and took a huge breath. "Ellen's been charged with first degree premeditated murder."

FORTY-FOUR

Mock trial practice had to happen Friday after school, even though Dorene was unavailable, wrapped up, as she was, in a real criminal case, one I absolutely wanted her to win. I left several messages, offering to assist, but she and I knew my entire legal education came from the extracurricular activity with my teenage high school students.

My mind couldn't focus on the rehearsal, and I watched the performance as if from afar, easily acquiescing when the team suggested Felipe take the plaintiff role of Captain Rostron of the *Carpathia*. However, as well as he acted, the general consensus was he not play the defendant parts of Maggie Murphy nor Molly Brown. Allie decided Felipe should play the lookout aboard the *Titanic,* Reginald Lee, because he tended to go off script. His well-prepared delivery differed from what the kids expected, and his revisions required them to react quickly and think on their feet. He never exactly changed the story, but his recitation took an unexpected turn and his emphasis deviated from the norm. After her initial irritation that he didn't follow the predetermined script, it seemed even Lorelei saw his modifications as advantageous. He could upset more than just our apple cart.

"Well? How're you feeling about the case?" Jane asked the students as they put my classroom back in order.

"It's like 'where no man has ever gone before'," said Lorelei, giggling, quoting from Brock's favorite show.

"And that's a good thing?" said Felipe with a guarded smile.

"Absolutely. This is going to be so much fun. And besides, you're on a roll." Brock didn't know his own strength and slammed two desks together. "Oops. Didn't mean to do that."

"What roll?" I asked, boxing up the remaining accoutrements of our makeshift courtroom.

The boys exchanged disbelieving looks. "You didn't tell her?" Brock said. "C'mon, man."

Brock beamed, catching Felipe turning beet red in probably his first honest reaction of the afternoon. I didn't think he could act that well. "I took first place in the distance category for the folded paper airplane contest."

It was about time for good news. "Congratulations. You earned that trophy. Did you beat the record?" I didn't know how long I could refrain from teasing Pete if one of my students knocked him out of first place after all this time.

He turned a deeper shade. "No, but I was close. Maybe next time."

Carlee finally stopped applauding and said, "We're wondering if we could meet tomorrow."

"If you think it will help make you feel prepared, I can be here, with or without Ms. Mackey."

"I'll be here." Jane snuck a peek at each student and added slyly. "Even if it's a long shot." She struck a pose I'd liken to Rodin's *The Thinker*. I'm not sure what the kids expected her to say. They started to protest until she added, "The national competition is in Georgia. I'm originally from Atlanta, and I'd love to visit, so, can we get together at ten?"

Felipe glanced at the clock. "Oh, man. I've got to work the dinner hour this evening. If you don't need me for anything else—" He grabbed the stack of papers in front of him and stuffed them in his backpack. "I'll see you in the morning—ten o'clock."

Jane and I followed the rest of the students out of the math department. "Felipe is not Allie, but he's still a great addition. I can't think of anything more we can do. Can you?"

"We may need to find another attorney coach. I don't remember seeing that in the rules, but we almost lost once when we didn't have the right representation." Jane's eye's glittered mischievously. "We could ask ZaZa." I opened my mouth to protest. "Luckily she's not a lawyer."

She hopped in her Ford Edge, and her laugher faded as she sped from the lot before I could even whisper my response, "Not in a million years, Jane Mackey."

My phone rang. Still lost in thought about Ellen, I picked up. All I heard was dead air. Worried about Ellen's predicament, I wondered how I would know if she called. For a fraction of a second, I considered the possibility I'd been wrong about her, but I knew she wasn't connected to the murder. Someone set her up. But who? And why?

And then an unresolved issue about time surfaced, but the harder I worked to bring the question to the forefront, the murkier it got.

Tired of thawing Ida's precious stores of delicious food, Dad ordered take out, and I stopped at Ho Wong's to pick up three carry-all bags.

"Are you certain this is all for Harry Wilk?" Each bag contained two white cartons. I didn't know if he was exceedingly hungry, planning two days' worth of meals, expecting company, or if he, too, had a bout trying to remember how many of us there were. Maybe Ida was home, or someone was stopping by.

The lovely woman behind the counter nodded and said, "Yes, miss."

Friday nights either hummed with frenetic activity or droned a relaxing restart for the upcoming week. Sniffing the delicious spices, I'd yield to either excuse as long as I could taste the sumptuous savories riding home with me.

Dad and I fumbled with the chopsticks, attempting to eat the smorgasbord of Asian specialties. He hadn't been able to limit his choices, and I expected leftovers, but every dish tasted better than the last, and we finished off four entrees. All that remained was an order of chicken chow mein, a half cup of fried rice, and six fortune cookies.

Dad leaned back in his chair and patted his stomach. "I'm stuffed. I'm saving my dessert for later so I can enjoy it. How about you?"

I finished off the last bite of my Kung Pao Shrimp and shoved my plate away. "I'm going to wait too, but I'm going to lock the cookies away in the cupboard. My canine companion has been licking his chops throughout our meal, and I'm sure he'd swallow them cellophane and all."

Maverick stared at the rice. "Nope, my friend. Not for you. There are onions in there." I did, however, sneak him one small scrap of shrimp. He stretched lazily but just before he settled in his kennel, he stood and barked. He always knew when Ida's doorbell would ring.

FORTY-FIVE

I answered the bell, and for an instant, I didn't recognize Redd behind the tendrils of hair blowing in the wind in front of her penetrating gaze. She brushed away the strands, flaunting her turquoise ring, and the familiar insouciance surfaced.

"They haven't released Ida yet, have they?"

"No, I'm afraid not, but Dad's going back to visit tonight. She's chomping at the bit to get home. Do you want to come in?"

She pondered for a moment but when four familiar raucous students turned onto the sidewalk leading up to the front door, hollering and waving, she shook her head and said, "Tell the missus I expect her to be seated at the piano tomorrow in her concert finery, fingers curled over the keys, and ready to make some music when I get here. I'll bring my implements and fine tune her piano just for her." She hefted her kit.

I smiled at the thought. "If they let her go, she should

be home by noon. She'll make it painful for someone if they keep her too much longer."

Redd lifted her chin and reminded me of a proud Scarlett O'Hara gathering her strength and intention from Tara, thinking, *after all, tomorrow is another day*. "We have a plan." She nodded. "Bye, Wilk."

Brock, Galen, Felipe, Carlee, and her dog, Renegade, scattered to the lawn, clearing the path as Redd swept by them. Felipe stooped to pick something up and watched as Redd slid into her vehicle and drove off.

"What's up?" I made a show of reading the time from the watch on my wrist as my students tittered and hooted, jostling each other and mounting the short flight of steps. "We don't have rehearsal for another fifteen hours and twenty-nine minutes."

"She another friend of yours?" Felipe asked with a bit of awe in his voice and held up a folded creation. "She dropped this paper plane. I saw her compete, and if she hadn't used the laminate, I think she'd have won the adult design category." He held out a shiny silver folded sheet with reverence. "Can you return it?"

"I must have missed her flight." I thought about what I'd been doing instead—finding Weber, and the hairs on the back of my neck stood on end. I took the airplane. "She'll be back tomorrow." The expectant faces glanced from one to another and focused on Felipe.

"Go on," said Galen. "Cough it up."

Felipe slowly drew a manilla folder from his backpack and handed it to me.

"What is it?"

"Open it," said Carlee.

I slid my finger under the flap and watched my students.

Carlee implored leniency. Brock and Galen sniggered, expecting push back of some kind, and Felipe's eyes were glued to his shoes.

I extracted a thin, blue, canvas-covered booklet and read the line at the bottom of the cover. My forehead scrunched, and I squinted in disbelief. "How did you come to have my gradebook?"

"The guys, I mean, these guys. I mean, Brock and Galen and Carlee came to Las Tapas to eat supper and stayed until the end of my shift. I asked about the past competitions and pulled out my script to highlight what they thought of as a few relevant passages. I found your grade book." The pace of his words picked up. "I must've picked it up with the stack of pages you gave me. Brock said if I got it back right away, I wouldn't be in too much trouble."

I stared at Brock, and he shrugged.

"I'm so sorry."

"My bad for leaving it out."

"I promise, I won't do it again. I didn't open it."

"You didn't do anything wrong. It was all my fault. I should have put it away."

"This mutual admiration society is going nowhere. Self-recrimination can go on forever and never resolve." I gawked at Galen, and he was grinning. "What? You didn't think I could learn new vocab for the SAT. So, Ms. Wilk, how about you accept Felipe's apology? You can claim equal responsibility, and you'll both experience absolution."

Felipe extended a hand. "I'll mind what I pick up from now on, Ms. Wilk."

"And I'll be better prepared for our practices."

"Where's that amazing dog of yours?" asked Carlee.

Renegade barked agreeably, and I heard Maverick's answering woof. "They're kind of an item." Carlee giggled as the kids followed me through the house to the back yard where the dogs played fetch, with the growing heap of tree parts, and keep-away in equally good form.

Dad joined the fun as Emma, our three-year-old next-door neighbor, tottered over with her mother. "Just two pats, and I'll go quietly, Mommy." She loved our dogs. Bookended by Maverick and Renegade, she methodically stroked their necks before saying, "See you Sunday," and fluttered her tiny hand as her dad loaded her into her car seat.

I returned the wave until the car edged onto the street and my phone buzzed with a call from Ellen's attorney. Dad entertained the kids, and I took the call inside.

"Hi, Dorene."

"That woman doesn't understand the severity of her position." She let loose a growl.

"She tends to go off on a tangent easily, especially when she's nervous. Is there some way I can help?"

"I won't ask her outright. I don't need to know, but I can't see her killing Falsch. That poor woman may have been struck by accident, but the medical examiner's report says she was run over a second time and that wouldn't be accidental. Ellen's motive is flimsy at best, but for the jury to acquit Ellen we have to find out what really happened. She has too much time unaccounted for."

Until I knew for certain, I couldn't bring myself to tell her Ellen might have been aware of Joette's role in Aurora's death. Not yet. "And how do we do that?"

"I don't know yet but keep your eyes and ears open." Dorene let the silence stretch a bit. "She'd like to see you."

I breathed in and out. "We're having a mock trial practice tomorrow—"

"I don't have time." There it was again, the mention of time, and I winced. "Will you need another attorney for the duration?"

"We'll let you know. Ida' s coming home tomorrow too, so I'll visit Ellen Sunday."

"See that you do. She won't let me contact her parents. You and Harry are all the family she has right now."

I wanted to assure her I considered Ellen part of my family too, but Dorene had already disconnected. I squeezed the phone so hard my nailbeds turned white.

A warm voice behind me said, "Anything I can do?" and made my heart palpitate. I spun around and rushed into Pete's arms. A warm, furry tornado wriggled between our knees and around our legs, knocking us even closer together.

"Did they hire someone new?" I mumbled into his collar and felt his chin pivoting atop my head—a negative response. "I didn't think you had time off this week. I'm so glad to see you." My voice began to quaver. I didn't know why, but I knew, wrapped in his arms, I didn't have to keep up the pretense of strength, if I ever had.

"Harry sent the kids home, and he and dad are off to see Ida, but ..." He rubbed his nonexistent belly, his chiseled abs rippling through the t-shirt. "I have a little time before I have to go back in. Harry thought you might have some chow mein left."

"I do." I reluctantly slid from his secure embrace. "Have a seat and I'll warm it up for you."

When his fork scraped the plate, I brought out dessert. I cracked my crisp cookie, peeled the tiny paper nestled inside, and read, "The darkest hour is just before dawn. That could mean anything." As I nibbled, crumbs fell to the table. I brushed them into my palm, clenching my fist so my food motivated dog wouldn't think of lapping them up. "What does yours say?"

After a long-drawn-out stifled yawn, he blinked a few times and squinted at the small print. "Love conquers all." The look from those hot milk chocolate eyes took my breath away, but the corners of his mouth worked so hard to smile, it looked like a weightlifter after pressing the barbell one time too many. He jerked his head from side to side, shaking off the tiredness. "We interviewed a candidate for the ER position today. I don't think we'll have long to wait."

"You do need another partner, but right now you need to get some rest."

This time the smile curled quickly, and he rose. "I'm not very fine company, and I've a few errands to run before I have to get back, but promise you'll stay out trouble."

"Me?" I snuggled close for another hug, and I was afraid, if he lingered, I wouldn't let go.

Pete left and as I watched the clock, I put together the time element that was bothering me. I dialed Drew, but he didn't pick up.

"Hi Drew. Carolyn Hall told me Weber was released only three weeks before he died, in which case he couldn't have been your burglar. I could've heard wrong, but I thought you said the thefts began six weeks ago. I thought you'd like to know."

I'd done all I could, so I flopped onto the couch and opened my new Tim Ellington novel. So tightly engrossed in the pages, when Maverick barked, rather than investigate,

I told him to be quiet. He continued intermittently, and I ignored him, but my thoughts took a turn.

Had we concluded the enquiry before answering all the important questions? Weber wasn't the only person new to Columbia. What did I really know about Ozzie? Weber wasn't the only one with access to Ida. Riley had done a number on her. Weber certainly wasn't the only one who could have manipulated the piano strings. Blake Hall was a professional pianist. And Weber wasn't even the only one with polyurethane footwear. But was he the only one with a grudge?

I hesitantly fanned the pages closed. Ellen's arrest had circumvented our investigation of Weber. Could I link the two events together? Joette Falsch, Sister Lawrence, and David Koskiniemi added another layer of questions.

But Redd. She was a new addition to Columbia, the last one to see Ida before her relapse, had questioned Ida about her relationship to the *Titanic*, and according to Felipe, she even had fashioned a paper airplane from reflective paper—perhaps after luring me to Weber's body. I grew uneasy and picked up my phone with every intention of speaking to Drew or Amanda or Ozzie, but my calls went to voicemail. Next on my list was Pete.

Maverick's obnoxious repetitive barking made it impossible to hear. "Kennel, Maverick." I repeated the cue, and when he reluctantly complied, I added a treat while closing the door. "Good boy. Quiet."

While he scarfed down his savory snack, I heard a ring tone play outside. Maverick barked in response and struggled to free himself, rattling the kennel, inching it across the floor. I opened the door to check out the sound and came face to face with Redd standing on the top step.

I forced a smile. "Hi, Redd. What can I do for you?"

She tilted her head in an oddly familiar way and said, "I came to do something for you."

"And what's that?"

I glanced down, noticing her footwear, and tried to reconcile the oversized sloppiness of the clogs on Redd's feet. My heart pounded. The clogs I found with Weber's body looked way too small in comparison. But she caught me unaware. The next thing I knew, she'd rammed a sweet-smelling cloth over my nose and mouth, and the night faded to black.

FORTY-SIX

I slowly regained consciousness and awoke with a rag crammed into my mouth. Redd tossed the end of the red felt strip wrapped around my wrists up into a tree and hauled my arms above me. I dangled below a limb, my toes brushing the grass. I swiveled and gasped when I saw Pete crumpled in a heap on the ground, thick, dark blood congealing on a wound at the back of his head. I veered toward him, but Redd pulled the strip taut, wrenching my arms straight overhead.

Curly, flaming cinnamon-colored hair exploded, unfettered from the light-brown tresses when Redd removed the wig. She shook her locks free and raked her fingers through it, caressing the coils. Her eyes shot daggers. And they were green.

"Gerhard and I weren't really at cross purposes," she said. "I could've let the idiot Weber finish the job, but what satisfaction would there be for me. The day you planned to trap him, I warned him off. The fool thought he had something on me. He actually threatened me. *Me*."

She circled, prowling like a tigress. Her cackle made my skin crawl. "He didn't commit suicide. He resisted until I stole his very last breath, which is better than what you can expect."

Memories and questions of the day I found Weber flooded my aching head. This woman lured me to Weber's death site using a page of foil laminate. Had she been behind the door I couldn't open? Why did she enter the folded reflecting paper in the airplane contest?

As if she could read my mind she glanced at the sky and paced. "I thought you might take the blame, but I set the stage too well."

My toe caught a tuft of grass and propelled me around so I could keep her in my sights. "But I only want justice." She stopped and took a step closer. She tipped her head parallel to mine. "You took my family."

"Who *are* you?" I tried to say. I grappled with the bonds at my wrists, jerking back and forth. The gag smothered my words. What I mumbled next sounded nothing like, "What are you talking about?"

She mimicked my garbled utterances, and my mind raced back to September, tied to a chair in a shack, having my words thrown back at me in a similar fashion. Then I knew who she was. I slowed, afraid to breathe. Terror chilled me. I stopped struggling. Rache was German for revenge. But Flanagan was Irish for red, and I'd witnessed the decimation of her family. I'd also seen her portrait the day one of her twins died in front of me. Tears clouded my vision. The real Maura Flanagan stood triumphant before me.

"Good. You understand. Everything is falling into

place." She raised her palms and shrugged, then turned her right hand over to gaze admiringly at her gaudy ring, a family bauble I should have recognized. I couldn't get my footing to rotate fast enough to keep up. She swiftly stepped behind me and looped a coarse cord over my head, drawing it tight around my neck.

I tried to shake it off, but she pulled me close and whispered, "How could none of you realize it was Weber who'd come back for Ida? It was obvious the moment I laid eyes on him. Poor man had worked on his devious scheme since the day he entered prison. The plan came to fruition the week he was released. He shoved Ida's cousin down some steps, causing just enough damage to warrant assistance and suggested she contact a relative. He helped her craft the request, and Ida came running. After making her and everyone around her doubt she was capable of living alone, he planned on tripping Ida down a much longer flight of stairs. He'd been so proud of his subterfuge until I told him the jig was up. He confessed all, blubbering about his losses in life."

"Revenge is a dish best served cold." Maura tossed her curls. "But I couldn't let him take what was mine. I intended your loved ones go before you. I thought you should watch them die."

She pushed me away and circled to the front to give me a pitiful look. "You don't have many, do you?" Her eyes narrowed and she smirked.

My toes dug into the ground, and, suspended by the rope tying my arms above my head, I bounced. Small reverberations travelled down my arms and tingled through my torso. I screamed behind the fabric, shoving my tongue against the cloth, hurling my head back and forth.

"I planned to sabotage your sister's car. Ellen should have been the first to die. She made it so easy, leaving her keys lying around all the time. Just in case, I made an impression of the keys the day I returned the missus's love letters." She said the last two words sourly and wrinkled her nose.

I screamed from behind the cloth. My tongue seemed to find more room in my mouth, and I worked the gag looser, opening my jaw to a painful dimension. I threw my head forward and the saliva-soaked projectile hit Maura on the cheek. She crinkled her nose and pursed her lips. She sneered and meticulously dragged the back of her hand across her face to wipe the spittle.

"Yes, I took her stupid scrapbook. It contained *Titanic* memorabilia I added to my collection to replace what you took from me and my family."

"And you've been taking items from others," I croaked. "Did you tune their pianos too?"

"A piano tuner's like one of the family." Drew had looked in all the wrong places. I shook my head, but she ignored me.

"Ellen told stories about her mother, your mother, and the ancestry connection. I researched Barbara Hale because she'd have to be on my list sooner rather than later. I tailed Ellen. Imagine my surprise when the woman I thought was your mother appeared from nowhere, running across the street, dragging a suitcase. I didn't even have to hotwire the car. I calmly sat in the driver's seat and turned the key. The car started right up."

"You killed Joette." My eyes teared up.

"The only glitch came when some buffoon took Ellen's parking space, but I pulled in close to the original spot and she never knew."

Ellen knew.

After a self-satisfied smirk, Redd said, "And now she'll spend the rest of her life in jail." Her voice took on a crazy crowing sound. "And she has no idea why."

"I figured it out. I won't be the only one."

She acted as if she hadn't heard me. "After you're gone, rest assured Harry and Ida will be devastated, but I won't let them suffer long. They'll be next, and there'll be absolutely nothing you can do."

Distant crashing and muted barking sounds pulled her eyes to the house. Her sneer concluded with a wicked shriek. "And your little dog too."

She'd threatened everyone close to my heart. I pulled with all my weight and imagined the branch above my head gave a little. I lifted my feet and dangled. The tree limb bounced again. Maybe it wouldn't hold. I bobbed. I forced my weight up on my toes and came down hard, repeating the action, swinging back and forth. The slight slack in the rope told me my efforts might be rewarded.

Maura leaned over Pete, caressing his chin, lifting his head ever so gently. She turned her gleaming green eyes to me, smirked, and went back to the task in front of her. "I'll take advantage of the opportunities given me. Your dad and Ida aren't here, but you are, and you'll watch your boyfriend die." She edged toward Pete with another noose.

"Leave him be. You want me. Come and get me," I screamed, and screamed, and screamed.

Maura narrowed her eyes and fixed her malevolent gaze on me. I thought Maverick and I might make enough noise to draw her away from Pete and maybe rouse any remaining neighbors, but with dexterity I didn't see coming, she rammed into me. To keep her from replacing the gag, I shook my head from side to side. She locked one arm around my neck and struggled to maneuver the noose tighter. I rose up on my toes, jumped, and with her added weight, the branch holding me cracked and crashed on top of us.

I'd been hopeful and ready and covered my head against the rain of timber. The bulk of the wood struck Maura and dropped her to the ground, folded over, one leg bent at an impossible angle. I dragged myself to Pete's side and brushed a lock of dark curly hair from his face with my tied hands. "Please be okay." I repeated the mantra as I carefully watched him breathe. I undid the knot around my wrists with my teeth, and I'm sure my dentist would have been mortified. My fingers ran lightly over Pete's injuries, assessing the seriousness, until I heard the rapidly growing rumble of the angry woman stirring behind me.

She bellowed and rolled from one side to the other. I didn't think she'd be able to move but felt a sharp jerk as she reeled in the cord tightening around my neck. I tried to fit my fingers between the cord and my skin, but I couldn't breathe and began to see stars.

I hoped to telegraph the words I couldn't speak. *I love you, Pete.*

FORTY-SEVEN

I heard my words echoed, "Please be okay," but uttered by a husky male voice instead. I peeled one eye open, and the vision elicited as much of a grin as I could conjure.

"She's ba-ack." Pete's bruised and battered face was the most beautiful sight I'd seen in weeks.

"Where is she?" I squawked in a raspy voice. Maverick thumped his nose on my hip, and I reached to scratch behind his ear.

"She's under lock and key at the hospital." He ran his thumb gently down my cheek.

"It was—"

"We know, child." I looked past Pete at Ida, sitting next to Dad, in her blue wingback chair, wearing a concerned expression. "Weber and Flanagan, out for revenge, and they didn't even have their stories straight."

I sat up too quickly and black invaded my peripheral vision. I shook away the wooziness. When my sight cleared, Pete rested in front of me.

"What happened?"

"I heard an angel say, 'please be okay,' and—"

My laugh sounded like a honk.

"I wasn't quite with it. I could hear, but I couldn't work my appendages. You called Flanagan off me. Thanks for that. I regained consciousness as she was dragging you across the lawn. I could barely get you out of the noose."

Carlee's voice came from behind me. "Renegade wouldn't calm down, so I took her for a walk, and she dragged me to your house. We'd never heard Maverick kicking up such a ruckus before. We rang the bell. No one answered and when Galen tried the knob—"

"The door opened. Carlee released Maverick," said Galen. "He really wanted to go outside so we let him, and he made more noise. He might have wanted to tear that woman apart, but I don't think vicious is part of his vocabulary. When we saw what happened, we called Chief West."

Pete pulled me into his arms and his forehead touched mine. We breathed in the same air. He leaned in for what might have been a kiss except his phone rang. He pulled it out and read the screen. His eyes said it all.

"Go," I said. "I'm fine. They need you, but make sure Susie cleans you up, and I only trust her to clear you for work."

* * *

The weather was perfect, blue sky, slight wind, temperatures in the high seventies. Word spread throughout town. We'd completed our Saturday morning mock trial practice, and our entire crew joined the crowd multiplying on the grassy area of Prada Park. Dorene had used her lawyerly know-how to get Ellen released, and Amanda had delivered her into Dad's care. She stood next to me, holding Maverick's leash while she continued to harass Ozzie about what the Z in his first name might stand for. Ida's laugh lines had returned.

Sister Lawrence brought Dad two pieces of jewelry she'd found among Barb's effects. Dad teared up as he gave a ring to Ellen and a necklace to me. Sister Lawrence and Ida sat in folding chairs in the front row, commiserating about piano students. Lance and Dad flanked Blake and Carolyn Hall who'd come out when they discovered their piano tuner might have had ill intentions toward Maverick. Amanda and Drew had uncovered the *Titanic* loot Maura Flanagan had stolen, and there was every possibility Maura had taken Carolyn Halls's sunglasses to plant and muddy the evidentiary water, but she'd yet to spill those beans.

One of the black-and-white striped attired student referees hit a gong, and Mr. Paul stepped up with a bull horn, which was the only sound to break Jane's loving gaze at Drew. Mr. Paul repeated his explanation of the engineering concepts used in paper airplane building and introduced the competitors, announcing the first-ever challenge from this year's student victor.

Felipe and Pete shook hands and lined up. They both inhaled and exhaled slowly. Mr. Paul blew his whistle, and they released the folded creations simultaneously. Two perfectly creased white paper airplanes gracefully soared and cut through the periwinkle sky. The slight, warm breeze caught the underbelly of the invented designs, gently guiding them accurately along the plot line, and for a moment they were lost in the glare of the sun.

Slowing, the paper constructs drifted, and no one moved, fearing to upset the smooth landings. From our perspective, it was too close to call. Armed with tape measures and protractors, the referees swiftly approached from the left, the right, and the starting block, but Maverick beat them to the goals, swooping in and fetching both planes.

My eyes flashed at a stricken Ellen as Maverick romped back to me. He'd done a marvelous job and couldn't be faulted. I knelt, and my retriever dropped the limp creations in my hand. I spent the next five minutes dodging sloppy dog kisses, laughing with my beautiful people, and wondering what new trouble he'd get me in.

Pear Martini
2 oz pear vodka
1 oz elderberry liqueur
1 oz simple syrup
½ oz fresh lemon juice

Mix in a shaker over ice. Pour into a glass. Drizzle 1 teaspoon of maraschino cherry juice into the mixture over the back of a spoon along the rim to get a bright red *layer* at the bottom. Gently add a maraschino cherry.

* * *

What's next for Katie and Maverick?

Stories abound in the weeks leading up to the Kentucky Derby, flooding the news feeds, and Katie Wilk has been given the task of studying the math involved in the equine industry. There are numbers related to the economic impact of jobs, money, statistics (which can be interpreted in many ways), racing, outcomes, and wagering. But while investigating local thoroughbreds, Katie discovers the finish line for one dead horsewoman, and you can bet she and Maverick will want to lend their expertise to solving the crime. But will she gamble her life on what she's told is the real thing or will she play the odds?

ACKNOWLEDGMENTS

What fun to have readers who love a thrilling cozy mystery. I appreciate all the supportive reviews and emails. I have so many people to thank for keeping my fiction as true as it can be: for legal expertise, Luke Seifert, Esq., Kindra Szymanski, Esq., and Adam Szymanski, Esq., and for pharmaceutical information: Matthew Smith, PharmD, and Anne Bruckner, PharmD. Our own piano tuner, Dennis Benson, gave wise insight as did my felt artist friend, Donna Brau. Note: the mistakes made under the guise of artistic license are all mine.

My helpful writer friends and readers made comments about inconsistencies and unknowns, and opened the door to other possibilities. For advice along the way, thank you Tim Ellington and my Cozy Thrills Group: Kate, Judy, and L.C. The words were corrected, polished, and ordered correctly under the eagle eye of Dennis Okland, Colleen Okland, and Lisa Donner. Michael Gehlen, Margaret Sullivan, and Michele Germscheid checked out the April Fool's jokes—stories our father told on his favorite day of the year. And thank you to our marvelous team of beta readers: Marcia Koopmann, Isobel Tamney, Donna Townsend, and Eve Osbourne.

The names Carolyn Hall, Kerstin Edwards, and David Koskiniemi were shared by reading friends. Look for more down the road, Dianne. Stephanie Dewey and Lee Ellison are always there with wisdom, guidance, and help. This wouldn't happen without them.

My family gave terrific insight, comfort, support, and unconditional love. Thank you, dearest John — you're always there, Kindra, Adam, Danica, Mitch, CJ, Thomas, Jack, Leo, and Emely. I couldn't do this without you.

Thank you, dear reader, for taking the time to read *Pranks, Payback & Poison*. If you enjoyed it please tell your friends, and I would be so grateful if you would consider posting a review. Word of mouth is an author's best friend, and very much appreciated. Thank you,

Mary Seifert

Get all the books in the Katie & Maverick Series!

Maverick, Movies, & Murder
Rescues, Rogues, & Renegade
Tinsel, Trials, & Traitors
Santa, Snowflakes, & Strychnine
Fishing, Festivities, & Fatalities
Diamonds, Diesel, & Doom
Creeps, Cache, & Corpses
Pranks, Payback, & Poison

Get a collection of free recipes from Mary— scan the QR code to find out how!

Visit Mary's website: MarySeifertAuthor.com/
Facebook: facebook.com/MarySeifertAuthor
Twitter: twitter.com/mary_seifert
Instagram: instagram.com/maryseifert/
Follow Mary on BookBub and Goodreads too!

Made in the USA
Middletown, DE
20 August 2024

59395134R00177